HEARTACHE
for the
SHOP GIRLS

Joanna read English at Cambridge University and worked on the production team of *The Archers* for ten years before serving as a scriptwriter for twenty. She has written several spin-off books about the long-running radio drama and on TV wrote for *Crossroads*, *Family Affairs*, *Doctors* and *EastEnders*. *Heartache for the Shop Girls* is her third novel.

Find out more about Jo and the next book in the series on Facebook.com/joannatoyewriter and on Twitter @JoannaToye.

Also by Joanna Toye

A Store at War
Wartime for the Shop Girls

HEARTACHE
for the
SHOP GIRLS

JOANNA TOYE

HarperCollins*Publishers*

HarperCollins*Publishers* Ltd
1 London Bridge Street,
London SE1 9GF

www.harpercollins.co.uk

First published by HarperCollins*Publishers* 2020
2

A catalogue record for this book is available from the British Library

ISBN: 978-0-00-829872-2

This novel is entirely a work of fiction.
The names, characters and incidents portrayed in it are
the work of the author's imagination. Any resemblance to
actual persons, living or dead, events or localities is
entirely coincidental.

Typeset in Sabon by Palimpsest Book Production Ltd, Falkirk, Stirlingshire

Printed and bound in the UK by CPI Group (UK) Ltd, Croydon CR0 4YY

MIX
Paper from
responsible sources
FSC™ C007454

This book is produced from independently certified FSC™ paper to ensure
responsible forest management.
For more information visit: www.harpercollins.co.uk/green

For Clara, with love from Shosho xxx

Chapter 1

The writing above the clock on the first floor of Marlow's read *'Tempus fugit'*. That, Lily had learnt, meant 'Time flies'. Well, if time was flying this morning, it was a bird with a broken wing, a Spitfire spluttering home with half its fuselage shot away, a bee drowsily drunk on pollen. It might be half-day closing, but with the sale over and many customers away, Wednesday mornings in August could seem longer than full days.

August was the strangest month, thought Lily as she spaced the hangers on the girls' pinafores the regulation half-inch apart. It had a sleepy,

1

droopy-eyelids feel, and it was still summer, but it often felt as if summer was over, with a blank white sky, shorter days, the leaves crisping and the shadows lengthening on the grass. And things happened in August – not always good things. The Great War had started in August, and so had this one, pretty much, with the wait for Hitler's 'undertaking' that had never come.

She looked across to Furniture and Household, hoping to catch Jim's eye, but he was with a customer. He was tipping a kitchen chair this way and that, demonstrating its sturdiness. He took his job very seriously. Jim took lots of things seriously – and plenty not so seriously. It was a combination that had first attracted her to him – but whether he was testing her or teasing her, Lily had accepted the challenge.

'Miss Collins! Customer!'

Lily snapped to attention and smoothed down her dress as Mrs Mortimer approached. She was one of the first customers Lily had served after her promotion from junior to sales, and a kind, tweedy soul so it had been a gentle dunking, not a baptism of fire.

Mrs Mortimer would only be looking – or 'doing a recce' as she put it – on behalf of one of her busy daughters or daughters-in-law before she, or they, returned with the essential coupons to make the purchase. But it was all good practice.

Lily began as she'd been taught.

'Good morning, Mrs Mortimer, how are you? How may I help you?'

On Toys next door, Lily's friend Gladys was dusting Dobbin, the much-loved Play Corner rocking horse, and thinking much the same about the time. When you had nothing to do on your afternoon off, a long morning didn't matter, but when there was something you were looking forward to, my, did it drag!

This afternoon there was a little party planned at Lily's, a welcome home for their friend Beryl's husband. Les Bulpitt had been invalided home from North Africa, to everyone's relief and delight, especially Beryl's, now a proud mother to baby Bobby. Les had been away for Bobby's birth, so hadn't seen his son as a newborn. Now he was home they could be a proper family.

Gladys sighed happily. Thoughts of contented married couples always led to thoughts of her fiancé, Bill, and how contented she would be when they were married, and especially when they started their family. A husband and children were all Gladys had ever wanted, and Bill was the answer to years of fervent prayers. Had it been wrong to pray for something like that, Gladys wondered now, when there were bigger things to pray for, like an end to starvation and cruelty and persecution? She probably

3

ought to pray for forgiveness for having been so shallow and selfish, but she was too busy praying for a speedy end to the war and for Bill to be kept safe in the meantime.

On Furniture and Household, Jim had made his sale.

'If you'll sign here, please, Mrs Jenkins, I'll send this up to the Cash Office to get your receipt.'

He stuffed the sheets into the little drum, rolled it shut and inserted it into the pneumatic tube. Off it whizzed upstairs. Jim smiled at Mrs Jenkins, another of the store's regular customers.

'I'm not sure when we can deliver, I'm afraid,' he began. 'With the new petrol regulations . . . '

Mrs Jenkins held up her hand. 'Don't worry, a few days won't matter. We've been without a kitchen chair for months – I had to give cook one of the dining chairs when the old one got past repairing. I'm grateful you had anything, even second-hand!'

'The Utility Scheme will help,' said Jim. 'We should get more regular supplies.'

Mrs Jenkins looked sceptical.

'Newlyweds get first dibs, though?'

'Oh, yes. And anyone who's been bombed out.'

The tube throbbed as the cylinder plopped back into the little cup at its base. Jim retrieved it and handed Mrs Jenkins her copy.

'I'll telephone,' he promised, 'with a date for delivery. I hope within the next week.'

'Marvellous – well, as good as it gets these days! Thank you. Goodbye!'

'Goodbye.'

Jim closed his sales book and looked across to Childrenswear, hoping Lily was looking his way, but she was with a customer. Lily's blonde curls bent close to Mrs Mortimer's grey head as they examined the smocking on a summer dress.

The clock showed half past twelve. Only half an hour to go before all four lights below it would be illuminated, the sign that the last customer had left the store and the commissionaire had bolted the doors and drawn down the blackout blinds.

Thirty minutes, then freedom . . . or was it? Jim had a funny feeling that there'd be a list of jobs for him ahead of the afternoon's little party. No change there, then! In a year as their lodger he'd realised that it was Lily's mother, Dora, who made work for idle hands. The devil never got a look-in.

'Really, Jim, is that the best you can do?'

'What? I'm at full stretch here, I'll have you know!'

'Come off it!' Lily scrutinised his efforts. 'What's the point of a banner if it looks like a drooping petticoat?'

Jim lowered his arms and the 'Welcome Home' banner he'd been holding up slumped dispiritedly to the floor.

'That's better.' He eased his neck and shoulders. 'My arms were nearly dropping off.'

5

He might have known he wouldn't get away with that.

'How can they drop off when they're above your head?' Lily retorted. 'Drop implies down, doesn't it? Tch! And to think you're the one with the School Certificate!'

Jim looked at her, head on one side, mouth twisted. Only a few weeks ago the two of them had finally admitted that their friendship had grown into more than just that. But their fledgeling romance didn't mean they weren't still friends first and foremost – friends who teased each other relentlessly.

To show she was on his side really, Lily dragged over a dining chair. Jim was over six feet tall but her mum had been adamant that the banner had got to be thumb-tacked to the top of the picture rail, not the front – she wasn't having it look as if it had woodworm. To say Dora Collins was house-proud was a bit like saying Hitler had simply got out of bed on the wrong side on the day he'd invaded Poland.

'Haven't you two finished yet?' Dora, pinny wrapped across her slender frame, hair bound up in a turban, appeared from the scullery, sounding stern, but only concerned that everything should be just so. 'There's lettuce to wash and tomatoes to slice, sandwiches to make . . . '

She was carrying a sponge cake on the best cut-glass stand. The icing and the little silver balls that Beryl had requested had of course been impossible, but it still looked delicious. Dora Collins wasn't to be beaten in the cake-making stakes, and thanks to the hens they kept in the yard, cakes in this house didn't have to be made with foul-smelling dried egg, either, even if it meant sacrificing sugar in tea.

Jim and Lily exchanged a 'that's told us' look and Jim scrambled up onto the chair, having first, of course, removed his shoes. Dora might have been turned away, setting the cake in the middle of the table, but she had more eyes in the back of her head than a whole platoon of snipers. Lily passed up the tacks, and soon the banner was in place to everyone's satisfaction.

Ivy and Susan, Beryl and Les, Gladys – Dora checked she'd set out enough plates. That was five, plus the three of them – yes, eight in total.

Banner fixed, chair replaced, Dora marshalled Lily and Jim into the kitchen.

'Now,' she instructed. 'Let's get a bit of a production line going. If I slice the bread—'

'Jim can spread the marg, and I can fill.' Lily finished the sentence for her.

Jim smiled to himself.

'The apple doesn't fall far from the tree,' was one of Dora's many favourite sayings and it certainly explained where Lily's organisational skills – he wouldn't have dared call it bossiness, not to her face, anyway – came from.

* * *

'Aw, you shouldn't have!'

'But we did! And it's all for you, Les!'

Beryl hung on to her husband's arm as they stood in the doorway, Les grinning at the spread. But he wasn't the Les that Lily remembered. He looked very different; thinner, and paler than you'd expect after months in the desert. But she'd been silly to expect him to look brown, Lily realised – most of his tan would have disappeared in the weeks he'd spent in hospital and a further few getting home on a troop ship. He looked older somehow.

'Me and Susan made the banner, Ivy and Dora's done the tea . . . '

Beryl steered Les into the room as his sister, Susan, carefully carrying baby Bobby, came in behind them.

Beryl had scribed the 'Welcome Home' in big fat letters, but she'd let Susan do the colouring, which was why it was all wonky and went over the lines. Les's sister was thirteen, but she'd been born with all sorts of difficulties, including a weak heart and poor eyesight. Co-ordination wasn't one of her strong points, and as the doctor had gently put it, Susan would always be backward in her development.

'How are you?' Jim was enthusiastically shaking Les by the hand, but Lily could tell he was just as shocked as she was by Les's appearance.

'He needs feeding up, that's what!' clucked Ivy. Still in her shapeless duster coat and even more shapeless hat, Les's mother was adding her contributions to the table – a plate of sausage rolls and a dish of junket.

'That's right,' Les agreed. 'Nothing a bit of home cooking won't put right.'

'Was it awful, the food out there?'

Lily was keen to know, as the story back home was that they had to do without to keep the Army marching on its stomach. Though frankly Les looked as if he hadn't eaten for weeks.

'Not bad. A bit repetitive, that's all.'

'Sounds like here,' said Gladys. She'd arrived earlier and was helping Susan, still holding the baby, settle herself in an easy chair. 'Anyway, it's lovely to see you home. And congratulations on being a dad!'

'Isn't he a little smasher?' Les beamed at his son. 'Hasn't Beryl done wonders?'

Beryl glowed as everyone showered praise on her, the baby, and the general miracle of creation.

'Don't you want to sit down, son? It's nearly wiped him out walking over here.'

As she spoke, Ivy was removing her coat and lowering her own sizeable behind onto the luckless dining chair that had drawn today's short straw. Dora nodded in agreement. Physical opposites, Ivy large and expansive, Dora neat and trim, they'd become fast friends since Les and Beryl's marriage, united by their unswerving devotion to their families.

'Pull him up a chair, Jim.'

Common sense and a desire to appear manly tussled in Les's face, but he gave in to the inevitable.

'Maybe I will.' He took the chair. 'Just for a minute or two. I'm a lot better than I was!' he added bravely.

'I think he looks awful, don't you?' Lily asked Jim under the hiss of the kettle. They'd been sent out to the kitchen to make the tea.

'Not great.'

The worry about Les had started after the battle for Tobruk back in June. Nothing had been heard of him, or Lily's brother Reg who was also out in North Africa, for weeks. Finally, Reg had managed to send a wire saying he was OK. From Les, though, there'd been nothing till Beryl got a letter saying he'd been in hospital – and nowhere near the fighting! He'd been taken with something called West Nile fever – from a mosquito bite.

'I don't like it,' said Lily. 'Do you think it was more serious than he let on?'

Jim shrugged.

'I can't think why else a simple fever case would mean him being shipped home and discharged for good.'

Lily sighed.

'Oh, Jim. This war! If so, where does that leave Beryl and Bobby?'

Chapter 2

It wasn't till after tea that Jim got the full story out of Les. Under the pretence of giving Bobby, newly fed and changed, some air, they went out into the yard where the hens scratched tirelessly if pointlessly in their run. Les was already looking a bit less peaky. He'd certainly eaten a giant tea.

'So, this fever . . . ' Jim began.

Beryl had already told them with a hint of pride that Les's records had gone to the Hospital for Tropical Diseases in London as an interesting case.

'I'd never heard of it,' answered Les, shifting his body slightly to protect the baby's eyes from the bright sky. 'It's not that bad in itself. But I had complications.'

'Right . . . ' So there had been something else – just as Jim and Lily had suspected.

'I carried on, see, thought it was gippy tummy or heatstroke – they were always warning us about that. By the time I came over real queer, it had taken hold. I had this kind of seizure, woke up in hospital and my legs had gone all floppy. You know how they hit you with that little hammer? Not a thing.'

'My God, Les. Scary.'

'It was. I thought it was polio or something. But they said . . . let me get this right . . . the fever had gone to . . . encephalitis, is it?'

Now Jim understood. Without telling anyone, even Lily, he'd gone to the library and read up on tropical fevers back when they'd first had the news that Les had been in the isolation ward. Encephalitis was a swelling of the brain.

'But you got the feeling back?'

'Yes, thank God, bit by bit. And I'm better now.'

'Are you? Really?'

'Well . . . ' Les looked shifty. 'I get the odd headache. My heart races a bit. But I'm properly on the mend.'

'They still invalided you out.'

'Yeah. And compared to some blokes, lost a leg, blinded, burns and what have you, I'm darn lucky. But the Army can't have me driving or handling machinery, let alone a gun. They can't take the risk, "in a theatre of war" was how they put it.'

'No, I should think not.'

'But I could kiss that mosquito!' The mosquito being unavailable, Les kissed the baby's head. 'Giving me a free pass home!'

This was more like the old Les.

'Well, maybe it's for the best,' Jim said thoughtfully. 'At least Bobby's going to grow up knowing his dad. There's plenty of kids who won't have that.'

They both looked down at the baby. At four months he hadn't quite mastered getting his thumb into his mouth but was happily sucking his fist. Les stroked his silky hair in disbelief and wonder.

'What was it like out there, Les? Really?'

Les puffed out a breath.

'What can I say? Like everyone tells you: heat, dust, sand, flies, more sand, more heat . . . What they don't tell you is wearing the same clothes for days, soaked in sweat, drinking water that tastes of petrol from a rusty can, lying in a scrape in the sand being strafed by the Jerries, seeing the truck ahead of you hit a mine . . . and the things you see . . . fellers blown apart, bits all over the place . . . digging them a grave . . . '

Gently, he touched Bobby's head again.

'But at the same time, the lads, we had such a laugh – you had to. And the guts of some of them – injured and carrying on, could have got a Blighty pass no trouble, but raring to get back to it – and that's officers and men. And not just us Brits. Indians and Aussies and New Zealanders . . . they've fought like lions.'

Jim was silent. He'd tried to join up when he'd turned eighteen but had failed the eye test. He still felt guilty about it, despite the fact that he did his ARP duty three nights a week and took his turn fire-watching on the roof of Marlow's.

'They should have kept you on – recruiting officer!'

'No thanks! But, look, Jim, I want to talk to you about that. What's the chance of my old job back?'

Until he'd been called up, Les had worked as a delivery driver at Marlow's. Beryl had worked there too. It was how they'd all met.

Jim had been waiting for the question and he knew the answer would disappoint. Les had never been replaced and the store was hardly going to create another driving job now, with petrol rationed even more strictly.

'Les. Be realistic. You can't go back to driving. The Army have got a point.' Les opened his mouth to object, but Jim carried on. 'No, listen. There is a job coming up. Not driving – it's warehouse-man-cum-porter. I know it's a step down for you. It wouldn't be quite as well-paid, and you'd still have to convince them you were fit enough . . . Would you be up for that?'

'With a wife and kiddy to support?' Les nearly bit off not just his hand, but his whole arm. 'I'd be up for anything! And I'll work on getting myself A1 fit. Get my chest-expander out!'

'Don't overdo it!' warned Jim. 'One step at a time. I'll have a word with Staff Office and try and get you seen. I should think they'd be glad not to have to advertise, and wade through a load of useless applications.'

'Thanks, Jim. I appreciate it.'

Lily, Gladys and Beryl trooped out now, Beryl saying they ought to get going and get Bobby to bed. She, Gladys and Les formed an admiring circle round the baby as Lily squeezed in next to Jim on the wall of the veg bed. He put his arm round her.

'Still on for the cinema?'

'You bet!'

They were going to see *The Magnificent Ambersons*. Lily had been all for seeing *Mrs. Miniver* again, which was still playing at the Gaumont, but they'd tossed a coin in the end and Jim had won. He was a big fan of Orson Welles. In truth, Lily didn't much care what they saw. It would just be a treat to be on their own, walking to the cinema, arms entwined, and having a quick smooch before the picture started – being Jim's girl.

When Lily had first shyly confessed to her friends that she and Jim had finally moved things on from being friends, Gladys had leapt ahead to suggest cosy double dates with herself and Bill, as Lily had known she would. Gladys and Bill were going to get married on his next leave, though when that would be, neither of them knew. Bill's ship was on escort duty in the Northern Passage so it might not be till well into next year. If the war lasted that long, of course.

Before Gladys could get to double weddings, though, Lily had firmly had to tell her that she and Jim were happy to let things unfold slowly – very slowly.

'We're no age, Gladys,' she'd protested. 'I know you and Bill aren't much older, but just because marriage and babies is right for you, it doesn't mean it's right for us. I mean, can you see me as a full-time wife and mother, honestly?'

It was generally agreed that Lily's attempts at knitting would have been useful colanders; Dora despaired of her daughter's anything-but-light touch with pastry.

Gladys had looked baffled by Lily's reluctance to swoon at the whiff of orange blossom and the idea of a ring on her finger, but Beryl, forthright as always, had weighed in on Lily's side.

'Look,' she reasoned. 'We all know Lily and Jim are marked out for something a bit better than the shop floor at Marlow's. It wouldn't affect Jim, but Lily could kiss goodbye to any idea of promotion if she got married, let alone up the duff.'

'Rubbish!' Gladys defended herself. 'There's loads of married women working now, and ones with children. In Marlow's and everywhere else.'

'Only because the men are away fighting! When they come home, they'll take back their jobs and shove us women straight back in the kitchen, you wait and see!'

Lily nodded, grateful for the support, but then Beryl wasn't a full-time wife and mother herself. She couldn't be called up for war work now she had the baby, and her old job in the Toy department at Marlow's, even if she'd wanted it, had been filled by Gladys. So, starting in a small way with her own wedding and bridesmaids' dresses, she'd set herself up in business hiring out bridal wear from home. Les's picture of himself as the family's sole bread-winner was a complete illusion: Beryl had a five-year plan for Beryl's Brides that would have had Stalin stroking his moustache.

'Did you get much out of Les?' Lily asked Jim quietly now. The adoring acolytes weren't listening, still worshipping the wonder child.

Jim kept his voice low, even so.

'It may not be quite as bad as we thought. He had a horrible infection, but it sounds as if he's going to be OK. Like he said, he just needs to build his strength up.'

'Thank goodness for that. Did you tell him about the job?'

'He jumped at it.'

'Good.'

Lily sighed contentedly. The worry had mostly

17

subsided; there was still the cinema to look forward to. After the long, dull morning, and the concern over Les, what a perfect end to the afternoon.

It was getting on for six by the time everyone had gone, the last of the crocks were put away and the banner could come down. Jim was shutting up the hens.

'It hasn't got Les's name on it,' Lily said as she folded the banner carefully. 'We can use it for Reg.'

She really was starting to think, or at least hope, two things – first, that the war might be over soon, and second, that both her brothers might get through it unscathed.

Reg was a mechanic with the Royal Electrical and Mechanical Engineers, attached to the Eighth Army. General Montgomery was leading them now, experienced, energetic, determined: everyone was hoping against hope that he was the one who'd finally drive Rommel into the sea. Lily had an even better reason to hope for the safe return of her other brother, the middle one of Dora's children. Sid had joined the Navy but an injury picked up in training meant he'd had to settle for a desk job. He was up in Scotland at a place called Largs, and though he wasn't thrilled at being a penpusher instead of a fighting man, he'd had to acknowledge that it took away some of the worry back home.

Dora, though, wasn't one to cross bridges or to

count chickens: hope for the best but take what comes was nearer the mark for her. She changed the subject.

'Hadn't you better get a wriggle on if you two are going out?'

'Yes! You're right. We should.'

Dora smiled fondly at her daughter. She was thrilled that Lily and Jim were courting. They were always discreet about it in front of her, but no one could fail to notice the even readier smiles, the even more affectionate teasing, the sneaked glances, the surreptitious squeezes. Lily had always been bright and strong-minded; she needed someone like Jim to catch her, and then to match her. He might seem the quiet type but he was no pushover. He was quick and clever too – Lily needed that.

'Off you go then. But see to your hair before you do!'

Lily's blonde curls, as strong-minded as she was, had a tendency to resist arrest, and the fact that her few precious hairgrips had long since lost their grippiness didn't help.

'Beryl says I should get a permanent, now I'm a salesgirl proper, but I'm not sure . . . Jim?' Lily broke off as Jim came in from the kitchen. He was ghost-white.

'The bucket,' he said blankly. 'I was taking it to the pig bin and I met him in the street. The telegram boy.'

19

Oh no, not Reg! Please, not Reg! Not today – not any time, but especially not today!

Dora held out her hand for the telegram, but Jim shook his head.

'It was for me,' he said. 'It's my mother. She's had a stroke.'

Chapter 3

Wasn't that just like life, thought Lily, as she stood and watched Jim fling a few things into a bag. At the start of the afternoon they'd been worrying about Les, and when she'd heard the word 'telegram', she'd automatically assumed it must be about Reg. Even then, when Jim had said it was for him . . . of his parents, the one you'd expect to get bad news about was his father, gassed in the Great War and left semi-invalided with a bad chest. Yes, just like life, to creep up and sandbag you from behind when you were looking in the other direction!

Jim zipped up his holdall and turned to face her.

'I'm sorry about the cinema.'

'Don't be silly. I'm sorry for you. And your mum. Will you go straight to the hospital?'

Jim's family home was in Worcestershire, in a small village, Bidbury. The telegram had said his mother was in the Cottage Hospital at Pershore.

Jim spread his hands.

'I don't know what I'll do. I've got to get there first.'

You couldn't count on the trains, when or if they'd run, and there was no direct train. Jim would have to go from Hinton to Birmingham, change there for Worcester, then for the branch line, a slow, jolting journey in a blacked-out carriage with long waits in between.

Lily put her hand on his arm.

'They wouldn't let you see her in the middle of the night anyway. Perhaps you'd be better going home to see to your dad. He can't manage on his own, can he?'

Jim pushed his hands through his hair, making it stick up in the way that flipped Lily's heart.

'Can you tell them at work? I haven't got time to write a letter.'

'Of course. Don't worry about that. Come here.'

She stepped forward and wrapped her arms around him. He rested his chin on top of her head and sighed. They both knew what this latest development meant.

The situation with Jim's parents had been complicated enough already. He was an only child, and was only here in Hinton because his mother, Alice, had traded on a never-before-exploited family connection to write to the store's owner, Cedric Marlow. She'd hoped that he'd help Jim through Agricultural College, but she hadn't dared to ask outright and instead Cedric Marlow had offered a Jim a position at the store. With neither of them feeling that he could turn it down, Jim had moved away to the town, and Marlow's – and Lily. His mother, frustrated at losing him, had spent the entire time since hoping that he'd return. In fact, she'd done more than hope – she'd as good as schemed to get him back.

Just a few weeks earlier, seeing that looking after his dad, the house and the garden was getting too much for her, Jim had started going back to Bidbury every other weekend, leaving after work on Saturdays and taking Mondays off unpaid to make the lengthy journey worthwhile.

The new regime had coincided with Lily and Jim confessing what they felt for each other, and if it was a brake on their relationship, at least it was better than the screeching full stop that Lily had feared. She'd had moments when she'd genuinely thought Jim was going to leave Hinton for good, and the fact that he was still there at all felt like deliverance.

But now this.

Jim pulled away and looked sadly down at her.

'I'm sorry,' he said again. 'We'll make things work, Lily, I promise.'

Lily stood on tiptoe and kissed him.

'I know.'

Jim held her tight and kissed her back. 'I'd better go.'

'You had.'

Lily saw him to the front door. He kissed her again, for longer this time.

'I don't know when I'll be back.'

'I'll see you when I see you,' she said, as brightly as she could. 'Give your mother my best, won't you?'

Jim smiled thinly. He knew that Lily's good wishes were the last thing that his mother would want and in her heart of hearts, Lily knew it too. The two of them were gambling for Jim's affections, and, though a stroke was hardly something you could fake, or plan, and she felt wicked for thinking it, it still seemed to Lily as though Alice had played an ace.

'Poor Jim!' Gladys, the next day, was sorry to hear the news. 'His poor mum, of course. And poor you, Lily!'

Lily shrugged the sympathy away.

'Don't feel sorry for me. I'm not the one in hospital.'

'And the telegram didn't say how bad it is?'

'No.'

Gladys pushed a bit of potato round her plate, trying to robe it in the thin gravy. The friends had managed to get off to dinner together, and the clatter of the Staff Canteen was all around them. The meat dish of the day was roast heart, which Lily couldn't fancy – a bit too much like her own. She was doing her best with a lump of grey fish in a heavy sea of white sauce.

'Who sent it anyway?' Gladys managed to transfer the dripping chunk of potato to her mouth. 'His dad never leaves the house, does he?'

Lily paused, knife and fork arched.

'I never thought. I never asked. A neighbour, perhaps?'

Gladys nodded. She was such a sweet soul; she was really feeling for Jim, Lily could see.

'I suppose so. Oh dear. And we'd had such a lovely afternoon.'

It was early afternoon by the time Jim got to the hospital. He hadn't got back to Bidbury till dawn, trains cancelled or diverted, stuck in a siding in Birmingham to let troop trains pass, then the sirens going, hearing planes overhead, straining to hear if they were German Dorniers, then realising they were Lancasters, probably on their way back to base from a raid of their own.

Exhausted, he'd had to walk the last few miles, letting himself into the darkened cottage to find his father asleep in the chair with the dog loyally at his feet. Jim had a couple of hours' sleep, washed and shaved his father and himself, and at nine had walked back into the village to get some food in. From the shop-cum-post office he'd telephoned the hospital to hear that his mother's condition was unchanged, and that visiting was from two o'clock till four.

Now he was standing nonplussed in the ward with its shiny lino and tidy beds, trying to see which pale figure, pinioned by the bedclothes, was his mother. A nurse came by with a cloth-covered tray, so he asked.

'Far bed on the left,' she said, swishing off on rubber heels to the sluice room.

Head down, uncomfortable and feeling out of place, Jim made his way past the other patients, who, apart from one jolly woman surrounded by a tribe of relatives, seemed to be largely elderly and unloved, or at least unvisited. But as he neared the end bed, he realised that wasn't the case with his mother – there was someone there already. A young woman was sitting at the bedside with her back to him.

'Margaret?'

The girl spun round and stood up rapidly, rattling the chair back. She looked almost as out of place as Jim in her cord breeches and shirt, with tanned arms and her brown hair cropped close into her neck.

'Jim! You made it!'

Jim caught the chair as it rocked.

'Yes, finally. How is she?'

He could see straight away there was no point in addressing the question to his mother. She was asleep, or seemed to be, her face white and her lips a thin mauve line.

Margaret motioned him to one side. She kept her voice low.

'The doctor was leaving as I got here. They've given her something to calm her down – she was getting what he called "agitated". She hasn't said much, so they can't really tell about that, but it's taken her movement, Jim, down her right side.'

'Oh, God.'

On the long journey Jim had speculated about how the stroke might have affected her. A mother, especially his mother, who could get about but not communicate was as bad as one who was physically impeded but still had the power of speech. Now it seemed his mother might have lost both. He reached for the only possible straw.

'People do get better, though, from a stroke? With exercises . . . ?'

Margaret lifted her shoulders minutely.

'It's too early to say. But the doctor did say the stroke was a relatively mild one.'

'That's something.'

It still left him with a heck of a problem, he knew.

'Look, Margaret,' he offered. 'I'll sit with her now. I can stay till she wakes up. It's good of you to have come. And thank you so much for sending the telegram.' His father, who seemed bemused by the whole thing, had told him that much. 'I'll give you the money.'

'Don't be silly. That's all right.'

'How did you . . . how did you even know it had happened?'

'Oh,' said Margaret. 'But I was there. I was with her.'

His mother showed no sign of stirring, so they went outside to talk. There was a small garden with a sundial and some benches where recuperating patients and their visitors could sit. Jim was too tense to sit down, so they walked round and round the narrow crazy-paved paths.

'I've been dropping in when I could,' Margaret explained. 'I know you've been coming at weekends, Jim, but I think your mum was lonely. Your dad sits in the chair dozing most of the day. She asked me to call if I had time, so I did. I think she just wanted company.'

'I see.'

That wasn't all his mother had wanted and Jim knew it. Margaret was the daughter of a local farmer. Both her brothers had been killed in the war and, unbeknown to her, she was part of Alice's scheme to get Jim back. If Alice could pair Jim off with Margaret, that was not one, not two, but three birds with one stone. Jim would be back home, with a wife on his arm and running the farm down the lane, country trumping town, her son secure and with a promising future.

Jim knew his mother felt she'd been dealt a rotten

hand in life. Now it seemed to have turned into a winning one, because if she didn't make a good recovery – and who knew? – he'd surely have no option but to come back to Bidbury for good.

While Jim had been thinking, they'd continued their aimless circuit of the garden, Margaret brushing her hand against the tall spines of lavender and releasing their scent. Jim's mother had claimed that Margaret held a torch for him – always had – and there was no doubt she'd make a wonderful wife for a farmer. She was milking her father's herd by herself these days, butter-making, delivering the churns, delivering and looking after the calves, too – and she had other talents. She'd wanted to go to Art School, but that had been scotched by the war and she'd taken on her new role uncomplainingly. Jim liked her very much, admired her, even, and felt sorry for what she'd had to give up. All in all, Margaret was a thoroughly nice girl and, if things had been different, they might even one day have made a match. But things were different. He had Lily now.

When Lily got back to her department after dinner, Miss Frobisher was waiting for her. Lily instinctively looked at the clock but Miss Frobisher held up a reassuring hand.

'You're not late, don't worry!'

'Good! Did you want me for something, Miss Frobisher?'

'Yes, I do. Not now, but on Monday. I want you to come with me to Ward and Keppler.'

Lily's mouth made a fair imitation of her dinnertime fish being landed.

Ward and Keppler were big manufacturers of children's and babywear – their Robin Hood brand was top quality and they chose their outlets very carefully. The only shops in Hinton favoured with their goods were Marlow's and their big rival, Burrell's.

'You may well look surprised,' Lily's boss went on. 'I was due to go with Miss Naylor, but she has to be at home that day for the ruins recorder.'

Miss Naylor was the buyer on Schoolwear. Her house was in a terrace that had been part-destroyed when a bomb had dropped on Hinton the previous year. The council's inspector had to make regular visits to make sure the houses still standing were safe to live in.

Poor Miss Naylor – but lucky Lily! Lucky Miss Frobisher too, though she'd never have let on. She and Miss Naylor were not the best of friends and Miss Frobisher had always felt her presence on the trip, on the basis of girls' gym knickers and boys' rugby socks, was superfluous.

'The expenses had already been cleared and the tickets bought,' Miss Frobisher went on, 'so rather than waste one . . . '

Her eyebrows signalled it might be a good idea if Lily made some response, and she found her voice.

'Miss Frobisher, that would be wonderful!' she managed. 'Thank you!'

'It's intended to be instructive,' said Miss Frobisher firmly, in case Lily thought it was to be a jolly day out – which she hadn't. 'Selling's only one aspect of running a department. This will show you where and how it all begins – the buying process.'

Lily knew she should be listening as Miss Frobisher explained how she'd cleared Lily's absence with the first floor supervisor, Mr Simmonds, when they'd need to leave and when they'd get back, but her mind was running ahead.

'One aspect of running a department?' *Of running a department*? Lily knew she wanted to progress and she knew Miss Frobisher thought she had it in her . . . but buying? Was her boss really implying she could see Lily going that far at Marlow's?

Things really did happen in August – and they weren't all bad, either!

Chapter 4

Lily hugged the news to herself for the rest of the day. She told Gladys about it as they left the store but made sure to talk it down as much as she could.

'I expect she just wants company,' she explained. 'You know what the trains are like.'

Lily knew from past experience – look at the way Gladys had reacted to Lily and Jim getting together – how her friend loved to build things up and she didn't want her reading any more into it than she only half-dared to herself.

She had to tell her mum as well, naturally, because who knew when she and Miss Frobisher would get back and she didn't want her to worry. But Dora wasn't to be fooled.

'She must think something of you, Lily!'

'Oh, well, maybe.'

Dora wiped her hands on her apron – she'd been peeling potatoes – and came to give her daughter a hug. She hadn't been very free with her hugs when Lily and the boys had been growing up – too busy keeping them fed and clothed after she'd been widowed. Her life was hardly any easier now she was living through the second world war of her lifetime, and she missed and worried endlessly about her sons – but if that had made her more demonstrative to the child she did have at home, Lily wasn't complaining.

'I did promise when I started at Marlow's that I'd try my hardest. But I'm so lucky with Miss Frobisher. Not all the buyers are like it, but she wants to help me along.'

'And up, by the sound of it!' Dora had a sudden thought. 'Lucky you got that jacket at the rummage the other week. And if you want to borrow my horseshoe brooch for the lapel, you've only to say.'

The only person Lily could really confide in about her hopes was Jim, but when he came back on Sunday, he was understandably preoccupied.

'Flying visit,' he said, surprising Lily and Dora by turning up as they were finishing their meagre, virtually meat-free stew.

Dora immediately fetched him a plate and served

out the rest – so much for Monday's planned cottage pie – and Jim answered their questions between mouthfuls. The answers weren't encouraging.

'I don't know what to think,' he confessed. 'Mother's hardly been out of bed, but they're chucking her out tomorrow.'

'That can't be right!' Dora protested.

'No, that's not quite fair. Someone's been coming to walk her up and down – her leg's not too bad, though she needs someone to lean on. But she can hardly move her arm. Still, they need the bed, apparently.'

'What are you going to do? You'll have to stay on, won't you?'

Jim turned to answer Lily, but she knew what he'd say.

'There's nothing else for it, till I can sort someone out to look after her and my dad. I'm only back to collect some clothes.'

He'd finished his stew in what seemed like seconds and Lily trailed upstairs after him to watch him pack for the second time in five days.

'I wish there was something I could do,' she said.

'There is,' said Jim. He produced a letter from his pocket. 'Take this in to work; it's telling them I'll need a bit more time off.'

He gave a huge sigh and sank onto the bed, pulling Lily down beside him.

'What a mess it all is.'

Lily put her arms round him and pulled him close.

'It'll get sorted,' she said, trying to sound convincing. 'Things do.'

Jim smiled thinly. He didn't tell her that Margaret had instantly offered to help, though he'd rebuffed that straight away – she had a more-than-full-time job on the farm. No, he'd have to find someone else in the village, though the only available candidate so far was Mrs Dawkins, a rather chaotic woman who cleaned – and frequently drank – at the pub. Jim couldn't see her meeting with his mother's approval. Still, she might have to put up with it.

Within the hour he was off again for another wearisome journey. Lily saw him to the door. It didn't seem the right time to start going on about her day out with Miss Frobisher, and what it might mean, but when Jim kissed her briefly, Lily did mention that she'd been invited on a buying trip with her boss.

'Oh, good,' said Jim distractedly. 'You'll still be able to get that letter to Staff Office, though, won't you?'

Lily didn't say that she and Miss Frobisher were meeting at the station, so she'd have to set out early to divert to Marlow's first. But it was the least she could do.

'Good morning! You're looking very smart.'

Lily, already a little pink from her detour with Jim's letter, blushed some more. She hoped it wasn't too obvious that her jacket was a black and white bird's eye check – Miss Frobisher had a bird's eye suit in navy – or that her black barathea skirt was not unlike the skirt of Miss Frobisher's black barathea costume with its back pleat. Fortunately her boss wasn't wearing either of them today, but a camel coat and skirt, and court shoes the colour of conkers. Lily surreptitiously wiped the toes of her own black lace-ups on the back of her legs to buff them up a bit. If only she could be as polished as Miss Frobisher.

Miss Frobisher flourished the tickets.

'Platform three. And wonder of wonders, they're not predicting any delays.'

Wonder of wonders, 'they' were right for once. Settled smugly in the train – they even managed to get seats – Miss Frobisher began to fill Lily in on what to expect.

'I deal with Mr Ward directly,' she explained as the train pulled out in a hiss of steam and a shower of smuts. 'It's a relationship I've built up over many years – in fact, I was the one who persuaded him to sell through Marlow's. I dealt with him when I was at Marshall and Snelgrove's.'

Lily gaped. 'I had no idea you'd worked anywhere but Marlow's!'

'I started out at Marlow's as a junior like you.' Miss Frobisher put out a hand against the window as the train jolted on the tracks. 'In Ladies' Fashions. Ran around unpacking boxes and ironing out creases and picking up pins. Then gradually worked my way up through sales.'

That explained it! Miss Frobisher always looked like a fashion plate. How she did it on clothing coupons had always fascinated Lily; perhaps she still had contacts in the trade.

'But at the time – before the war, before the staff shortages we have now – there was no movement above me. No progress that I could see in any department. And then . . . one of the reps recommended me and I was made an offer I couldn't refuse. Junior buyer – in London.'

'London!'

'I only came back to Hinton because of the war. I . . . well, I had my son by then, I didn't want to risk it.'

Lily knew Miss Frobisher was married: it was one of the store's quainter conventions that its women employees were addressed as 'Miss'. Her son, she also knew, was only about four – a neighbour looked after him during the day. As for her husband, he was serving abroad. That was all anyone knew. Miss Frobisher never talked about him and she was hardly the kind of person you could ask. It wasn't their place, Lily and Gladys had agreed, and it wasn't uncommon; it was the way some women coped with the separation. But at the same time they'd convinced themselves that he couldn't be talked about anyway because he was engaged on some kind of secret hush-hush work – he'd obviously be doing something glamorous, in keeping with his glamorous wife.

Now Lily knew Miss Frobisher had lived in London, which was presumably where she'd met him, it turned the speculation into certainty. London was another world, exciting and different. Anyone Miss Frobisher might meet there – over champagne at the Café de Paris, no doubt – was bound to be too.

But Miss Frobisher had gone as far as she intended with her personal revelations – further perhaps – and she drew the subject to a close.

'We're not here to talk about me. Let me show you some figures.'

She produced a sheaf of papers from a small attaché case and spread them out on the little table between them.

The miles and the minutes flew by hand in hand as Lily tried to absorb costings and profit margins and sales by volume. She asked scores of questions – how did you decide what to buy in the first place? How could you ever estimate demand? Though that was easy these days – it always outstripped supply.

Before Lily knew it, the train clanked in to Nottingham. On the jostling platform, Lily kept her eyes fixed on the back of Miss Frobisher's smooth French-pleated head as they threaded their way through soldiers, airmen and civilians, women porters yelling 'mind your backs' and guards blowing their whistles. Outside, Miss Frobisher hustled her into a taxi – the extravagance! Dora would have died! – which wove through the streets and dropped them at a huge red-brick building; a proper old Victorian mill, long and low with tall chimneys.

Inside, Mr Ward's secretary led them up to the management offices, built on a sort of platform on cast-iron pillars overlooking the massive factory floor. Lily blinked in wonder. Not just the platform but the air itself seemed to vibrate. Looms rattled and clattered as the shuttles wove from left to right and back again, transforming loose skeins of thread into smooth sheets of cloth. The noise was deafening and it was a relief when the secretary left and closed the office door behind her.

Miss Frobisher made the introductions: it had been Lily on the train, but she was Miss Collins again now. Mr Ward, small, bald and so stout he looked as if he'd been blown up with a bicycle pump, shook her by the hand.

'Pleased to meet you! You couldn't have anyone better than Miss Frobisher here to teach you what for, but I expect you know that already!'

He kept up the merry chat as tea was brought in and poured. He didn't get much of a response – Miss Frobisher wasn't one for small talk – but it didn't seem to bother him. He answered his own questions about the trains and the weather and the state of the war while Lily surreptitiously eyed the plate of ginger biscuits. She'd never seen Miss Frobisher eat, nor heard her stomach rumble, as her own often did so humiliatingly during a long morning and, as she expected, Miss Frobisher politely waved away the plate when Mr Ward wafted it in front of her. Lily had no such qualms. She knew Miss Frobisher was keen to get down to business, but surely one wouldn't hurt? She extended her hand and Mr Ward beamed.

'Take two!' he urged. 'Spoil yourself!'

Lily didn't need telling twice. Aping Miss Frobisher's clothes and trying to copy her poise was one thing, but there were limits.

Miss Frobisher was flourishing her sheets again, and as Mr Ward squeezed himself into the chair behind his desk, she produced another on which she'd logged all the customer requests for Robin Hood babywear that she'd been unable to fulfil.

'I realise you're under pressure with government orders, but . . . '

'Long Johns and combinations,' Mr Ward confirmed. 'Bandages, blankets, and now they're talking about webbing and camouflage nets.'

Busy trying to eat her biscuit as unobtrusively as possible, Lily looked up; Miss Frobisher seemed shocked.

'Goodness! That's a lot more than I realised.'

'A lot more. In fact, things have got so bad that . . . ' Mr Ward sat back, light through the taped-over window glazing his bald head. His tight waistcoat had a big gold watch inserted even more tightly into the pocket. 'Mr Keppler and I have discussed it and we've decided to stop producing Robin Hood baby-wear altogether.'

Shot with a poisoned arrow, Miss Frobisher reeled back in her chair.

'You can't be serious!'

Lily had never seen her so discomposed.

Mr Ward held up a podgy, but pacifying, hand.

'Raw materials are so hard to come by, there's no choice. We can't guarantee the quality and we don't want to compromise the name.'

'But . . . you can't do that! If you can't send us your best, can't you at least send us something? And . . . well . . . call it something else?'

Genius, thought Lily admiringly. That's where Miss Frobisher's years of experience came in.

Mr Ward beamed.

'I knew you'd think of that – and it's exactly what we plan to do. And keeping with the Sherwood Forest theme, we thought we'd call the different lines after trees. Maple for underwear, Olive for baby blankets and pram covers, and so on.'

And so on? thought Lily. Maple, maybe, but since when were there olive trees in Sherwood Forest? What next? Coconut palms?

Privately she and Jim had joked about the Robin Hood name – robbing people with their exorbitant prices – but surely the point was for customers to make the connection with a label they'd trusted in the past? On top of which, not using native trees was hardly patriotic!

Miss Frobisher had emphasised that Lily was there to observe, not to intervene, but as always, she couldn't help herself.

'Why those trees, Mr Ward?' she asked.

Now she was the one pierced with a poisoned arrow – a poisonous look, anyway – from her boss. She scrambled to apply an antidote.

'I only thought, Miss Frobisher, that if a customer happened to ask, it'd be good to know.'

Mr Ward beamed again.

'That's a fair point,' he said. 'It's personal, really. My son's doing pilot training in Canada, hence the maple. And olive was Mr Keppler's suggestion, for the homeland his people have long wanted in Palestine. But if you're worried about them not being thoroughly British, we've got oak, beech and pine as well.'

'Does that answer your question, Miss Collins?'

Lily nodded dumbly, but Miss Frobisher didn't seem cross really. She was too relieved, probably, that she was going to have something to sell.

'So when will the new lines be ready?' she asked. 'And in what quantity?'

Before Mr Ward could answer, there was a rat-a-tat on the door and a head poked round.

'You asked me to pop by, Mr Ward. If it's convenient . . . ?'

'Perfect timing, Frank. Come in.'

Mr Ward extracted himself from his chair – not an easy process – and Lily swivelled in her seat to get a better look at the arrival as he crossed the room. He had a broad, open face, a head of dark curly hair, very blue eyes, and a cheeky smile.

'Miss Frobisher, I presume?' he said in a soft Irish accent, speaking as if he was greeting Dr Livingstone in the jungle. 'Frank Bryant.'

Miss Frobisher shook the extended hand without a word.

'And this is . . . ?' Frank turned to Lily.

'A colleague,' replied Miss Frobisher coolly.

'Miss Collins,' Mr Ward supplied helpfully.

Frank shook Lily's hand too.

'How do you do?' he said formally, obviously noting that the temperature in the room had dropped by ten degrees.

Mr Ward, insulated perhaps by his fleshy covering, seemed oblivious.

'Frank's our new Midlands representative,' he beamed. 'Of course, he won't be calling as frequently as Mr Harris did.' Mr Harris had been the previous rep, now a stores orderly in the RASC. Lily wondered why Frank wasn't in the Forces himself, but Mr Ward was continuing. 'Petrol and so on. But he'll be round as often as he can to check you're happy with the goods and to let you know in advance of any new lines.'

Lily stole a glance at Frank. He was straightening

his tie and trying to look serious, but not succeeding very well. He caught her looking at him and winked.

Lily looked away rapidly, but though Miss Frobisher seemed to have her head bent over her paperwork again, Lily could tell from the set of her shoulders that she was more Queen Victoria than Dr Livingstone. Definitely not amused.

Chapter 5

Frank excused himself after that, ('Invoices!' he said with a comical grimace), and Miss Frobisher and Mr Ward began an intense round of haggling. Lily watched, intrigued, as they danced around each other like hares boxing before Miss Frobisher yielded slightly on quantities and Mr Ward gave a little on price. Lily could see that it was important that neither of them lost face, but the handshakes at the end were warm enough, and as they left, Mr Ward even pressed a couple more biscuits on a delighted Lily. She secreted them in her gas mask case, knowing she should take them home for another day, but knowing too that she was bound to give in and eat them on the train.

'Were you happy with how it went?' she ventured as she and Miss Frobisher waited for their taxi.

'Reasonably,' was all Miss Frobisher said, but Lily could tell the meeting had been a success because at the station bookstall Miss Frobisher bought two fashion magazines and a bar of chocolate. On the train, she broke the bar in two and handed one half to Lily. As the train clanked and swayed, Lily munched happily – she could save the biscuits after all – and they leafed through the magazines together, Miss Frobisher pointing out how even proper couturiers like Hardy Amies and Norman Hartnell were adapting to Utility requirements. She even unbent enough to eat a square of chocolate in front of Lily: the remainder she tucked away – presumably a treat for her little boy.

When they arrived back in Hinton, so late that the station was half deserted, Lily thanked her profusely.

Miss Frobisher simply smiled her measured smile. 'Look and learn, Lily. And don't be distracted. That's all I ask.'

On Wednesday, just a week after the excitement of the party and the dismay of Jim's telegram, Lily was seated at the kitchen table sorting silver paper for salvage. Gladys had suggested their usual half-day treat of a cheese roll at Peg's Pantry and a matinee, but Lily had had to disappoint her.

'I'm sorry,' she told her. 'I can't. I just want to be at home – in case.'

'*In case Jim comes back*,' was unspoken but understood – and dear Gladys did.

'I'd be the same,' she said, 'if I thought there was half a chance of Bill turning up off his ship. Some hope! But I still want to hear all about Monday – I know you haven't told me the half of it!'

'You will, I promise,' said Lily, but she knew it wouldn't mean much till she told Jim. He'd understand the significance of it all.

She'd almost finished with the bottle tops – some people hadn't even bothered to wash them, disgustingly – when she heard the latch on the back gate click. Could it be . . . ? She jumped up, bottle tops skittering to the floor, and skidded to the back door, flinging it wide. There he was. She'd have flung herself at him too but, pale and pinched, he looked as though the force would knock him flying. Instead she took his hand and led him inside.

'Sit down,' she ordered. 'You look all in. Tea and toast coming up.'

Lily was her mother's daughter, all right – and as always, Dora's prescription was right. As he ate, Jim revived enough to tell her what he'd left behind.

'A right lash-up,' he sighed. 'But it's the best I can do. Mrs Dawkins is coming in early, to help Mother wash and dress. She'll make breakfast for her and Dad, do some chores, make them a sandwich, then come in again at night to help Mother make some kind of meal—'

47

'Help her? I thought she could only move one side of her body?'

'Her leg's not too bad. It drags, and she won't use a stick, of course. She can sort of get around by holding on to things.'

'With her good arm, so how can she possibly do anything else?'

'She's got exercises to get the muscles in the bad one working again.'

'Is she doing them?'

Jim pulled a face.

'What do you think? Says she'll only get better by actually doing things.'

'Oh, Jim! She should! It's going to be very frustrating – the things she can't do. And if she overdoes it—'

'Do you think I haven't said? You try telling her she can't do things for herself in her own house. I'd rather argue with an angry rhino. Or you!'

Lily grinned – even a fed-up Jim could make her smile. Jim grinned too, but sadly. He took his plate and cup to the sink and spoke facing away from her.

'Look, Lily. I'll have to go back every weekend now. I'm not going to be much fun. If you want to call it a day – between us, I mean—'

'What?'

He came back to the table, sat down and took her hand.

'This isn't how I thought it would be. If you wanted me to – what's the phrase? – release you from your obligation—'

Lily burst out laughing.

'Hah! Nice try, but if you think you can get rid of me that easily, think again!'

'Really?'

'For goodness' sake, Jim! We're not in the nineteenth century! You'll still be here most of the time, anyway!'

'Yes, but we'll be at work all day, in the evenings there's ARP and fire-watching, and all these ideas I've still got to work up with Mr Simmonds—'

Jim had been given a project by Cedric Marlow. As a result, the staff were doing more for the war effort, and to compensate, there were sports and social clubs to boost morale. The next phase was to think up ways to bring in more custom.

'Jim!' Lily took his face in her hands and made him look at her. 'Stop it! We'll be fine.'

He leant forward and touched his lips lightly to hers.

'Thank you. Thank you. And I promise I'll try and put my folks out of my mind the days I am here. Because there's one good thing . . . Margaret says she'll keep an eye.'

'Margaret . . . ?'

'You know,' said Jim. 'Ted Povey's daughter from Broad Oak Farm.'

Broad Oak Farm had come up in conversation on the one occasion Lily had visited Bidbury.

'Oh, I remember. That's good of her.'

'It is. It's some reassurance anyway.'

There was no more to say. It was how things were, and how they'd stay till Jim's mother improved. The alternative – that she didn't – was something Lily didn't want to think about. For now, Jim would be here some of the time, and that was lots more than most people had of the person they cared for. She leant forward into his hug.

Later that afternoon, across town, Dora was settled in at Ivy's enjoying one of what Sid called their 'tea-and-tattle' sessions.

Dora had dispensed the news, such as it was, on Jim's mum; now it was Ivy's turn.

'There's some good news, anyway,' she announced. 'Les has been for an interview – and it looks like he's got that job at Marlow's!'

'Oh, I am pleased!' exclaimed Dora. 'That'll put a spring in his step!'

'Already has! Him and Beryl were straight out to the pictures last night, and a drink afterwards at the White Lion, if you please!'

The White Lion was Hinton's smartest hotel.

'That's good, isn't it?' Dora sipped her tea, wondering why Ivy sounded a little sour. 'He must be feeling better. He certainly looks it.'

'Oh, he is, twice the lad who came home. And in his oil tot about the job; all smiles! And her!' Ivy sniffed. 'Not home till gone eleven, if you please, and me up and down to the babby all evening, and only half an inch of gripe water in the bottle! My legs are killing me!'

'Ivy . . . ?'

Ivy inserted two thumbs in the top of her corset and loudly expelled some air.

'That's better,' she said. 'Oh, take no notice of me, Dora. I've got one on me today.'

'Come on. What's up?' Dora persisted.

'It's this business of Beryl's,' sighed Ivy. 'Taken over the entire front room, she has. Taken down my *Stag at Bay* and the sampler my mum made and instead we've got wedding dresses hanging from the picture rail. Display, she calls it! And to cap it all there's a notice in the front window, didn't you see? "Beryl's Brides – Wedding Dresses, Bridesmaid Dresses and Occasion Wear for Hire—"'

'Occasion Wear?'

Ivy took a long gulp of tea and clattered the cup back on the saucer.

'You know what Beryl's like for wearing a high hat. Says she's branching out. And you haven't heard the best. Then it says, "Enquire Within"! The liberty!'

'What about when she's out?' Dora frowned. 'Taking Bobby for some air, or to the clinic?'

51

'It's Muggins here that has to answer the door! And I'm to be polite, mark you, she's told me all the patter. Name and address, telephone if they've got it, all got to be written down in a little book!'

'She's very business-like, Ivy. You have to hand it to her.'

'Do I? I could show her the back of my hand sometimes.'

'You don't mean that,' chided Dora.

Despite their forceful personalities, Ivy and her daughter-in-law had got on surprisingly well when Les had been away, but with him coming home and Bobby getting bigger – he'd be crawling soon – the house was obviously starting to feel crowded. Ivy's husband, Eddie, was in the Merchant Navy, and rarely, if ever, at home, but there was Susan to think of as well, of course.

'It's all for the good, isn't it, Beryl's little enterprise?' Dora soothed. 'Les has got a job again, and the more she can make, the sooner they can get a place of their own. Then they'll be out from under your feet and she can do what she likes with her own picture rails and front windows.'

'And when will that be?' challenged Ivy. 'You seen many houses going begging round here? Or flats? Rooms, for that matter? They're all full of people that's been evacuated! There's folk come from Croydon and Mitcham and Hackney – lots from

Hackney, they're over the back from us. A right rowdy lot, they are, and all.'

'Well, yes, but when they've been bombed out and got nothing, and London's the mess it is, what's the authorities to do? They've got to go somewhere. We're lucky still to be under our own roof.'

Even in the worst of the Blitz, Hinton had got off pretty lightly – it had no major factories to bomb. They'd had their fair share of incendiaries, of 'tip and run', but serious damage had been limited to a few high explosives that had landed near a smallish factory making aircraft parts, and a hit on a row of houses and a pub. Of course the sirens still went off at night, and it was a toss-up whether to head for the miserable damp darkness of the Anderson in the neighbours' garden or to crouch under the kitchen table or under the stairs. Dora was too superstitious ever to stay in bed with the covers pulled up, like some people, or to let Lily or Jim do the same. Whatever you did, there was the straining of your ears for the planes, let alone the shrill whine of a bomb, the dropping off exhausted and jerking awake seconds later, the bone-weariness the next day . . . but for all that, they still had a home to call their own. Some of these displaced families had been bombed out not once but twice, buried alive, their houses wrecked then looted, even their poorest possessions gone.

But Ivy tossed her head and swirled the dregs of her tea.

'Perhaps we'd better change the subject,' she said. 'Heard from your Reg lately? And how's Sid getting on?'

September was usually one of Lily's favourite months with its gentle warmth, but not this year. She was still delightedly pinching herself at the thought of having a young man of her own, but he was hardly ever there. They managed an occasional walk or night at the pictures around work and ARP and fire-watching but it wasn't the same. He wasn't the same. It seemed to take all his time in Hinton for Jim to unwind and for Lily to draw him back to her after his weekends with his parents, and just when she had, it was time for him to head off again.

She knew it must be grim, his father uncom-plaining but his mother finding fault with everyone and everything. Alice had been as proud a house-keeper and as good a cook as Dora, so every slapdash dish, every non-dusted surface, every grimy window she must see as a reproach. And as Lily had predicted, trying to do things herself, with or without help, only meant that she got more frus-trated and cross. There was no improvement in her mobility. If anything, Jim reported glumly, her arm seemed weaker.

He was preoccupied at work, too. He'd talked

Cedric Marlow into a monthly staff newsletter, *The Marlow's Messenger,* and had produced it in his spare time. Except now he didn't have any.

'Hand it over to someone else,' Lily urged him. She wouldn't have minded having a go herself, but Jim was as stubborn as his mother, she was discovering.

'Not likely!' he said, though he did let her choose the 'Suggestion of the Month' (every employee to get a day off for their birthday – controversial stuff) and to write up the triumphant rounders match between Marlow's and Timothy Whites in which Lily had scored four rounders.

Then he was back to poring over plans of the store, deciding where best to site the escalators he was hoping for once the war was over, and wondering if he could use the Timothy Whites match to revive his campaign to shunt Marlow's into the twentieth century by dropping the apostrophe from the name.

Every Monday evening, though, Lily pinned on her brightest smile as she left the store in case Jim should have come back early and be waiting for her. She knew how important it was to present a cheerful face to your young man whatever you might be feeling – that's what Beryl's *Woman's Own* kept telling her, anyway. Jim tried just as hard, but how could he be cheerful when the situation at home was so gloomy?

Then one Monday, there was a boy with a big grin waving to her when she emerged from the staff entrance. Lily waved back automatically – but it wasn't Jim.

It was Frank Bryant.

Chapter 6

'What are you doing here?' she gasped as Frank took her elbow and steered her to one side so that the departing swell of Marlow's staff could get by.

'This is my patch, remember?'

'Yes, but . . . Miss Frobisher didn't say you'd been in today.'

The reps never came to the sales floor. They saw the buyers in the management offices or, if there was a problem, in the stockroom.

'Very good, Miss Marple!' Frank wagged his finger at her. 'I've been in Birmingham, at Rackhams and Lewis's, if you must know. I'll be calling on Miss Frobisher tomorrow.'

'Oh! Right. Do you want me to give her a message?'

Frank shook his head, laughing.

'No! Of course not! I want you to come and have something to eat with me.'

'What?'

'It's no good pretending. I know you eat. Someone had been at those ginger nuts in Mr Ward's office. It can't have been him because he's got sugar diabetes and he's not allowed. And Miss Fro doesn't look the type to smudge her lipstick. So, call me Sherlock, but I conclude, Miss Lily Collins, that it was you.'

He had some nerve. And talk about the gift of the gab!

'I can't just go off with you!' she protested. 'I don't know you!'

'So let's get to know each other over a nice cup of tea and . . . hmm, I could rather fancy a Welsh rarebit. At Lyons. See? All perfectly harmless and innocent. Not some backstreet dive, not a pub – where's the harm?'

Lily frowned. There was no harm, of course. The reality was that Jim wouldn't be back till midnight at the earliest, because he never was. Monday was Mrs Dawkins's day off, so he cooked the evening meal for his parents, ate with them and, though it was highly embarrassing for both of them, helped his mother into bed. Only then could he begin the long trek back to Hinton.

'Oh, come on,' wheedled Frank. 'Take pity on me. A new boy in town . . . all on my lonesome, you're not going to consign me to a miserable supper and a lonely evening reading a penny dreadful in my digs, are you?'

Lily relented.

'All right then. A cup of tea. A quick one.'

'Don't do me any favours, will you?' said Frank, but he was grinning. 'Good girl. Come on.'

Lyons wasn't one of Lily's regular haunts. She and Gladys favoured Peg's Pantry, which was cheaper – if nothing like as swish. As they queued for a table, Lily looked around – in part for the atmosphere, but mostly checking for anyone from Marlow's – she didn't particularly want to be seen with a stranger. Thankfully, there was no one she recognised. Then Frank spotted a couple leaving a table for two by the side wall and pointed it out to the hostess, which meant they could leapfrog two groups of four ahead of them.

'Got to have your eye to the main chance,' he said as they sat down. The waitress was still laying the new top cloth. Frank smoothed it and helped her to reposition the cruet and the little vase.

'While you're here,' he said to her, 'you may as well take our order. Save your legs, eh? Tea and Welsh rarebit for two, please.'

The elderly waitress gave him a 'Get on with you!' look but was clearly charmed as she scribbled the order on her pad. Lily was dumbfounded.

'When exactly did I say I was going to eat with you?' she demanded as the waitress walked away.

'Oh, don't start all that again,' said Frank, leaning forwards with his elbows on the table and chin on his hands. 'Tell me something interesting about yourself. I'm sure there's lots.'

'I'm not in the least interesting,' said Lily. 'Like everyone else, I get up, I go to work, I go home to my mum . . . '

'Right,' said Frank. 'Tell me about that, then.'

Exasperated but amused, Lily told him about Dora and Sid and Reg, and how long she'd been at Marlow's, and how she loved it.

'I can see you do.' Frank sat back, pulled down his cuffs and adjusted his cufflinks. They were oval with a blood-red stone. 'You're a bit in love with Miss Fro as well, aren't you? Still, Mr Ward thinks a lot of her, so as a role model, you could do far worse.'

'She's taught me a lot,' said Lily frostily, annoyed at being so transparent. 'And I've got lots more to learn yet. But what about you?' she probed. 'Why are you repping? Are you filling in time till you're called up?'

'That's a sore point,' said Frank. 'I tried to join up. Last year, the minute I could. But they didn't want me.'

'Why not?'

'Promise you won't laugh? You've got to promise.'

Lily nodded.

'Flat feet.'

Laugh? Trying not to, Lily spluttered.

'Oh dear!'

'Yes, yes, I know, it's like a music hall joke! They'd never been a problem, not once! I hadn't a clue till I went for the medical.'

Lily was about to say it had been the same with Jim and his eyesight, but somehow she didn't. Frank was carrying on anyway.

'They'll get desperate enough to take me in the end and I hope they do! My feet are fine – football, running, the lot; I was regional under-sixteen boxing champion!' He extended an arm. 'Want to feel my muscles?'

'No, thank you!'

'Your loss.' Frank was unperturbed. 'Ah, here's our tea. Are you going to be mother?'

And so it went on. Frank might say he'd rather be doing something different – he didn't see himself as a babywear rep all his life, he declared – but there was no doubt he was in the right job. He was so persuasive and talkative – cheeky, too. Lily had to laugh at some of his stories – he could have sold sand to the Arabs.

Try as he might, though, as they left Lyons, having insisted on paying for them both, he couldn't persuade Lily to join him for a drink.

'I don't mean some spit and sawdust pub,' he

coaxed. 'You're worth more than that. The White Lion's the place to go, isn't it, round here?'

The White Lion was utterly respectable, but Lily stood firm.

'No,' she said. 'I don't think so.'

'Oh, come on. Not even a Tizer? Or a cordial? Would that be demure and ladylike enough for you?'

'That's not the point. I'm late as it is. My mum will worry.'

'All right, you win,' Frank conceded. 'I'm not in the business of putting girls' mums' backs up. Not when I hope to see them again.'

This time Lily didn't falter.

'It's out of the question,' she said. 'I've got a boyfriend.'

'I'm sure you have,' said Frank easily. 'Someone as attractive as you. Away in the Forces, is he?'

'No, actually—'

Her reply was irrelevant. Frank was continuing, smoothly, smiling.

'Well, whatever. He's obviously not around at the moment, or not all the time, or you wouldn't have entertained the possibility of spending the evening with me.'

'I did try my best not to!'

'Well, I'm glad you changed your mind.' Suddenly he sounded sincere. 'Very glad. I am grateful, Lily. It's the bit of the job I don't like, the evenings on your own in some strange place.'

'Hinton's not that strange.'

'Well, it is if a girl can't go out for an innocent cup of tea and a bite of cheese on toast with a colleague, don't you think?'

A colleague . . . was that what he was? She supposed so. And maybe . . . there were things she'd learnt from him tonight, like making yourself think up good points in an item you don't think much of, and what he called 'linking the benefit to the customer'. There was a lot more she'd be interested to find out about his side of the business. Then perhaps she could really impress Miss Frobisher.

Frank could see her mind working and he let it work. He wasn't a salesman for nothing.

'I have to go,' she said finally. 'But . . . maybe. When you're next in town.'

'Attagirl! It won't be for a while, you heard what Mr Ward said. But think of me in the wilds of Wales with the autumn gales blowing.'

'Oh, I'm sure you'll survive.'

'You reckon?'

'Get some of those Army combinations that Ward and Keppler are making.'

Frank threw back his head and laughed.

'You've got a very strange image of me if you think I'd be seen dead in those!'

Lily blushed and turned her face away. She wasn't sure she wanted to have any image of Frank Bryant, let alone one of his muscled torso in his underwear.

'Bye, then,' she said. 'Thanks for my tea.'

'You're very welcome,' grinned Frank. He tipped an imaginary hat at her. 'Till next time, Miss Collins.'

Jim spooned the stew he'd made onto plates. His father had already shuffled to the table, but his mother was hovering behind him, watching critically as Jim pulled the scraps of meat apart and mashed down the vegetables into the gravy. Both his parents needed soft, mushy food; almost what you'd feed a baby. Jim thought, not for the first time, how dreadful it was – for everyone – when you had to parent your own parents.

'Go and sit down, Mother, I'll bring the plates through.'

With a grunt, his mother obeyed – she was more compliant at the end of the day, when she was tired. In the mornings she was querulous and demanding, and barely a month into the new regime, Mrs Dawkins had twice threatened to walk out. Jim didn't think she was serious – the money was too useful – but it was another pressure. He wondered if he dared to ask his mother to be a bit more patient with her.

The meal dragged. No one spoke, both his parents laboriously eating. Jim's father had never been a talkative man, and nowadays breathing was so much of an effort that he had no energy for using his voice.

Jim had one eye on the clock, wondering if he'd make the 9.35 from Worcester. If he struck lucky and thumbed a lift straight away, he might. Last week it had been nearly two when he'd got back to Hinton, and he'd had to be up at seven for work the next day. But, Army life, Navy life, certainly life in the RAF was far more demanding, night after night with little or no sleep, and no break in sight, which at least Jim got from Tuesday to Friday. Count your blessings. Like everyone, he'd become practised in making the best of things.

His mother put down her spoon and tugged at the napkin Jim had tied round her neck.

'Like a two-year-old!' she muttered, or something like it. Officially her speech had been unaffected; in reality it was indistinct because the whole side of her face now drooped.

'Come on, Mother, you've hardly touched it. It's got to be better than Mrs Dawkins's offerings!'

His mother gave a snort.

'You get with Margaret, we'd be rid of that slut!'

Jim winced. The stroke hadn't taken his mother's powers of speech, but it had certainly made them cruder. The old, proper, Alice would never have used a word like that.

'That's not going to happen,' he said firmly. 'Margaret's a very nice girl, but as I've told you, Mother, Lily and I are courting.'

His mother mumbled something under her breath

which Jim feared was 'hussy', then pushed her plate away as if it was something from the cesspit.

'Bed. Now.'

Jim sighed and stood up. At least once she was in bed, he could safely go. She still insisted on sleeping upstairs, painful as it was to see her haul herself up. His father slept on the settee, the stairs being too much for him. He was a much more compliant character, and Jim thanked his stars for that.

In her room, he settled Alice, looking away as he stripped off her dress and petticoat and handed her the flannel to wash herself, then quickly slipped her nightdress over her head before unrolling her stockings. She fell heavily back on the pillows, and Jim made sure she had a glass of water and her stick beside her to bang on the floor if she needed anything.

'I'll pop up again before I go,' he told her, as he always did.

With any luck she'd be asleep and he could avoid having to kiss the grooved forehead, see the distorted mouth. Alice turned her face away.

Downstairs, his father was already unwinding the first of the mufflers he wore, the start of his bedtime preparations. Jim smiled ruefully at him and got on with clearing the table. In the scullery he scraped the leftover stew into a dish and put a plate on top of it while a kettle boiled for the washing up. There was something infinitely depressing about the greasy plates and he shook more washing soda than was needed into the sink, plunging his hands in the too-hot water in penance.

He was drying his stinging hands when there was a tap on the back door. No one ever called at night, and Jim stiffened. Not long ago the navigator from a crashed German reconnaissance plane had knocked on a cottage door in a neighbouring village, tied up the occupants and then stole money, food and clothes before being captured.

'Who is it?'

'Only me!'

'Margaret?'

'I came to see how you were getting on,' she explained as he let her in. 'I thought if I put your mum to bed, you could get off a bit earlier.'

'You're very kind,' said Jim, moved. She was a nice girl, turning out like this after a long day of her own. 'But she's gone to bed early, thankfully.'

'Oh.'

'I'm leaving myself soon. I'll walk you back. You shouldn't be out on your own.'

'It's all right. Dad's going to pick me up, he's gone to an NFU meeting. So I'll stay anyway and sit with her. And – look – I wanted to give you this.'

From the pocket of her old mac she produced a brown paper parcel.

'For me?'

'It's nothing. Honestly.'

As she was talking, Jim was unwrapping the parcel. He brought out a dark blue knitted scarf, beautifully made with a tasselled fringe.

'That's . . . you shouldn't have!'

Margaret blushed.

'I noticed the one you had was a bit . . . tatty. In fact, your mum said it was a disgrace, and as she can't knit any more . . . '

Jim grimaced. There was some truth in his mother's opinion, but if she or Margaret thought the holes were wear and tear, they were wrong. That was just Lily's knitting.

'Now the nights are getting colder,' smiled Margaret, 'it'll be chilly on those station platforms. I don't like to think of you catching cold.'

'I'll wear it tonight,' said Jim. 'Thank you.'

He leant forward and gave her a peck on the cheek. She really was a very nice girl.

The journey back was no more lengthy or tedious than usual, but Jim's mood was low. From what she'd said at supper, he knew his mother would never give him and Lily her blessing, and as her only son, that mattered to him, especially now she'd been robbed of so many other things in life.

As he sat on the final train, with Margaret's scarf tucked against his chest, he felt complete despair. Even if Margaret had made it in all innocence, his mother had goaded her into it and made her a partner in her conspiracy. With every turn of the wheels, Jim worked himself up into a frenzy of guilt. He should never have accepted it. It was deeply disloyal to Lily. But it was very warm . . .

Exhausted, he dropped off to sleep, only woken by the train slamming against the buffers when they arrived in Hinton. Outside the station, he tore off the scarf as if it was choking him and stuffed it in the inside pocket of his coat. He extracted Lily's holey offering from his knapsack and wound it round his neck. He felt the difference straight away: it was spitting with rain and the night air pierced his throat, but he set off walking smartly and swung his arms to keep warm.

Chapter 7

'Who was that well-set-up fellow you swanned off with last night?' demanded Gladys the next morning as she and Lily put their things away in the staff cloakroom. Gladys had been deep in conversation with Brenda from Books on their way out the previous evening, but Lily had felt her friend's eyes on her like searchlights as she'd set off with Frank. She'd been expecting an interrogation.

'His name's Frank Bryant,' she answered evenly. 'He's the new Ward and Keppler rep. I met him – well, he introduced himself – when Miss Frobisher and I went over there.'

Gladys made saucer eyes, agog.

'You never said!'

'Yes, I did. I said the new rep had looked in.'

'You didn't say he wasn't much older than us! I thought you meant someone about fifty!'

'Well, if that was your assumption, I'm sorry.'

Lily spoke more tartly than she'd meant to. But why hadn't she said, actually?

'So what was he doing looking you up here?' persisted Gladys.

'He's on his rounds,' shrugged Lily. 'He's seeing Miss Frobisher today. And calling on Burrell's as well.'

'So what did he want with you?'

Honestly, some days Gladys could have given the Secret Intelligence Service a run for their money. Lily shoved her gas mask case so fiercely into the back of her locker that the whole row rattled.

'A bit of company, that's all. We went for a cup of tea at Lyons.'

'Company? Well!'

Gladys managed to invest the final 'Well!' with amazement, admiration, curiosity and a large pinch of scandal. Lily turned on her.

'There's no need to say it like that! He was on his own in a strange town. He simply wanted a friendly face.'

'Are you sure that's all he wanted?'

Enough was enough. Lily slammed the locker door.

'Gladys! Not long ago you were walking me up the aisle with Jim! Who do you think I am, Mata Hari? We just went for a cup of tea, I'm telling you.'

71

'He's very good-looking.'

'Is he?' said Lily offhandedly. 'Well, if he is, he knows it. He's certainly rather cocky. Not my type at all.'

'Even so. Are you seeing him again?'

'I doubt it! I expect he went on to the pub. Someone like him'll have hundreds of friends in Hinton by now.'

'Hmm!'

'There you go again! Why don't you fold your arms and put a scarf over your curlers? Then you can really act like some scandalised old biddy. I'm not going to keep it from Jim, if that's what you're thinking.'

'I'm surprised you went in the first place, that's all. What time did Jim get back?'

'I don't know,' said Lily firmly, beginning to move away. 'Middle of the night, I suppose. He'd already left for work when I got up this morning, but his things were downstairs. Now come on, or we'll be late on to the floor.'

Gladys followed obediently as they joined the throng making their way up the worn back stairs that the staff used, but still she wasn't letting things drop.

'Why did Jim have to get here so early this morning?' she asked, trotting up a step behind.

To the annoyance of the staff surging up behind them, Lily stopped dead on the half landing.

'He'd got stuff to do on *The Messenger*, all right?' she said. She was fed up about it herself: she'd hoped they'd walk to work together. 'He left me a note. Now you know as much as I do, OK?'

'I was only asking!'

Shocked by her friend's vehemence, Gladys went quiet, leaving Lily feeling guilty, needled and resentful. It was the closest she and Gladys had ever come to having words. And over something completely innocent! That's what was so unfair!

Jim was trying not to yawn as his boss, Mr Hooper, droned on about developments in the Utility Furniture Scheme. On another day Jim would have been alert to the possibility of a piece for the next *Messenger*, but after typing up the final article of this month's onto a stencil, then turning the handle of the mimeograph in the tiny cubby hole with the stink of printing ink, and all before his working day had begun, Jim never wanted to think about *The Messenger* again. He'd change his mind, he knew, and next month's edition would have a tantalising piece entitled 'Are You Sitting Comfortably?' but for now, all he wanted was to do was crawl into a corner and sleep till kingdom come.

What's more, his uncle was on his rounds.

Cedric Marlow toured the store every day. He greeted customers as they came in at the doors, then made his way through every department, speaking to staff, giving praise where it was due and with-holding it when it was not. Rumour had it he'd once written his name on a cosmetics counter that hadn't been properly dusted after a spill of face powder.

Worse still, today he had his son, Jim's cousin Robert, with him. Robert had been first floor super-visor before Peter Simmonds but had left to work in the Birmingham stockbroking firm owned, conven-iently, by his fiancée, Evelyn's, father. He still occasionally popped back 'for old times' sake' he said, but as he'd had no feel for shopkeeping, Jim always felt it was to keep an eye on his inheritance.

Jim watched out of the corner of his eye, but from Gramophones, Cedric and Robert proceeded to Radiograms so the fact that Jim hadn't had time to polish his shoes to the mirror brightness his uncle required might not be noticed.

As soon as Mr Hooper had finished his tale, Jim signalled to Lily, who'd been watching for a sign since she'd arrived on the sales floor. Armed with a boy's jacket she could claim to be brushing, she sidled over to where their departments butted up against one another.

'Thanks for your note. How are you?' she asked quietly.

She could see he looked drained, but that was standard after two days at home.

'Ever felt like your eyeballs have been rolled in sand and put back upside down?'

Lily tutted sympathetically.

'How were things?'

'The usual.'

'I'm sorry. You got *The Messenger* sorted?'

'Thankfully. It should be coming round with the afternoon post.'

'Well done. Early night for you tonight.'

There'd be no walk along the canal in the twilight, no scramble down the railway embankment for the clutch of blackberries she'd spotted on Sunday, no stroll to the cinema while the starlings circled.

'I've got ARP.'

'Oh, Jim . . . can't you get out of it?'

'I can't let them down. I'm still paying back the nights I missed when Mother was first taken ill.'

He was so conscientious, drat him! But would she have wanted him any different? Not really.

'If you say so,' she conceded. 'Look out, Mr Marlow and Robert are heading this way. We'd better get back. I'll see you at half five.'

At least they could walk home together.

There'd been rain all afternoon, or so various damp customers told Lily, but it was mercifully dry when at last the long day was over and Lily and Jim could step into the street. Jim wound Lily's scarf round his neck.

'That's a bit of luck, anyway,' said Lily, determined to be cheerful. She tucked her arm through his.

'Another rib on my umbrella broke at the weekend. I'll have to see if I can get it mended, though I don't hold out much hope.'

Jim gave a grunt of acknowledgement and Lily fell silent. She'd looked forward so much to seeing him, his lanky frame and his thoughtful face, but he was obviously tired out, and she couldn't think of much to say. She didn't think he'd want to hear about the only thing that had happened at work in his absence, a delivery of shampoo that had caused such a stampede in Toiletries that the commissionaire had had to come inside to keep order.

'Nothing much to report at home,' she said as they walked. 'Not a peep from Sid or Reg.'

Another grunt.

'Monty doesn't seem to be making much difference in North Africa yet. That push to retake Tobruk came to nothing.'

Silence.

Of course, there was one other thing that had happened at work, or through work, but somehow Lily didn't feel the time was right to mention her encounter with Frank.

They passed a jeweller's, a tobacconist's, a grocer's. The shopkeeper was pulling down the blinds and it obviously reminded Jim of something.

'Drat. There was some butter I meant to bring back.'

When she'd been well, Alice had always sent Jim back from the country laden with largesse – jams and jellies, rabbits, pigeons, cream. That was another thing that had disappeared at a stroke, so to speak.

'Never mind,' said Lily reassuringly. 'We'll live!'

They stopped at the corner to cross the road into the park and Lily noticed a fresh poster on a hoarding. 'Is Your Journey Really Necessary?' it barked. It gave her an idea.

'Look, Jim. Why don't I come with you next time?' she suggested. 'I could book the Monday off. I'd like to—'

'No,' he said abruptly, starting to cross. 'It wouldn't work.'

'Why not?' Lily hurried to keep up. 'I'm sure there's something I could do for your mum – and take the pressure off you. Anything. Clean the windows, scrub the floor, pick the apples, they must be past ready—'

'No, Lily.'

They were inside the park now – or rather, the allotments it had been turned into – and he stopped to face her, unlinking their arms. A gust of wind shook the chestnut tree above them and a clutch of conkers thudded to the ground. Their cases looked, Lily thought, like naval mines.

'I'm sorry,' he went on. 'It's not a good idea. I . . . I don't think it would help.'

'Really? Why not?'

Jim looked as if he was about to say something,

then he turned his face away. Lily felt something boiling up inside her, something she'd felt for ages.

'Your mum doesn't like me, does she?'

Jim turned back to face her.

'It's not that—'

She'd started now, so she might as well spit it out.

'I think it is. I've been to your home precisely once, and that was a year ago. I don't think I did anything to offend her – I don't see how I could have – but I've never been asked back.'

Jim lifted his shoulders.

'She wouldn't want you to see her like she is.'

'But she doesn't mind Margaret seeing her?'

Where had that come from? Lily hadn't thought about Margaret Povey since Jim had mentioned her weeks ago!

He looked startled.

'Margaret?'

Suddenly he had a hunted look and Lily scented blood.

'Did you see her?' she asked. 'Did you see her when you were home?'

'Yes, I did as a matter of fact.'

He sounded almost shifty. Lily went in for the kill.

'So she's welcome, and I'm not.'

'Lily, she called round. I didn't invite her.'

'Oh, that makes all the difference!'

'You know she offered to keep an eye on my parents.'

'Yes, when you weren't there! She'd got no business being there when you are!'

'What? Now you're being ridiculous! What am I supposed to do, put her under curfew?'

'Well? What's the answer? What was she doing, coming round then?'

'You answer me! I'm not going to tell her when she can and can't call in, all out of the goodness of her heart!'

'Oh, I get it! I'd been seeing her in the dairy, in a white coat and a hairnet. But she's Saint Margaret in a white robe and a halo! No wonder I don't measure up! No wonder you don't want me to come!'

'Lily— Lily, please.' Jim reached out and touched her arm. 'Why are we arguing? I don't want to. You coming home with me or not has got nothing to do with Margaret. It's just . . . trust me . . . it's better if you don't get involved.'

Trust him. She always had, implicitly. But . . .

She looked at him and his eyes held hers, pleading. He moved as if to reach out and hug her but she flinched away. Silly, maybe, stubborn, certainly, but she couldn't let him touch her, not while she felt like this.

Suddenly it began to rain; big, fat drops that spattered on the leaves. It was a shock, but it was a relief. Now, thought Lily, they'd have to shelter under the tree and Jim would put his arms round her and tuck her inside his coat and tell her she was being silly, which she was, and everything would be all right again.

'Damn,' he said. 'I'll have to run for it.'

'What?'

'ARP. I can't be late.' Jim spread his hands. 'I'm sorry, I have to go.'

'Fine. Of course you must,' she said stiffly. 'Off you go.'

She stretched her mouth into a shape that was like a smile but wasn't. Jim gave another hopeless little lift of his hands. He made no attempt to kiss her or even to touch her. Sadly she watched him lope off, his hair getting plastered to his head.

She hadn't told him about Frank Bryant. And something told her she wouldn't, now.

Chapter 8

Splashing her wet way home through the park, cold and umbrella-less, her jacket held over her head, Lily felt remorse for the second time that day. If Margaret's presence gave Jim one less thing to worry about, she should have been glad. It was mean and childish to pick fights when he was already at the end of his tether.

'Never let the sun go down on a quarrel' wasn't just one of Dora's favourite sayings, it was the advice regularly dished out by the agony aunts in women's magazines. Beryl and Ivy read *Woman* and *Woman's Own* from cover to cover, then passed them on, though Dora only ever looked at the recipes and the knitting patterns. She didn't need an agony aunt's advice, thank you very much!

Joanna Toye

Lily didn't need it either. She knew her instinct was right, and Jim's mum had taken against her, but there was no point in rubbing it in. He was obviously not happy about it either, and as for Margaret Povey – well, she did, after all, live close by, and she had promised to look in on his parents, look after them, even . . .

By the time she got to the corner of Brook Street, she'd composed the note she was going to put on his pillow. But when she got in, he'd beaten her to an apology. His note was on hers.

'I'm sorry,' he'd written. 'I hate us arguing – it's just I'm so dog tired. I'll make it up to you. Flicks tomorrow night?' It was signed 'J', with two kisses.

So next night, they went to the pictures. *In Which We Serve* was supposed to be uplifting, with its rallying cry at the end, but Lily found it depressing, and it didn't seem to do much to lift Jim's spirits either. She had a sneaking feeling he hadn't been watching the film anyway, or even been in the cinema with her, despite idly stroking her fingers throughout. He'd been thinking about all the things he had to do that weren't getting done because he was sitting there with her.

But then, next day when she got back from work, like a shaft of brilliance into this drab time, came Sid, or at least, a letter!

If Lily had been going to admit to anyone how fed up she was about her and Jim's situation – and how guilty she felt about feeling that way – it would have been her favourite brother. She hadn't, though, keeping her letters determinedly cheery. But knowing her like he did, Sid hadn't been fooled.

Hello Sis, he wrote.

Well done for keeping your chin up, but I can tell the business with Jim and his mum is getting you down. But never fear, Dr Sid is here! He recommends a change of scene. They're sending me on a two-week course – in Bootle, can you believe! Why not come and see me on the middle Sunday? I could come into Liverpool and meet you at the station. How about it?

Lots of love,
Sid xxx

When she'd read it, it was all Lily could do not to fall on her knees right there on the kitchen floor and shout 'Hallelujah!' If Jim didn't want her to go to Bidbury with him at the weekend, then why shouldn't she have her own day out? On the way to work the next day, she went to the station and checked the trains, then wrote back to Sid. If it hadn't been a waste of paper she'd simply have written in capital letters YES PLEASE! But instead she told him it was a brilliant idea and, all being well, the time she reckoned she could arrive into Lime Street station.

Sid checked for trains and buses at his end too and his next letter confirmed the date. They were on!

After her recent journey with Miss Frobisher, Lily felt almost confident as she set off on Sunday morning. Jim had encouraged her to go, and though Dora had obviously been disappointed that Sid wasn't coming home, she'd guessed his offer to Lily was to cheer her up and contented herself with using her personal sugar ration for the week to make him a plum cake.

It was all going far too well, so Lily wasn't surprised when she learnt the train she'd planned to get had been commandeered for troop movements. All she had to do now was make sure she got a place on the replacement train, supposedly due in half an hour. A woman next to her grumbled, but Lily didn't care. As long as she got there sometime today . . .

When the train finally pulled in after fifty minutes, it was packed and the resulting journey so uncomfortable it could have been deliberately designed to make people decide their journey was distinctly unnecessary. But as far as Lily was concerned, the answer was definite and defiant – yes it was!

She'd arranged to meet Sid by the station bookstall, but when she approached the ticket barrier, head still booming and her body vibrating from the train, she could see him, tall, and broad-shouldered, with hair the same blond as hers, waiting for her there. He waved and grinned and tapped his watch as if to say, 'About time!' and Lily waved happily back. Then, as she got to the barrier, she saw his face up close.

Before she could speak, Sid had her in his usual bear hug, but Lily wriggled out of it.

'What happened?' she demanded. 'I thought you weren't on active service! What is this course you're on?'

Sid was sporting a nasty gash on the bridge of his nose, another above his eyebrow, and the beginnings of a proper shiner of a black eye. And was that a bruise on his jaw?

'Advanced Accounting Practice,' he grimaced. 'It's amazing the damage an inky pellet and a ruler can do.'

'Sid,' admonished Lily. 'I'm not that daft. You haven't . . . you haven't been in a fight?'

'Let's get something to eat,' Sid replied. 'Then I'll tell you.'

They went to the Kardomah Café on Church Street. Behind the taped-up plate glass, some of their famous cakes were on display – in plaster of Paris and cardboard. The waitress gave Sid's injuries a hard stare, but he smiled winningly and shrugged as if to say 'war wounds', and since the other customers included a soldier with his face scored with vivid scars and another with a stump for a hand, Sid was hardly the worst sight in the place. Only Lily knew that he couldn't have got his injuries from flying shrapnel or being flung across a deck by a depth charge – and not from an inky pellet flipped by a fellow clerk, either.

Sid demanded the news from home, so she told him quickly, such as it was, while they were served with a pot of tea and – at Sid's insistence – sandwiches *and* cakes. As Lily went to pour the tea, she asked what she really wanted to know.

'So . . . tell me how you ended up looking as if you'd done five rounds with . . . ' Lily faltered. Sport was not her specialist subject, violent sports in particular. 'I don't know. Name me a boxer.'

'Come on, Lil. Can't you guess?'

Lily paused, the teapot hovering. She put it down carefully.

Good-looking and full of fun, Sid had always had much more success with girls than the quieter, more cautious Reg, so Lily had been stunned when Sid had confided in her that he wasn't attracted to girls at all. It was men he had feelings for. At first Lily had been disbelieving, devastated, confused – all of those things at once. She'd gone back over all the years they'd grown up together, wondering if she should have seen some sign. But of course she hadn't. That was the point. Men like Sid had to hide it. It was against the law.

Bit by bit she'd realised that it didn't change anything: Sid was still the same person, still the same adored brother, who teased her unmercifully, but who'd always waited for her when she'd trailed behind him and Reg as a child and had even sometimes let her win at cards.

Now, Lily feared what had happened to Sid's face was something she'd been dreading. There were plenty around who saw men like him as abnormal, unnatural, perverted – sub-human even. And who didn't wait for the law to punish such 'perversion' – they exacted their own rough justice.

'Oh, Sid,' she said. 'Because of you being . . . ?'

Sid lifted his shoulders but winced as if they hurt him.

'I've been waiting for it to happen. The irony is, it wasn't down the docks, or in some rough pub. It wasn't even on Queen Square here – that's where, well, men like me go. I'd been to the cinema. In Bootle. On my own!'

'And?'

'Pour that tea and I'll tell you.'

Lily did as she was told. Sid lit up a cigarette, blew the smoke towards the intricate plasterwork ceiling, and began.

'It was last night. A filthy night as well. I come out of the cinema, turn my coat collar up, and that's enough to set off these two blokes that are lounging about. Said I did it like a pansy.'

Lily flinched.

'That's the least of it. "Pansy", "Fairy", "Faggot",

"Queer". Look, I'm sorry, Lil, but you have to face it.'

Lily nodded. They were just such horrible words, and so unfair. Sid rested his cigarette on the ashtray and took a sandwich.

'Come on, eat up!'

Lily didn't feel like eating at all, listening to Sid, but she took a sandwich and took a bite. Once she had, she realised how hungry she was. Sid was chewing carefully; that bruise was coming out.

'So I say nothing and walk off, but I don't know where I'm going, and once I got off the main road, well, I could have been anywhere. I'm walking fast, just to get away, I look behind, they've gone. Great, so I double back to get to the main street again, and they pop out from an alleyway. Well, I'll spare you the rest. But I put up a good fight! Those Charles Atlas exercises I do morning and night have paid off!'

Lily shook her head. How he could joke about a thing like this?

'So how did you get out of it? Did you see them off?'

'I'd like to say I did . . . ' Sid admitted. 'But in a bit of luck a copper came by, and they scarpered. Shouting the odds about what I was, but the copper either didn't hear, or didn't take any notice. Asked *me* if I wanted to make a complaint! As if! I told him I was OK and he sent me on my way.'

'Oh, Sid . . . '

'No, I'm almost glad it's happened.' Sid took up his cigarette again and looked at it before taking another long draw on it. 'It's been like waiting for a shoe to drop.'

'It doesn't mean it won't happen again.'

'It means I'll be even more on my guard. This desk job's turned me soft.'

Lily put out her hand and covered his. His knuckles were swollen.

'What are you going to say to them on your course? You'll be in trouble, won't you? For getting in a fight? And you can't tell them the truth.'

'I can, Lil. I'm going to tell it like it was, that two blokes set on me for no good reason. That is the truth.'

He was right. There was no reason at all why Sid should be persecuted, just because he was different, and had been born that way. And despite his poor face, despite the shock it had obviously given him – his hand, lighting his cigarette, had been shaking, he needn't think she hadn't noticed – Lily had never been more proud of him.

They managed to talk about other things after that, and when Sid had paid the bill, he took her down to the Mersey where the seagulls wheeled and tumbled around the equally tumbled façade of the once-elegant Custom House, bombed in the Blitz. But the air was fresh and salty, and Lily could feel the cobwebs blowing away.

Sid walked her back to the station in good time for her train. Under the huge blacked-out glass roof, he hugged her again and she touched his sore face.

'You could do with some steak on that eye,' she told him.

'Huh!' he grinned, then winced again. 'I'll be lucky. A rissole, maybe. But hey, we've hardly mentioned you and Jim, and that was the whole reason I asked you up here.'

'Oh, there's nothing to say, really,' said Lily.

Their situation paled into insignificance beside what Sid had been through – and would continue to go through for the rest of his life.

'You were right,' she went on. 'Just getting away for a bit has put it in better perspective. I'm lucky he's still in Hinton at all, and not in the Forces. Lucky he's alive, not dead, lucky that we all are. And I do know that.'

'That's my girl,' said Sid. 'And he's treating you right when he is around, is he? Or he'll have me to answer to. Don't forget I've had some practice with my fists lately!'

'He is,' smiled Lily. 'I'm fine, truly. We're fine.'

Chapter 9

'Hello? Excuse me? Could I get a cup of tea?'

Dora was down on her knees with a cloth, mopping where the urn dripped onto the floor. She looked up to see a face peering over the counter of the tea bar.

'I'm sorry.' She got to her feet, wiping her hands on her WVS overall. 'Of course you can.'

'I wasn't sure there was anyone here,' the man said. 'Thought it was a phantom tea bar.'

Dora lifted the heavy pot and began to pour. His accent was strange, like an American, but softer. One of the Canadians, then, stationed at the big house a few miles outside the town. From the pips on his tunic, an officer. A major, if she wasn't mistaken.

'There's only me till the afternoon relief gets here,' she explained. 'The other helper's had to take her dog to the vet.'

At the mention of the word 'dog' there was a sudden yelp from the vicinity of the man's feet. He looked down.

'Quiet, Buddy!'

'You've got a dog?'

Dora pushed his cup towards him.

'Trust me, ma'am, I'm no ventriloquist. Look, I've a few errands to run in town. If it wouldn't be too much trouble . . . any chance he could have a drink of water?'

They couldn't help themselves, could they, these Americans and Canadians, thought Dora. Never backwards in coming forwards. Still . . .

'Well, let's see . . . ' she cast around. There was an old veg dish they used for wet tea leaves. If she put those in the pail . . . 'Just a minute.'

'I'd be most grateful, ma'am. And Buddy would be too.'

Tea leaves dispensed with, Dora passed him the dish filled with water, and he bent to place it on the ground. Enthusiastic lapping sounds told her it had been well received and, intrigued despite herself, she leant out under the flap and over the little ledge where people could rest their cups. A half-grown cocker spaniel was slurping away, giving his curly ears a dip in the process. Dora watched, amused.

'How do you come to have a dog, if you don't mind me asking?'

'Ah.' He sipped his tea. 'If you hadn't guessed, I'm with the forces stationed up at Nettleford Manor.'

His light, bouncy way of talking made it sound like a question, even though it wasn't. His pronunciation, too, was different. The locals called it 'Nettlef'd'. The way he said it was 'Neddle-ford', with the emphasis on the 'ford'. Dora couldn't help another smile. Hadn't some clever writer or other said something about America and Britain being two countries divided by a common language?

'Sorry, that's not really an answer, is it?' He was smiling now. 'There's a farm on the estate.' He said it 'ess-state' of course. 'One of the farm dogs had pups, and somehow this little guy found his way onto our firing range. Lucky we weren't practising on moving targets that day, but we gave him a scare and . . . I guess I felt sorry for him. There's something about those eyes.'

The dog looked up at that moment, his eyes the sort of melting chocolate that in pre-war days Dora might have poured over a cake. His owner had nice eyes too, a very pale blue, and sandy hair, thinning and brushed back. She wondered what he saw, and was pleased she'd washed her hair – still brown, hardly any grey, amazingly – and put on a bit of powder before leaving home. Shocked at herself for even thinking it, she straightened up and, to give herself something to do, began pouring milk into cups. She couldn't think of anything more to say, but he carried on regardless.

'I'm not the only one. Your Guy Gibson, he's got a dog.'

Guy Gibson, one of the RAF's ace pilots, had a Labrador that he supposedly took with him on training flights.

Dora conceded.

'True. Even so, your Buddy's fallen on all four paws with you.'

She was thinking of the rations – there'd be no living on bread crusts and rats for Buddy as there would have been on the farm.

'And he knows it, don't you?' The dog gave a little whine which, if you were fanciful, you could almost take for agreement. 'All done, boy?'

This time the dog didn't answer. His owner stooped to retrieve the dish and handed it back, then drank down his tea.

'I must be getting along.' He laid sixpence on the counter and replaced his hat. 'Thanks very much, ma'am. Just what I – we – needed.'

Dora pushed the coin back towards him.

'You don't need . . . that's too much—'

But he was gone, sucked into the crowd that had just disembarked from a train and was surging towards her.

'Two teas, please.'

'Tea, no milk. Can you make it quick, I've got a connection in five minutes?'

'No biscuits?'

'Any sugar?'

Dora pushed the sixpence to one side.

'One at a time! I'm on my own here!'

Her day resumed.

She didn't get away from the tea bar till nearly five: the volunteer taking over from her had been delayed by a visit from the water board about a pipe that had finally ruptured after being damaged by one of last year's bombs.

Now Dora needed to get home. She'd boiled up some cow heels before she'd left and wanted to thicken the soup into something a bit more appetising, which would do for her and Lily with a few slices of the National Loaf that everyone moaned about so much. Dora didn't mind it, though brown flour, which was all you could get now, was hopeless for baking. Good job she'd laid in a stock of white before it had disappeared, otherwise there'd have been no cake for Sid . . . Thinking with satisfaction about that, and wondering how Lily had got on, she was miles away – practically in Liverpool, which had had its own Blitz, of course – there'd been that picture in the paper of Lewis's with all its windows blown out . . .

She was so far away from the streets of Hinton that when the siren began blaring she thought at first she'd conjured it up to go with the images she was seeing in her mind. But suddenly people around her were stock-still and staring, or running in panic, and she was torn between the two. It was months since they'd had an air raid warning, longer still since an actual raid – how could it be happening? And why? No one had thought the German planes would come so far inland again; they'd been concentrating on the south east and the coast.

She stood transfixed, occasionally buffeted along by people heading for the shelter. A policeman appeared, blowing his whistle and urging people to take cover; a warden approaching from the other direction shouted the same. But Dora wasn't keen to be trapped in a public shelter with Lily either stuck on a train, or back home and worrying about her. She needed to get home. She was nearly halfway there, after all. She began to hurry, but she was hurrying too much. The next thing she knew, she'd tripped on a loose slab and the pavement was coming up to meet her. It had already met her knee and was about to meet her outstretched hand when—

'Hey, careful!'

An arm shot out to grab her and Dora felt herself being hauled upwards until the same strong arm was pressing her against the khaki serge of a uniform tunic. Gasping, both from the shock of her stumble and her equally sudden rescue, she blinked and swallowed.

'Are you OK?'

A voice she recognised. It was the major from the tea bar – she'd seen the pips on his tunic close to now – rather too close.

Dora nodded weakly. She felt a bit giddy. And sick.

The arm's pressure lessened and she stepped back unsteadily. He didn't let go, though – he held her by her upper arms and scrutinised her carefully up and down.

'That knee doesn't look too hot.'

Dora looked down. She had a nasty graze, but even worse, 'My stocking!'

He laughed. 'Women! You nearly go flying and that's all you worry about!'

Indignation brought Dora back to herself. She spoke without thinking who she was speaking to, or that she barely knew him.

'It's all very well for you men! No one sees a darned sock!'

Mind you, as if he'd ever darned a sock in his life, the Yanks and Canadians were so well kitted out he could probably afford to throw his holey socks away!

He looked as if he was about to defend himself but the policeman jostled past, shouting over the sirens.

'No time for chatting! Hurry along, you too, sir. Get to the shelter!'

If she'd been that sort of person, Dora could have

cursed: it would have to be the shelter now. Her knee was throbbing; she wouldn't be able to walk fast enough to be sure of getting home safely. But apart from gently releasing his grip on her arms, the major didn't move.

'Take no notice,' he said.

The sirens were still wailing but he seemed completely oblivious.

'Pardon?'

'It's fine. It's a false alarm.'

'How do you know?'

Was he privy to some military intelligence?

'Buddy told me.'

'Your dog?'

In reply, he dipped his head to where the dog was sitting calmly in a newsagent's doorway, the shop the major must have come out of in time to save her as she fell.

'You're telling me he's got a sixth sense?'

'No, he's got very acute hearing. He can hear the planes.'

'Over the sirens?'

'Before they start. He can sense some kind of change in the air.'

Dora looked sceptical. Dogs that could scent trouble, yes, but dogs that could hear trouble? Still Buddy didn't move but sat there happily panting. He almost looked as if he was smiling. As well he might be, because as suddenly as they'd started, the sirens faded and were replaced by the long steady drone of the all clear.

'See?' the major grinned. 'We can cut the shelter, but look, you've had a shock. There's a pub back there. Let me buy you a drink.'

'Oh no! No, thank you!'

'Teetotal?'

'It's not that. I have to get back. My— my family will be expecting me.'

It wasn't quite true; there'd most likely be no one there, but now she was over the initial shock, Dora was flustered for a different reason. She didn't know the man; she didn't even know his name, but she'd been fleetingly crushed against his chest. And in the street! With a torn stocking and her hair all mussed up! If anyone passing hadn't seen her fall, what must they have thought! To cover it, she blushed and looked down at her knee. She could already see the swelling. He looked too.

'Well . . . if you insist. I'm afraid I can't offer to drive you, or even escort you. I'm being picked up back in town.'

'Oh, I wouldn't expect . . . ' Dora began. The very idea! The neighbours'd love that!

He patted his pockets.

'Take my handkerchief. For a bandage.'

She wasn't having that, either.

'You've done more than enough! I could have broken my wrist! I'll bathe my knee when I get in and put something on for the swelling.'

Focus on the practical. Take back control. Forget

that he put his head on one side when he was posing one of his statements-that-sounded-like-questions or that she was still aware of the imprint of his fingers on her arms. He smiled again. He did a lot of smiling.

'Ah, the bulldog British spirit we're always hearing about. "That's the ticket" – isn't that what you say?'

She wanted to tell him that the British spirit was a case of needs must but was sure he'd simply file that away as another example of 'stiff upper lip' or whatever else he and his men had been told to expect from their hosts in this strange, proud, stubborn country. Instead she held out her hand, formally.

'Thank you for stopping it being any worse,' she said. 'I'm most grateful.'

He shook her hand solemnly. Why did she get the impression he was laughing inside?

'If we're doing this properly,' he said, 'we can't part without an introduction. My name's Hugh – Hugh Anderson.'

'Dora Collins.'

'Pleased to meet you, Dora.'

Buddy gave a whine. Dora was grateful; she didn't know what to reply. 'And you,' seemed a bit . . . bold? Hugh turned to the dog.

'He's feeling left out,' he grinned. 'C'me here, boy.'

Buddy trotted over.

'Sit!' commanded Hugh. 'Now shake hands.'

The dog lifted his paw and Dora – unable to believe she was doing this – meekly bent and shook it.

'Honour satisfied,' Hugh concluded. 'All round.'

The all clear had died away; the street was filling up again.

'I really must be going,' she said.

He touched his forehead in salute.

'Take care now,' he smiled.

Chapter 10

When Lily got in, Dora told her about the air raid that wasn't, but she didn't say anything else about her afternoon. Lily was full of her day in Liverpool anyway and Dora was glad. Major Anderson – Hugh, if she could learn to think of him like that, instead of 'the Canadian' – Hugh's quick thinking had stopped the graze from being anything more than superficial, but a nice bruise was forming. Dora had dabbed it with witch hazel, then changed her skirt to a longer one to cover it. She'd lived her whole life not drawing attention to herself, putting the family first, and that wasn't about to change now. In any case, she wanted to know all about Sid.

On Lily's side, it wasn't the first time she'd had to

conceal something Sid had told her from her mum. She didn't like it, but Sid didn't want Dora to know about his tendencies. There'd come a time, he said, when he might have to confess – because that's what it felt like – but that time wasn't now, when they all had so much else to think about. 'What the eye doesn't see, the heart doesn't grieve over' as Dora herself might have said.

So Lily told her mum about the Kardomah and their walk down to the river. She told her Sid was doing fine on his course and had stopped fretting about not being on active service: she didn't add that Sid was seeing plenty of action of his own.

Later, in bed, Dora allowed herself a secret smile as she thought back over her afternoon. She wondered what Lily would say if she told her she'd been picked up by a strange man in the street – she wouldn't have to say it was literally – and had been held against his chest. And she couldn't ignore the little pulse that began to beat because of the sensation of being held by a man again after all this time.

September slid into October. Jim came and went to the countryside, where he said the fieldfares had arrived. In Hinton, the swallows had long gone but there were flocks of starlings – the war couldn't touch the birds, thought Lily, which was cheering at least. The nights were drawing in, though: a lower sun than before played on the bronze leaves of the beech trees and the citrus colours of the birch.

Sid, back in Scotland, wrote and told Lily how much he'd enjoyed seeing her. To Dora he wrote that he was the most popular bloke on the course thanks to her cake. Naturally, he didn't mention his battered face – or the reaction of his course tutor – to either of them.

When he was in Hinton, Jim was as busy as ever with work, his war work, *The Messenger,* the accounts for the Fowl Club he'd set up on the store's roof and the weekly pow-wows with Peter Simmonds. He was fed up because Cedric Marlow had scotched their latest proposal for enticing in the customers.

'It was such a great idea,' Jim told Lily as they pulled down the runner bean wigwam one Wednesday afternoon; at least they had that time together. 'Simmonds was this close to getting Pierre and Lavelle.'

They weren't quite Fred and Ginger, but Monsieur Pierre and Miss Doris Lavelle were famous and popular Latin American dancers.

'And Mr Simmonds suggested it? I wouldn't have thought the rumba was his sort of thing!'

It didn't seem a very likely interest for a former Army PT instructor.

'Anything that keeps people fit, he admires. And we'd got it all worked out,' said Jim bitterly. 'Clear a space in Model Gowns and Exclusives – there's not much in there anyway – and tie it in with a promotion on Wireless and Gramophone. But it's all gone for nothing.'

'They're not coming?'

'They needed a fee, and expenses, obviously, to come from London, but Uncle Cedric, honestly, these days he's tighter than the seal on a submarine door.' Jim slashed at the last of the runners. 'Whatever happened to "speculate to accumulate"? Think of the customers it would have brought in! And the publicity!'

'Well, yes. Not to mention the glamour!'

Lily told Gladys about it the next day when they found themselves on the way to Goods Inward at the same time, chasing long-awaited deliveries.

Gladys's shoulders sagged, as Lily had known they would.

'That would have been so lovely!' she exclaimed. 'Just what we could do with!'

'I know,' Lily agreed. 'But it's not going to happen. You'll have to get your fix of romance at the cinema, I'm afraid.' Talking of romance, she asked, 'Any news of Bill?'

Gladys shook her head. 'Nothing. It's been five weeks now.'

As far as they knew, Bill's ship was still escorting merchant convoys – possibly even Eddie Bulpitt's ship. Thinking about Eddie Bulpitt reminded Lily of Beryl – more guilt.

'I feel bad, not going round so much,' she confessed, as they pushed through the swing doors by the loading bay. 'But I have to make the most of Jim when he's here.'

'Beryl understands,' Gladys reassured her. 'I

popped round a few days back. She's busy with her wedding dresses anyway. She's got a new one that she reckons might do for me! The style anyway, it's not my size.'

'Oh, yes?'

'I'll see it on Saturday. I'm babysitting. Beryl says she and Les could do with a night out.'

'Where are you and Beryl going?' Gladys asked, pulling on her gloves as she and Les left the staff entrance of the store at closing time on Saturday.

Les gave his cheeky chappy grin.

'Down the Palais,' he said. 'Beryl's been itching to get her dancing shoes on ever since I came home. And I've got my old chalk stripe out of mothballs. Fits me again now; it was hanging off me when I first got back!'

'Very nice.' Gladys tried to keep the envy out of her voice. She checked her bag to make sure she had her writing pad and pen with her for yet another letter to Bill once Bobby and Susan were settled. It was important to keep writing, she knew, even if you didn't hear back for months.

'I'm a bit rusty, mind.' Les executed a nifty two-step on the pavement, then grabbed a startled Gladys and waltzed her round. 'Better practise!'

Gladys shrieked and a passing bus hooted as they nearly fell off the kerb.

'Idiot! You'll get us killed!'

'No danger!' Les tipped her backwards over one arm and doffed his cap with the other. 'Who needs Pierre and Lavelle?'

Gladys thumped him on the arm as he returned her to the vertical, but she was grinning. It was so nice to have Les back, and back to his usual self.

He was full of his new job and the tricks the lads got up to in the warehouse, the dartboard they'd made out of an old packing case and the bush telegraph that worked when the Foreman was on the prowl, so it could be hidden away. He was explaining the finer points of gin rummy as they turned the corner into Alma Terrace, when the door to number twenty-six opened and Beryl ran towards them, her face white and streaked with tears.

'Les! Thank God you're here!'

'Beryl? What is it? Is it the babby?'

'No!' Beryl was shaking, Gladys could see. 'It's Susan!'

Les hustled Beryl towards the open front door.

'Is she took bad? Let's get inside, see what's going on.'

'She's not there!' wept Beryl. 'That's the point! She's gone and I don't know where she is!'

Inside Beryl stuttered out the sorry tale. Ivy had left for her cleaning job at half five as usual. Bobby was in the playpen, safe, and Susan was at the table, colouring, with a milky tea and a slice, when the doorbell had rung. Beryl had gone to answer it, only to find a prospective customer on the step.

'I took her in the front room, to show her what I had,' she sniffed. 'She was really taken with the ivory, the slipper satin – asked me how much, told me when she wanted it for, I checked the diary, it wasn't booked out, she said she'd come back with her mum and try it on—'

'How long did all this take?'

'Not long, Les, I swear! Five minutes . . .' She faltered. 'All right, ten.'

'And when you came back through—'

'Gone. Back door open, back gate open, no sign of her in the alley, I ran all to left and right but I couldn't go any further 'cos of Bobby. I was about to put him in the pram and go looking when you got back. I'm sorry, Les, I'm so, so sorry—'

But Les was already on his way out. Horrified, Gladys ran after him and stopped him in the scullery.

'Les! Shall I come with you? Can I do anything?'

'Yes. Go round the neighbours, ask if they've seen her. I'm going to the rec. There's nowhere else I can think of that she could get to.'

'Oh, not the rec!' Beryl sank onto the kitchen chair and covered her face with her hands. 'There's that stream . . . '

But Les had gone.

* * *

Gladys did as Les had asked, but no one had seen Susan. She wasn't surprised. Most Hinton families lived on the back of the house – the front room was for visitors and the laying out of bodies – so she doubted anyone would have been standing at the window, looking out. What did shock her was the way a couple of householders, hearing who she was looking for, simply tossed their heads and shut the door in her face. Susan might have been backward and looked a bit strange, with her pebble glasses and her mouth perpetually hanging open, but none of that was her fault. She was still a human being, and a child! These people would have shown more compassion if Gladys had been asking after a dog.

Disgusted, she hurried on to the rec. It wasn't a recreation ground as such – it would have been allotments by now if it had been – but an untidy weed-strewn wilderness of builder's rubble where a house had been demolished. People dumped things there – things that even the salvage men weren't interested in – though children were. They made dens with anything they could find and when Gladys and Beryl had once walked by, there'd been a gang of scabby-kneed boys who'd set up bits of pot on a broken pipe and were shooting at them with catapults.

Gladys saw Les at once, over on the right with his back to her. Stumbling, she sped as best she could over the stony ground.

'Susan! Susan! Can you hear me?' Les was calling.

'Susan, sweetheart! It's me! Come on out, darling, if you're anywhere.'

'No luck?'

'Gladys. Thanks for coming on. No one's seen her?'

Gladys shook her head. Les sighed.

'I'm working my way front to back,' he said. 'I'll go down the far end now, work along the stream. You keep working back and forth from here.'

'Don't worry, Les. We'll find her.'

'If we don't, I'm going to the police. It'll be dark soon.'

If not for double summer time, it would have been dark already, thought Gladys, but she nodded and started making her way over the rubble to the other side, calling Susan's name. The stones were going to wreck her good work shoes, but too bad.

She'd hardly had time to criss-cross the area more than three or four times – was this what it was like for the rescue men, she wondered, picking their way over bomb sites? – when she heard Les shouting. She couldn't see him at first – he was in the hollow dip where the stream ran across the bottom of the area. Not knowing what to expect, she hurried to where she could see him.

'I've got her!' he called, waving. The relief in his voice steadied Gladys's lurching heart. 'She's all right!'

She was, but when Gladys got there, Susan was a sorry sight. Filthy dirty, dress stained and torn, and bleeding from scraped knees and a cut on her head,

Susan clung snottily to her brother. She'd been hiding in a sewer pipe.

'What's happened to her?'

'All she's said is "nasty boys".' Les looked grim. 'But I know who it is, those little tykes that have been rehoused on Inkerman Street. We'll take her home, and then I can tell you, I'm going to give them what for.'

Chapter 11

There'd be no tripping the light fantastic at the Palais for Beryl and Les that night.

Gladys followed sorrowfully behind as Les helped his terrified sister home. When they got there, Susan clung so tightly to his neck that Les had to sit in the armchair with her nestled on his lap while Gladys boiled kettles and lugged the hip bath in from the outhouse and Beryl put another precious lump of coal on the fire. Once Susan had been peeled off her brother, they persuaded her into the water, bathed her knees and rinsed her matted hair. Nothing, though, could wash away the terror of the experience and she was still visibly shaking as they tugged her nightdress over her head. Les, his mouth a grim line, had gone out again to deal with the culprits.

Out of the bath, Susan clung to Gladys, who was forced to sit with her as Les had done. Bobby had fallen asleep in his pram, so Beryl crept upstairs to put him in his cot.

'Ivy's going to skin me alive,' she said when she came back down. 'And she's got every right. We haven't been getting on that well as it is, and now . . . And I can't say it wasn't my fault, because it was.'

'Oh, Beryl.'

Gladys was still appalled by what she'd seen of Susan, crouching like a wounded animal in that awful pipe.

'Les'll have something to say to me and all,' Beryl added. 'And just when the business is getting going!' She jutted out her chin. 'I'm not giving it up, though, I don't care what either of them says!'

Gladys shook her head, not knowing what to say. People didn't half get themselves into scrapes. That was the thing about the war. You'd think you could rise above the little things of life, the accidents and misunderstandings and fallings-out, with so much else that was bigger and more important happening, but they still went on, and why wouldn't they? Life went on, and people would always be people.

Gladys laid Susan, now half-asleep, gently in the other chair while Beryl made a pot of tea, and they sat quietly at the table drinking it. They both jumped, and even Susan stirred, when they heard the back door open, then crash to again.

'Shh!' Beryl warned, indicating Susan, as Les appeared in the doorway.

'Sorry,' mouthed Les. He looked even more grim than when he'd gone out.

'Well?' asked Beryl quietly.

'B—' Les moderated his language as a concession to Gladys. 'Flipping waste of time.' He snatched off his cap. 'Those lads – there's three of them, brothers, and two other little devils they've palled up with, but they're just hangers-on. They were all out playing in the street – at this time of night! Anyway, I went to the brothers' house, raised hell on the knocker, the mother comes to the door, fag in her mouth, baby on her hip, beer bottle in her hand—'

Gladys's eyes widened. Nobody in these streets was well off, but barring one or two, it had always been a respectable area, where the women whitened their steps and polished their door knockers. If they drank or smoked, they did it on high days and holidays, and if it was in the house, then on the quiet.

'I told her what her lads had been up to, but does she care? She gave me a right mouthful, asked what she was supposed to do with them, and how I'd like to be bombed out – twice – and start again with nothing in some god-forsaken town where they don't know a soul and everyone's taken against them. I wonder why!'

Gladys tutted. Her parents had sent her to live with her gran in Hinton as soon as the Blitz had started, so she hadn't been at home in Coventry when it was bombed, and she'd never been back. The city had been devastated, her own parents just two of the five hundred-odd killed, but it was one single night of destruction. Londoners had endured the bombs day and night for months non-stop. It'd turn any child wild. It had been easy to see the boys as pure evil for attacking Susan, but things were never that simple.

'What did you say?' asked Beryl.

'Told her it was no excuse! And if anything like it happened again – anything – I'd be round and belt them. She slammed the door in my face. The other two had gone in, but her boys were still playing out, creating merry hell with a couple of tin cans and a stick. Filthy dirty they are, don't look like they've had a bath in months. Or much to eat, come to that . . . And the language – makes the Army look tame! I told them what for, got another earful.' He shrugged, frustrated. 'There was no talking to them. I had to come away else I'd have done something I'd regret.'

'Where's their dad?' asked Gladys. 'Away fighting?'

'Hah!' said Les scornfully. 'A neighbour came out to walk his dog. He'd seen which house I'd been to. He's in the Scrubs, isn't he?'

Gladys frowned. Was that a nickname for one of the Army regiments, like the Paras or the Desert Rats? Beryl saw her face.

'She's an innocent, isn't she? He's in prison, Gladys, that's it, isn't it, Les?'

'At His Majesty's pleasure,' Les confirmed. 'He's been in and out for years.'

As Gladys took this in, Susan stirred. Les looked fondly down at her.

'I'll put her to bed,' he decided. 'Then I'll walk you home, Glad.'

Gladys tried to say there was no need, but Les was insistent – one casualty a night was enough, he said.

'Les—' Beryl began, as Gladys went to fetch her hat and coat from the front room. 'Ivy'll be back soon—'

'No.' Les held up a warning finger. 'You can face Mum yourself and explain. I don't want to be here. She'll only try and make me take sides.'

'If I could change anything—'

Les calmly removed her pleading hand from his arm.

'This is what I mean,' he said, but his voice was gentle. 'I know you only took your eyes off her for a bit, but our Susan's . . . well, you've learnt the hard way. It's more of a risk than taking your eyes off Bobby, 'cos she can get about and he can't. But their understanding of the world is about the same. Maybe you get that now.'

Beryl sat back, defeated. Gladys came back in and Les offered her his arm.

'Shall we go?'

'Take care,' said Beryl with a wan smile, standing up. 'Thanks for your help, Gladys.'

'I'm glad I was here,' said Gladys earnestly. 'All's well that ends well, eh?'

Beryl nodded, but Gladys didn't think she looked very convinced.

'It was awful,' Gladys told Lily next day.

Gladys was religiously (ho, ho, as Sid had noted) attending the church where she and Bill were going to get married and, as her bridesmaid and with Jim away, Lily had started going with her. She enjoyed the hymns, at least.

'Ivy's been going on about that family,' she sympathised, as they walked away after the service. 'But I never thought they'd go this far. Poor Susan.'

'They haven't had the best start in life, those boys,' said Gladys reflectively.

'You're sticking up for them?'

'Not what they did,' replied Gladys. 'But maybe why. Their dad's in prison, they've been bombed out, I don't suppose they've been in school for years—'

'It's not perfect, but their mother's not the only one coping without a husband. Most mothers are these days!'

'I know. But those dads aren't in prison. It's not the best example.'

'True.' They walked for a while in silence, itself unusual for Gladys. Lily was thinking about it too.

117

First Sid, now Susan, picked on just because they were different – what a world. She took her friend's arm. 'It's really bothered you, hasn't it?'

'I just feel so lucky. Bill had a rotten start too, brought up in a children's home, no mum or dad . . . But he's turned out all right.'

'Of course he has. And he's more than all right now he's got you,' said Lily loyally.

Their little awkwardness over Frank Bryant was long forgotten. Frank himself was almost forgotten, though Lily had had a funny moment the other week when a part-delivery had arrived from Ward and Keppler. Unpacking it in the stockroom, she'd suddenly had the crazy notion that Frank might have concealed a note inside and had to admit to a surge of disappointment when she got to the bottom of the box and even raising the cardboard flaps revealed nothing tucked away.

'Hm!' Miss Temple, an older sales lady who was with her, held up a tiny garment. 'I'll say it's not such good quality! You can practically see through this vest! No wonder they wanted to change the name!'

Lily thought she was exaggerating – the way Miss Temple was stretching the fabric, of course you could see through it, but then Lily had been exaggerating herself – exaggerating her importance to Frank. He was touring the Midlands on his rounds – with a girl in every port, no doubt!

Gladys brought her back into the moment.

'And you're all right too, you and Jim?' she asked. 'I know this business with his mother's a bit of a trial, but—'

'You needn't worry about Jim and me,' she said firmly, and just as she'd said to Sid, 'we're fine.'

In Bidbury, Jim hadn't got time to go to church. A tree had come down in the copse up the lane, or so the postman had told his dad, and Jim was out with a barrow to salvage what he could. Most of the easily portable branches had been taken but he attacked what was left. Beggars couldn't be choosers and it was satisfying to wield the axe. He could work off some of his frustration.

There was no improvement in his mother. Every weekend he looked for a sign – a bit more movement, clearer speech, a brighter look in her eye, and every weekend he was disappointed. She was still spurning the exercises from the hospital, still finding fault with Mrs Dawkins, still dragging herself around, dropping cups, spilling things.

In his darkest moments, Jim wondered if she really wanted to get better. Her disability on top of his father's only boosted her campaign to get him home for good. And with the evidence in front of him, it was becoming harder and harder to resist.

He shook his head, trying to get the thought out of his mind. His shoulder ached from his exertions with the axe but somehow he enjoyed the pain. He stopped to set up another section to quarter, and a movement to his right caught his eye. Pheasant, probably – but no . . . he could see something else . . . someone was watching him.

Propping the axe against the barrow, he stepped quickly to the side and parted the thick branches of a laurel bush. He was faced with Margaret.

'Hah! Are you spying on me?'

She blushed as red as the chequered pattern on her jumper.

'Not really. I came to sketch the big beech before it loses all its leaves. But then I heard someone working . . . '

Jim noticed her sketch pad lying on a little canvas stool.

'Good story, but I'm not falling for it,' he grinned. 'There's a roll of microfilm or some secret message in that old tree trunk, and you've come to pick it up. I hope you're on our side! You're not a double agent, are you?'

'Very funny. If you want proof . . . ' She picked up the pad and began to turn over the top sheet.

'Yes, show me your fake identity card, why don't you?' Jim teased, then stopped her hand. 'Hang on, turn back over.' With slight reluctance, Margaret did. 'Never mind beech trees. That's me!'

'It's not very good. That's why I gave up on it.'

Jim took the pad and studied it closely. She'd somehow managed to capture the muscularity of his movement, the action of a moment, and put it down on paper. How had she given the sensation of his arm swinging, the swish of the blade? He wouldn't have known where to start. It was uncanny.

'It is! This is damn good, Margaret,' he said.

She reverted to her usual diffidence.

'Not really. I don't often do people, only still life, nature studies mostly. So you were a double challenge, the way you were going at that poor old tree.' She paused. 'I could do a much better one if you'd sit for me.'

'If I had the time!'

'You could be doing something else as well. But something less active. Like . . . your mother had me write down a list of jobs . . . I know, having a look at the radio.'

'That *will* be a still life!' groaned Jim. 'I haven't the first idea how to fix it.'

'It's probably just a loose wire.'

'Sounds like you should do the repair and I'll sketch you!'

Margaret smiled ruefully.

'If you don't want me to, that's fine.'

'No, no.' Jim relented. It would be nice to have someone to talk to while he had a go at the wretched radio – if he was allowed to move a muscle while she drew. 'Look, go on, then, if you really want to. I expect Mother would like to see you anyway.'

'I don't want to impose—'

'You won't be. I'm nearly done here. Walk back with me and I'll have a go at the radio. But on one condition.'

'What's that?'

'You sign it for me, and I hang on to it. Then when you're famous, I'll be quids in!'

Margaret grinned.

'Deal.'

'OK. I'll finish here, then let's go!'

Chapter 12

'Sit still, can't you!'

They were in the cottage kitchen; his parents were dozing next door by the fire.

Jim looked up from the muddle of wires that had greeted him when he'd taken the back off the family's old set. So much for 'wireless'!

'I am sitting still!' he objected. 'I'm frozen in horror looking at this cat's cradle. I wish I'd never started this!'

'You may think you're still,' Margaret scolded. 'But you're twitching and pulling faces like someone at a flea circus!'

Jim got up and moved round the table to where she was sitting. Margaret's back was to the window and the pale October sun threw diamonds through the latticed panes onto her pad.

'You got a pretty good likeness when I was swinging an axe. I can't see how a slight frown can be—' He broke off. 'Margaret, you shouldn't be so hard on yourself. That's really good!'

Margaret rubbed away impatiently at her sketch.

'No, it's not. Your forehead's far too prominent. You look like Shakespeare.'

'Thanks! Big brain.'

Margaret huffed.

'It's throwing your whole face out of proportion.'

'All right, I'll sit still. I don't know where to begin with this wireless anyway.'

Jim went back to his seat.

'Now you're in a completely different position!' Margaret turned over another sheet. 'I shall have to start again!'

Jim's mother was delighted, of course, to find that when she woke and banged her stick on the floor, it was Margaret who came to see what she wanted. Jim, following, saw his mother's drooping mouth flicker into the nearest thing to a smile he'd seen since she'd had her stroke.

Margaret sat with her while Jim got going on the dinner, and it was a relief not to have his mother watching his every move, disapproving of the way he scrubbed the potatoes or chopped the carrots. As he waited for the vegetables to come to the boil, he took a look at the sketch that Margaret had finally declared herself happy with. It was another brilliant likeness – she'd somehow caught the sense of his despair at the task he was contemplating without making him look completely gormless. Instead he looked flatteringly like a philosopher pondering a particularly knotty problem. To his surprise and in a complete fluke, he'd even mended the wireless: he'd somehow fiddled with the right wire and tightened the correct screw to stop its persistent spit and crackle. All in all, the day was passing far more pleasantly than usual.

'How was it?' Lily asked him, also as usual, when he got back on Monday night.

Thanks to the progress he'd been able to make on Sunday – Margaret had stayed and kept his mother company until it was time for milking – Jim had caught an earlier train and was back at the Collinses' by eleven. Dora had already gone up to bed, and Lily had been on her way when she'd heard Jim's footsteps clattering down the entry. Now she was making cocoa for them both.

'Not bad,' said Jim, unwinding Lily's scarf from round his neck. Again, he'd exchanged it for Margaret's once he was back in Hinton.

'Not bad?' Lily turned from the stove. 'That's a big improvement!'

'Not in my mother's health,' conceded Jim. 'Still no change. But – look, Lily, I'm going to tell you because of . . . of what happened between us before. I don't want a repeat performance.'

The milk was starting to catch at the sides. Lily used it as an excuse to keep her eyes fixed on the pan.

'Oh, yes?' she said as nonchalantly as she could, though her heart had picked up its pace.

'I ran into Margaret yesterday,' Jim began. 'I'd gone to collect some firewood, and she was out sketching. She came back with me to the cottage, and she kept my mother company while I got on with some jobs. That's how I'm back so early.'

The milk was starting to heave. Lily turned off the gas and concentrated on pouring it into the cups. She knew what her reply had to be.

'Well, that's good,' she said evenly. 'I can see it was a help to you.'

'It's a help to both of us,' said Jim. 'I'm back earlier, after all.'

He came and stood behind her and slid his arms round her waist. He bent and kissed her neck where her bent head exposed it.

Lily put the pan into the sink and turned round to face him. She knew that what she said next was vitally important. She couldn't say what she really thought, which was that it wasn't such a great bargain from her point of view, and possibly a price she'd rather not pay, because that would sound mean and petty and – yes, jealous. Instead she smiled and reached up and put her arms round his neck.

'Thank you,' she said. 'For telling me.'

She could say that much, at least.

At work, the days passed. The sales floor was quiet, but behind the scenes, Marlow's was gearing up for Christmas.

Mr Bunting, the Toys buyer, had secured some Chad Valley jigsaws and farm sets, while for Childrenswear the visit to Ward and Keppler had yielded a half a dozen extra fleecy pram covers. From other manufacturers, there were some smocked velvet party dresses and for boys, little bow ties and matching pocket squares. Even on Jim's department, there were a few enticing items. Pride of place, he reported, would be given to a couple of brass companion sets, a log box, and a fender stool. The fact that they were second-hand, salvaged from houses in Exeter that had been bombed in the Baedeker raids, wouldn't stop a stampede.

On Friday, Jim treated them to rock and chips and the mood was good at the Collinses' as they sat round the small fire; Dora had decreed the end of October was far too early be eating into their rationed coal.

'I'll hear the news, then I'm for bed,' she declared, as the laughter and applause faded at the end of *It's That Man Again*. 'I'm not going to start another sleeve tonight.'

Her one-woman output of scarves, mittens and

pullovers for the troops must by now, Sid joked, have left a lot of sheep feeling the chill.

Jim was poring over what he called his 'proofs' of the next edition of *The Messenger* and Lily had been trying to darn her work stockings – darning a darn, basically. Her eyes felt sore and gritty, and her finger throbbed where she'd jabbed the needle down the side of her nail.

She really would be a hopeless housewife. It was a constant joke between her and Jim, who claimed after her clumsy attempt to darn one of his socks that he was going to set up a Society for the Prevention of Cruelty to Hosiery. With Lily, though, it had become almost a badge of honour – she'd far rather progress at work, anyway. Leave the housekeeping to the Gladyses of this world.

The BBC newsreader waited for the last note of Big Ben to die away before starting the bulletin as usual: 'Here is the news, and this is Alvar Liddell reading it.' He took a breath. 'A new offensive has begun at El Alamein in the Western Desert,' he announced.

That made them all sit up.

'Operation Lightfoot has been launched by General Montgomery with the aim of breaking through the Axis lines. No reports have yet been received of its progress.'

He took a breath.

'Addressing Members of Parliament earlier, the Prime Minister stated that . . . '

Lily turned to look at her mother. Jim raised his eyebrows.

Letters from Reg were few and far between. He'd never been as good a letter-writer as Sid, and with the distance they had to travel, ages could go by before three letters arrived at once, dated weeks apart. The latest, received last week but written in September, had said that he'd had a couple of days' leave, which had been welcome, and that one of his mates was keeping a pet scorpion in a jam tin. Hardly informative about where he was or what he was doing, but what did they expect? It would only have been scored out by the censor. And anyway, it would have been weeks out of date.

Reg had started out with REME but men went where they were needed, and did what they had to, and for a big push like this, every man would have to play his part. So as they sat there under a dim lamp, Reg could very well be under fire, and firing back, the desert sky lit up like a firework display.

But worried as they were, sick as they might feel, there was nothing they could do. The only news they were going to get was what the BBC and the newspapers could tell them day by day, which was not very much. Sid wrote twice during the week but there was no news from, or about, Reg – which, they tried to tell themselves, was a good thing.

* * *

'Penny for the guy, Miss?'

It was a Friday night and Lily was walking home alone: Jim was staying late at the store to do a stocktake. A scruffy boy was sitting on the pavement beside a crude-looking dummy.

'That's a daft place to sit. I could have broken my leg! No, I'm not giving you money for your horrible guy! You won't be allowed to burn it, anyway!'

Bonfires and fireworks had been banned since the outbreak of war.

'Going to hang it from a lamp post, ain't I? Best place for 'im.'

The dummy was, inevitably, Hitler, with mad eyes and a moustache drawn on an old bit of rag.

Lily walked on. She usually loved Hallowe'en with its games of Snapdragon and then the Bonfire Night fireworks, but there'd be none of that this year, and she wasn't in the mood anyway. Still . . . Christmas was coming. She'd had a fountain pen put aside for Jim at Marlow's, which with her staff discount, she could just about afford. For her mother, she had her eye on a black cat brooch – Dora already had a lucky horseshoe, but didn't they need all the luck they could get? At the thought of how pleased her favourite people would be with their presents, she shook off her mood. Jim had said he wouldn't be late – the lack of stock making any stocktake speedier – and Dora had promised them sausage plait for tea.

But when she opened the back door, there was no

Dora in the kitchen and no smell of anything, let alone something as delicious as sausage plait. Lily went through to the living room, groping her way in the dark. The blackout was up, so she put on the light and saw her mother sitting at the table.

Dora indicated a piece of paper lying beside her. A telegram. Lily snatched it up.

REGRET TO INFORM YOU YOUR SON CORPORAL REGINALD ARTHUR COLLINS POSTED AS MISSING ON 27TH OCTOBER 1942. PLEASE ACCEPT MY SINCERE SYMPATHIES. LETTER FOLLOWS.

Chapter 13

When Jim got in, blithely unaware, he found Lily sitting as Dora had been: her mother had gone upstairs. At the sight of Jim, Lily's courage dissolved: all he could do was hold her while she cried. When Dora came down, having heard the door, she made no reference to the telegram and brushed away Jim's sympathies.

'It's how it is,' she said flatly. 'We've just got to wait for the letter. I'm sorry there's no tea. I'll make you a sandwich.'

Jim said to leave it to him, but Dora insisted: she'd rather be doing something, she said. She went off into the kitchen. It was as if she had aged not even ten, but twenty years, and her eyes were rimmed with red.

For the first time almost since the start of the war, they didn't listen to the news – what was the point? What did any of it matter? Dora went to bed at ten to nine. On the landing, Jim hugged Lily extra tight before they went to their rooms.

'Missing may not mean the worst,' he reassured her, not for the first time that evening. 'He really might just be—' Even as he said it he knew there was no 'just' about it. 'He might have been taken prisoner.'

In her head, Lily knew he was right, and it was the better option when you considered the alternative. In time, she knew she'd see it like that if – please God – that was the news that came. But at this moment, anything that wasn't Reg tired and dirty, hungry perhaps, battle-weary certainly, but safe behind Allied lines, was no consolation.

The next day was Hallowe'en, and Lily was even less in the mood for it now. She looked like a spectre herself, hollow-eyed with lack of sleep. She still had to go to work, though: Miss Thomas didn't work on Saturdays and Miss Temple only for half a day. But when she presented herself on the department, her boss could see at once that something wasn't right. When Lily explained, Miss Frobisher didn't hesitate.

'I appreciate your coming in, Lily, but you shouldn't be here,' she said crisply. 'If you're waiting for a letter, you should be at home with your mother. Off you go.'

Lily stuttered her thanks and raced home, hoping against hope that she could be there before Freda, the post girl, delivered the letter with the War Office franking. But Freda must have been early on her rounds, and when Lily got back Dora handed her the single sheet. She didn't even ask what Lily was doing home.

Dear Mrs Collins,

I regret to inform you that a report has been received to the effect that your son Corporal Reginald Arthur Collins was posted as missing on 27th October 1942.

The report that he is missing does not necessarily mean that he has been killed as he may be a Prisoner of War or temporarily separated from his Regiment.

Official reports that men are Prisoners of War take some time to reach this country and if he has been captured it is possible that news may not be received for some months. Regrettably, given the hostilities between us and our enemies it is impossible to expedite such reports.

Please accept my sincere sympathies for the anxiety this situation will doubtless cause you. As soon as any news is received, rest assured I will communicate it to you.

In the meantime your son's personal effects

*will be collected and returned to you via the
official channels.*

   Yours sincerely,

It was signed with a squiggle – some captain or
other.

Suddenly Dora seemed to realise that Lily was
standing in front of her, and not at work.

'Miss Frobisher sent me home,' Lily explained.

'I see,' said Dora quietly. 'But there's no point you
being here. I'm at the Clothing Exchange today.'

'Mum, what? You can't go and do that when—'

'I'm not letting them down. You can do what you
like, love. But I shan't be here.'

Equally quietly, Dora fetched her hat and coat,
pinned her hat on in front of the living room mirror,
and left. Lily was left staring at a closed door and
the typewritten words she didn't want to read again.
If only she could be as strong as her mother.

If she could have seen Dora at that moment,
sitting in the little rustic shelter in the park, rocking
and clutching at the bench, inconsolable, she might
have thought very differently, but Lily never would
see it. To the world, and even to her family, Dora
would put on her coping face again. That was
strength.

Lily went back to work. What else could she
do? Miss Frobisher said nothing but kept her away
from customers and gave her mindless tasks in the

stockroom, sorting hangers and checking for lost price tickets.

All day, telling herself that the news was not – yet – the worst, Lily stayed strong for Miss Frobisher, but walking home with Jim, her voice wobbled.

'You haven't seen it, but I've been thinking about that letter all day. It was so . . . it has to be the worst, doesn't it? Why else would they send back his things?'

Her voice cracked. What would they be? Their letters to him, a few pairs of socks, his gilt cigarette case? Would that be it? That and the few snapshots in the album, taken as they were growing up? That and her memories of her brother?

'It's procedure, Lily,' said Jim. 'Bureaucracy. Officialdom. That's all it is.'

Lily didn't believe him, and he wasn't sure he believed it himself. He pulled her closer against his side.

'Look. I won't go to Bidbury this weekend. I'll send a wire. And one to Margaret, to ask if she can go over instead, or get Mrs Dawkins to, and to tell her I'll pay her the extra.'

Lily stopped dead in the middle of the pavement. Pedestrians bounced into them, bounced off, tutted and pushed past. Jim drew her into a doorway.

'Oh, Jim, would you really?'

'Your mum may not think she needed you today, but you need me. Maybe you both do. I want to be here, anyway.'

Lily threw her arms round him and he held her tight.

'Thank you! Oh, thank you! Gladys promised to come round tomorrow, but . . . '

She sniffed. She was going to cry. It was always the same when you were upset and someone was nice to you.

'I'm here,' said Jim soothingly. 'Shh. Shh.'

'I don't know,' Beryl reflected as she and Ivy put the baby's nappies through the mangle on Monday morning. 'All this worry for them on top of Jim's mum.'

Ivy fed another napkin into the rollers and shook her frizzy curls. 'Well, they do say that misery loves company.'

Beryl stopped turning the handle for a moment. The nappy dripped onto the yard.

'It just makes me grateful all over again that Les is home,' she said.

Les hadn't held what had happened with Susan against her: he wasn't one to sulk or bear a grudge, but there'd been hard words, and plenty of them, from her mother-in-law for Beryl. Eventually, Les had had to get drawn in to defend her, and eventually, whether she truly believed it or not, Ivy had seemed to accept that Beryl's lapse had been momentary and born of ignorance, not wanton neglect. The two women had reached a truce, but it was an armed truce and Beryl knew that Ivy was ready to fire off a salvo at the slightest provocation. The effect on Susan, meanwhile, had been marked. She cringed when anyone knocked the door, had to be dragged out of the house to go anywhere, shrank from strangers and froze when she saw any boy, however blameless. She was wetting the bed almost every night.

'Everyone's so miserable!' Beryl said to Les when he got in from work that night. 'And no wonder!'

'I keep telling Lily, they mustn't lose hope,' said Les, lifting the lid on the saucepan to see what was cooking. 'You didn't hear from me for weeks after Tobruk and I was OK, wasn't I?'

'That was different, you weren't even there! And we never had a telegram from the War Office!'

'I know, but look, Reg is missing, not dead or even missing presumed killed. I know it sounds harsh, sweetheart, but they've got to hang on to that.'

'And they have been!' Beryl fired back. 'But you don't understand, Les. I had a bit of it with you. They'll be on edge every day, waiting for the wire that says he's copped it. And if they don't get that, if he's been took prisoner, they might not hear anything definite for months! It's torture!'

Les put the lid back on the pan.

'Did you make this stew?'

'Don't change the subject,' said Beryl tartly. 'No,

you're quite safe, your mum did. And even *she* had a bit.'

She nodded towards Susan, who was sitting at the kitchen table. That was another thing. She followed you round the house like a shadow. Beryl found it wearing, but she could hardly complain.

Les beamed at his sister.

'Did you, lovey? Had some nice stew? Well done!'

Susan went on sucking her thumb.

'Anyway, I think it's up to us to cheer everyone up,' said Beryl, putting two plates to warm. 'Or at least take their minds off it. Help them pass the time.'

'And how do we do that?' Les fetched a couple of glasses of water. 'A knees-up with,' he held up the glasses, 'council pop? And one lump of coal on the fire?'

'Don't be such a misery! I *was* thinking of a party actually. A bonfire party.'

'Nice one! Since they're not allowed,' scoffed Les.

Beryl flicked a spoon at him.

'Indoor fireworks, clever dick. No noise to scare Susan, and bright lights for Bobby to watch. Why not?'

Les put the water glasses down on the table.

'Come here, you,' he said. 'And give us a kiss. You're a caution, you are, Beryl Bulpitt.'

Beryl left the stew to simmer and moved into his arms. She smiled her most winsome smile.

'Is that a yes?'

'It's not a no,' said Les. 'And I didn't hear a "no" to that kiss, either, did I?'

When Beryl got an idea in her head, there was no stopping her, and before everyone quite knew what they'd agreed to, the get-together had been planned. And planned to the last degree.

'Thursday at our place,' she announced. She'd called round to Lily's that same night. 'It'll have to be early 'cos of getting the little ones to bed, so come straight from work. Don't worry about your tea, I'm going to do us,' she brought out the term proudly, 'a finger buffet.'

'A what?' queried Lily.

'I'm going to get Gladys to have one for her wedding instead of a plate tea,' said Beryl smugly. 'They're all the rage in America. Try to keep up, Lily.'

Jim was told of the plan when he came in from the extra ARP shift he'd been able to fit in since he was in Hinton on a Monday for once. It had been a comfort to Lily to have him there on Sunday, though. Like Dora, he thought work was the answer and he'd kept her occupied mucking out the henhouse, getting rid of the old chaff and making the hens a bed of leaves – straw, like so many things, was a long-forgotten luxury. Margaret had wired to say she'd look in on his parents on Sunday and for the rest, Mrs Dawkins had jumped at the chance of a bit more pocket money.

'I know Beryl's only trying to be kind,' Lily admitted to Jim when Beryl had gone. 'But I can't say I feel like a party. And Mum isn't thrilled either.'

'I know,' Jim agreed. 'None of us is. But we can't let Beryl down. She's only trying to help – in her usual clod-hopping way.'

That night as usual they gathered round the radio for the nine o'clock bulletin. They'd gone back to listening to the news. It was still all about North Africa and El Alamein, as more facts emerged, and there was always the ridiculous hope that, in a news-flash, the announcer might tell them that all telegrams and letters received last weekend had been a Hallowe'en hoax. Instead, on Wednesday:

'We suggest that listeners stay close to their sets until midnight. Good news is coming.'

The only news the Collins household wanted to hear was that Reg had been found alive and well, wandering about in the Qattara Depression, having survived for ten days on a tin of bully beef and dew collected in his helmet. Knowing the good news wouldn't be that, Dora went to bed, but Jim decided it was worth staying up. Lily said she'd stay up with him.

When they were sure Dora was safely upstairs, Jim moved to sit in the big armchair and Lily snuggled into his lap. There they dozed till midnight and after more chimes from Big Ben, the news began. Unable to contain his excitement, the regular newsreader departed from his usual formula, and began instead:

'Here is the news – and cracking good news it is too!'

He then informed them that the Eighth Army had triumphed. The Axis forces had been 'routed' and the town of El Alamein was back in the hands of the Allies!

'Now we really have got an excuse for a party!' said Les when he ran into Lily in the subterranean corridor of Marlow's next day.

'Sorry,' he added awkwardly. 'I didn't mean . . .'

'I know you didn't. And it's wonderful news, I can see that.'

'It is, Lily. You mark my words, the tide's turning at last – not that they have tides in the middle of God knows how many million miles of sand!'

But for Lily, the victory, wonderful as it was, only made the telegram and the letter about Reg harder to bear. She had moments when she was convinced her brother was alive – he had to be, somehow. Then reality would kick in and she was back in the usual round – the dread and then the refusal to believe that he was dead, and the hope, if hope was the word, that he'd been taken prisoner. He was retreating with the enemy, forced along at gunpoint, beaten, hungry, maybe wounded – perhaps forced on pain of death to fight his own side – but alive.

The promised evening of 'celebration' hung over her like a sword.

Chapter 14

Beryl had done her best, she really had. She'd hung up some Chinese paper lanterns and strips of lametta ('Why wait for Christmas?') and the promised 'buffet' – fish and meat paste sandwiches, a cold sausage each, some baker's rock buns and some home-made fairy cakes, was laid out on the table. She'd borrowed a card table from a neighbour and on it, on a tin tray, the famous indoor fireworks were on display, with a box of Vestas to light them once the lights were turned out.

'First time ever the blackout's a good thing!' Les remarked cheerily, echoing what Jim had said about the lack of stock cutting his stocktaking time in half. Talk about looking on the bright side!

A letter from Sid had arrived that morning. They'd written straight away to tell him the news and he'd obviously gone straight to his Chief Petty Officer but leave, compassionate or otherwise, was 'off the agenda' for the moment – there was, he said, 'a lot of work' on. Jim, reading between the lines, said it must mean some rapid deployment – Sid's job was to re-calculate the pay and allowances for men boosted up the ranks or put to different duties. Sid promised he'd come home as soon as he could, but in the meantime he quoted the family motto – 'head down, chin up'.

So now, in response to Les, they all tried to raise a smile.

The fireworks, to be honest, were something of a damp squib. The 'Vicious Viper' was more like a somnolent slug and the 'Fierce Fountain' spurted for a few seconds then dried up. Susan panicked and clung to Ivy, and Bobby was fretful, wanting his bedtime feed. Les put a good face on it for Beryl's sake, blaming the Army for nicking all the sulphur and phosphorus, while she took the baby off upstairs. Feeling sorry for her, and as a favour to a weary-looking Ivy, Lily and Gladys said they'd put Susan to bed. She was fond of them both and went off willingly, clutching her favourite Noddy book. Les revealed that he'd laid in a few beers for himself and Jim, so they repaired to the kitchen. Ivy and Dora were left alone with the empty plates, which Dora automatically began to stack.

'I'll fetch a tray,' she said.

'You sit down,' said Ivy firmly. 'Me and Beryl can do the dishes when you've gone. The boys are out there, anyway. They don't want us clattering around.'

She lowered herself onto the cracked leather seat of one of her dining chairs. Defeated, Dora did the same.

'I'll sit down on one condition,' she said. 'I don't want to talk about Reg. There's no point. We don't know any more, and we won't – if he's a prisoner – probably not for months.'

Ivy nodded. 'I know. But you're doing a grand job, Dora. It's not easy.'

'Well, no use moaning,' said Dora. 'It doesn't get you anywhere and no one wants to hear it.' She took a breath. 'Now let's talk about something else. Take my mind off it. How's your Susan, really?'

Ivy's jowls wobbled.

'If you're not allowed to moan . . . '

'Go on . . . I did ask.'

'Oh, Dora,' Ivy sighed. 'Those lads . . . it hasn't stopped.'

'What's happened now?'

'I had to take Susan out with me the other day, up the chemist to get her prescription. Madam—' she jerked her head upwards, meaning Beryl, 'she'd taken a headdress round to a customer. I had a hell of a game getting Susan in her coat, and it was like she knew something, because when we got to the end of the street, there they were, those lads, waiting. Pelted us with mud and – well, some of it was mud.'

'Oh, Ivy!'

'Susan went rigid, wouldn't move, which only egged them on. I was trying to deal with her, telling them to clear off . . .'

'Didn't anyone come and help you?'

'No one wants to get involved with those lads. They don't want the same happening to them, do they?'

'I see.'

'I only got rid of them 'cos the salvage cart came by and they ran after it to see what they could nick. I had to drag her the rest of the way, and when we got in the chemist, he had to give her something to calm her down. I finally managed to get her out again, but when we got home, they'd been here.'

'The boys?'

'Daubed muck all over the front door and written on the wall "Susan Bulpitt's yampy" and "Susan Bulpitt wets her knickers." She couldn't read it of course, but,' Ivy shook her grey curls dejectedly, 'I can't see how I'll ever get her out of the house again.'

'What did Les have to say about it?'

'I never told him.'

'What?'

'I cleaned it all off. What could he do?'

'Give them a good hiding! That's what he said he'd do!'

'It wouldn't help.'

'I'm sorry, Ivy, but that doesn't follow,' protested Dora. 'You can't let them get away with it! You have to stand up to people like that.'

'You don't understand,' said Ivy quietly. 'I had it with my brothers. They used to torment me, but if I went crying to my mother and my dad leathered them, they only stepped it up 'cos I'd been telling tales. I know the type.'

This was a revelation to Dora, and perhaps explained why Ivy had chosen the seemingly obliging Eddie as a husband, who'd given up his home life to go to sea to support the family.

'I still think you're wrong,' she insisted. 'If you leave it, it'll carry on – and they'll think they can do it to other people! If you don't want Les involved, go to the police.'

'The police?' Ivy scorned. 'You think they'd take any notice? They're that short-handed, they've more than enough to do with forged coupons and stolen ration books and pickpockets in the blackout! No, it's the same as you with Reg. We've got to soldier on.'

'That's completely different. There's nothing I can do about that. But you can!'

'Maybe. But as Hitler's beginning to find out, you can't fight on all fronts and I haven't the energy, not with this dress lark as well.'

'That's still a problem?'

'Course it is! She's obsessed. I'm minding Bobby

far more than was ever agreed and I wouldn't mind a bit more towards the rent if my front room's her blasted showroom! But Les'll only take her side, like he did in the end over her letting Susan wander off, which was the start of all this!'

Ivy's considerable bosom, encased in a too-tight sweater of dizzying chevrons, quivered with indignation. Dora opened her mouth in an attempt to pour some oil, but Ivy hadn't finished.

'I know it's all for her and Les's and Bobby's good, and I'm not saying she hasn't got her head screwed on right. All the profits are going into buying more dresses – another reason I can't ask her for a bit more towards the rent. But I'm telling you, Dora, what with one thing and another, cooped up here 'cos Susan won't go out, I'm not sure how much longer we can go on under the same roof!'

This time, Dora waited to make sure Ivy was done.

'Well,' she said. 'You've got that off your chest anyway!' Ivy's bosom heaved again and Dora realised it was an unfortunate phrase. She went on more quietly, 'That's all very fine, Ivy, and I'm sure they'd love a place of their own. But as you've said yourself, half the housing stock is boarded up, or bombed to bits, or taken by families with nowhere else to go.'

'I know, I know.' Ivy lifted her pudgy hands and dropped them again into her lap. 'We've all just got to get on with it.'

* * *

149

The party broke up soon after. Everyone kissed Beryl and thanked her for making the effort, even if they secretly thought the fireworks had been a washout and the 'buffet' no more than a pretty average Sunday tea.

Beryl stood on the doorstep to wave everyone off. Les was walking Gladys home, and Jim offered an arm each to Lily and Dora. The night was clear, which was a help in the blackout, and though they could see searchlights scanning the sky in the distance, there was no sound of planes or ack-ack guns, and no sirens. There hadn't even been any alerts since the day of Dora's encounter with Hugh: as Ivy had said, Hitler really was fighting on other fronts now.

Back home, Dora had barely put her key in the lock when their neighbour's front door opened: Walter Crosbie must have been waiting to pounce. A self-important little man in his fifties, he liked nothing more than poking his nose in where it wasn't wanted.

'Thank goodness you're back!' he said. 'Someone was knocking on your door like billy-o, about seven o'clock it was. I says to Jean, what the heck's going on, raising that racket? And when I saw who it was . . . of course, they're only supposed to deliver to the addressee. But I stressed that I was a shelter warden, so he knew he could trust me . . . '

A telegram! It had to be! Lily's heart started doing acrobatics only matched by those of her stomach.

Fish paste and fairy cakes churned. Silently Dora held out her hand.

'There's two!' said Mr Crosbie, producing them in triumph, as if this was somehow his doing and they'd multiplied in his pocket. 'Not just the one!'

He stood there expectantly, as if they were going to open them right there in front of him: he'd have loved that. But Dora turned the key in the lock.

'Thank you very much, Walter,' she said firmly. 'Goodnight.'

He continued to stand there as they trooped in. Lily glared at him and shut the front door firmly in his face.

Inside, Dora fumbled her way along the wall and Lily groped shakily along after her; only Jim had the presence of mind to find the light switch. Sitting down on the stairs – her legs were obviously on the point of giving out – Dora handed him both telegrams.

'Why two?' asked Lily.

But Jim was already opening the top one. Lily could see the word 'PRIORITY' on the envelope.

There was a pause of a moment, which lasted all eternity, then Jim looked up.

'You're not going to believe this,' he said. And read, '"Your son Corporal R Collins alive and well. Regret anxiety caused."'

'Oh, Mum! Mum!' Lily dropped to her knees in front of her mother and threw her arms around her. 'He's alive! And well! Oh, Mum!'

Dora didn't say anything, but Lily could feel her mother's whole body shaking with sobs – all the grief and relief coming out at once.

'Shh,' she said in the same soothing tone that Jim had used so often to her recently, the same one her mother had used to her as a small child. 'Shh. Don't cry, Mum. He's all right. There. Shh. Don't cry.'

It was probably only seconds, but it seemed another eternity that she and her mother rocked back and forth before she realised that Jim was still standing there, saying nothing. She scrambled to her feet.

'Jim? What's the other? A duplicate? Or a bit more detail?'

'Neither.'

He handed it to her.

MOTHER PASSED AWAY. DAD.

Chapter 15

They'd been looking in the wrong direction again, just like the last time this had happened.

'I'll have to go,' he said. 'Tonight.'

'Of course.'

Lily watched him pack as she'd done so many times in the past few months. She could tell he hardly knew what he was doing, moving blindly round his room, opening drawers and closing them again without taking anything out. She went downstairs and fetched his toothbrush and shaving things from the shelf in the pantry. Jim took them and stuffed them any old how into his knapsack: Lily wanted to reach out and touch him but though he was barely a foot in front of her, he had moved far away.

Guilt ate away at her insides. Jim had stayed with her last weekend when he'd normally have been at home. When he could have seen his mother one last time. Rationally she knew that it wouldn't have changed anything – if Alice had taken sick at, or since, the weekend, someone would have let Jim know, so it must have been sudden. The doctors had warned that after one stroke, the risk of another, more serious, one was higher.

For Lily, that wasn't the only risk.

He was fastening the straps on his knapsack. Soon he'd be gone.

'Jim,' she began. He turned and his lovely, much-loved face was already worn. 'This . . . it changes everything, doesn't it?'

'I don't know,' he replied. Even his voice sounded battered. 'I don't know what to think. I can't think about it now.'

'No, I didn't mean . . . I didn't expect an answer.'

She knew anyway; they both did. He'd surely have to move back to the countryside. He'd have to support his father.

Jim went to the wardrobe and took out his heavier coat, the old tweed overcoat he wore to Bidbury. Dora had acquired it for him when she'd been sorting jumble – her good works had their perks. Jim shrugged it on and from an inside pocket produced a scarf which he wrapped round his neck. It was navy blue, hand-knitted, well-knitted. It looked quite new.

'I haven't seen that before,' said Lily. 'Where did that come from?'

What a thing to say at a time like this! As if it mattered!

Jim looked confused.

'What? Er, no . . . haven't you? Look, I have to go. Sorry.'

They stood in the hall where half an hour ago, he'd opened two telegrams carrying such very different news.

'I'll tell them at work. Don't worry about anything here.'

'No . . . Um, thanks.'

He seemed so distracted Lily wasn't even sure he'd have kissed her if she hadn't reached out and kissed him first.

'I'm so sorry, Jim. Please tell your father too. I know you'll do your best for him. But look after yourself as well, won't you?'

He forced his mouth into the thinnest of smiles and opened the door a crack. Lily turned out the hall light so he could open it fully and step out. The night was still clear and their breath clouded around them.

He looked at her once more, then turned and set off along the street.

There was no point in Lily even thinking about going to bed. She knew she wouldn't settle. Instead, she looked in the back room for the telegram about Reg

– short and uninformative as it was, she wouldn't have minded reading it again – seeing was believing, after all. But it wasn't on the table, only letters to Sid and to Reg himself in her mother's handwriting – she must have dashed them off while Jim and Lily were upstairs. Lily realised the telegram must be upstairs too: it was probably under Dora's pillow. She crept back up but her mother's light was out. Lily was glad. It would be the first decent night's sleep her mother had had in ages.

She turned away, but not into her own room, into Jim's. She straightened the eiderdown that had slipped when he'd snatched up his knapsack, then crossed to the chest of drawers. Jim had left his sock drawer hanging open, and no wonder; it always stuck on the return and went back with a squeal. Lily tried to ease it back as quietly as she could, not wanting to disturb her mum, but in the end she had to give it a shove, sending the balled socks skidding to the back and a piece of paper sliding to the front. Curious, Lily pulled it out. It wasn't lining paper – there was something on it.

When she saw what it was, her heart, which had surely taken enough punishment, was in for another beating.

She was looking at a pencil sketch – a portrait – and of Jim. He wasn't looking up, but slightly down and to one side, which only showed the lovely planes of his face, his straight nose and the absorbed expression he often wore. He must have been doing some kind of close work because he hadn't got his glasses on. It was dated the middle of last month. And it was signed, 'Affectionately, Margaret.'

The room was spinning and Lily had to shake her head and swallow hard to make it stop. She counted back on her fingers. The date was a Sunday, of course, the Sunday she'd been to church with Gladys, and Gladys had told her about Susan's nasty experience . . . the Sunday that Jim had told her, when he'd got back, that he'd 'run into' Margaret and she'd come back with him to the cottage and 'kept his mother company while he got on with some jobs'. Nothing about her sketching him while he did them!

Sick, shocked, Lily laid the sketch carefully back where she'd found it. Her hand hovered over the drawer below. What else might she find? No, she couldn't. She couldn't go snooping on Jim. There was no reason to. There'd be an explanation. There must be. Maybe . . . yes, the sketch was to have been a present from Jim to his mother. That was it. The 'affection' from Margaret was meant for Alice.

The relief the thought gave her lasted precisely five seconds – or would have done if she'd had a stopwatch. Because then Lily remembered the scarf. The hand-knitted, well-crafted scarf that Jim had produced from his overcoat pocket. At once she knew she'd been kidding herself. The sketch wasn't a present for Alice, it was meant for Jim. Like the

157

scarf. And that was from Margaret too! In a blinding flash, she knew that Jim wore it every time on his trips to Bidbury, even though he would set off in the one Lily had made, the holey, hopeless one that hung on the peg downstairs with the mac he wore every day to work.

If Lily had thought she couldn't sleep before, she certainly wouldn't now.

The dawn came, or she supposed it did, it was impossible to tell through the blackout. All night Lily had tossed and turned, churning with fear and jealousy – there'd be an explanation, there had to be, she just had to ask Jim . . . but Jim wasn't there, and he wouldn't be for days. There was no way of contacting him except to write – and say what? I went through your things and found something I shouldn't have – and that you shouldn't have either?

Alice's death had receded; even the good news about Reg had receded. All Lily could think about was Margaret Povey, what kind of claim and what kind of hold she had over Jim.

She didn't even know what she looked like. Was she tall, short, dark, fair? She was artistic, so she should have been pale and slight; but she managed her father's dairy herd, so she must be strong and lithe. One question, though, was answered. It explained Alice's attitude. Jim and Margaret were closer than he'd let on and Alice had been all in favour of it.

This was no good. Lily pushed back the bedclothes: they'd never felt so heavy. Downstairs, the haggard face she saw in the little mirror over the sink shocked her. She splashed it with cold water and hurried back up to pat some colour into her cheeks and scramble into her work clothes so she could get out of the house before Dora stirred. Her mother would assume that she couldn't wait to get to work to tell Gladys the good news about Reg, even if it would have to be followed by the less good news that had come for Jim. Then there was the even less good news of her own.

The newsstands were still trumpeting the triumph of El Alamein. 'TROOPS' GLORIOUS ENTRY INTO CITY' was the headline on one placard. Everyone's mood had lifted. Strangers were smiling at each other and saying, 'Good morning!', shopkeepers opening up were whistling. Lily felt as if she was the only miserable person in the world.

At Marlow's, she lingered outside the staff entrance. She couldn't tell Gladys in the bustle of the cloak-room, with the clanking lockers and the excited babble of chat. Finally she saw her come round the corner and darted to meet her.

'Oh, Lily, isn't it marvellous?' Gladys was holding a morning paper. 'It says here they're going to ring the bells in celebration! Imagine that – church bells again! You will come with me to St Mary's, won't you? I've written to Bill . . . Lily, what is it?'

Tears were coursing down Lily's face.

159

'Oh, Lily, is it 'cos of Reg? I'm sorry—'

'No,' Lily managed. 'No. We had a wire when we got back. He's all right, he's safe!'

'Oh, that's wonderful!' Gladys threw her arms around her. 'Oh, I'm so happy for you! I'll write straight away and tell him how relieved we all are!'

Lily sobbed some more.

'Shh, shh,' soothed her friend. 'It's a lot to take in, I know . . . '

'It's not just that!' Lily was sobbing into Gladys's shoulder. She pulled away and wiped her eyes on her sleeve, and then her nose, leaving a snail trail of snivel. 'There was another telegram – for Jim. Oh, Gladys, his mother's died! And he's gone straight there – and he'll be seeing that Margaret! He's been seeing a lot more of her than I knew! And she's been . . . oh, Gladys!'

Bit by bit, in the washroom, Gladys got the story out of her.

'There must be an explanation,' she said as Lily mopped her eyes.

'That's what I think . . . thought . . . ' sniffed Lily. 'But what? I can't come up with anything.'

'You mustn't let two and two make seven. Margaret might not even have knitted that scarf.'

She was right, of course, and she was trying to be kind. But to Lily, it was as useful as someone giving out earplugs after an air raid.

'Well, who else? It looks new, and his mother can't knit now! And if it's all innocent, why's he been so secretive about it?'

Gladys shrugged, but helplessly.

'Through . . . not wanting to hurt your feelings.'

'Well, that didn't work very well, did it?'

And she was off crying again.

'It's just not possible,' insisted Gladys. 'I can't believe Jim'd carry on with someone else behind your back. You'll have to talk to him.'

'I know that! But when? How? His mother's died! Even when he comes back, his head'll be full of . . . I can't go making it all about me!'

Gladys had no answer to that, but the ten-minute bell answered for her. It was the call for staff to get to their departments.

'We'll have to go,' she said. 'Dry your eyes.'

Lily scrubbed at her face with her useless, soaking hanky, and then the roller towel.

'Look at me!' she wailed. 'I can't go on the shop floor like this!'

'You'll have to.' Gladys was unusually firm. 'Just tell everyone they were happy tears about Reg.'

Gladys was right. There was nothing else to do except carry on, but getting through the next few days was the hardest thing Lily had ever done.

She forced a smile as staff from all over the store sought her out and told her how pleased they were that Reg was safe – news about loved ones in the Forces, good or bad, always spread like wildfire. Jim's absence was noted and the few people who knew that he and Lily were sweethearts asked her to pass on their condolences, so she had to nod and smile about that as well, choked by the traitorous scarf and with the memory of the sketch floating fuzzily in front of her eyes. She'd forbidden herself from going into Jim's room to look at it again, but it tormented her every time she passed the door.

On Sunday, the bells rang out all over Hinton. Dora, smart and pretty in her best dress, went to church, which she usually didn't – she preferred her relationship with her maker to be private. Lily didn't go with her, grateful for the couple of hours alone that her mother's absence gave her. She knew Dora had noted how subdued she'd been, though nothing had been said, and Lily hoped her mum would put it down to simple concern over Jim. Which it was, though there was nothing simple about it.

Chapter 16

Monday came, and then Tuesday. The mood in the country had undergone a sea change. The weather was dull and gloomy, but people's spirits were sunny and warm. Relief – happiness almost – radiated from them as more news from North Africa came through. Rommel was on the run, his broken troops driven westward by the Allies, and in a pincer movement, British and American forces had landed in French Morocco and Algeria. They'd meet them as they fled.

'That Monty, he's the business,' Les declared when Lily met him in the basement corridor with a rattling cage of stock. 'Almost makes me wish I was back out there! There's talk they're going to make him a full General, and he's going to be knighted! Any more news from your Reg – or from Jim?'

Lily shook her head.

'Nothing. From either,' she said.

'Up to their eyes in their different ways, I expect.'

'Probably.'

Les peered at her.

'You look a bit peaky, Lil.' It was dim in the corridor, but not dim enough, evidently. 'Not going down with a bug, are you?'

'I'm fine,' lied Lily. 'Too much excitement, that's all.'

'Get used to it,' grinned Les. 'Our boys'll be in Berlin before you know it!'

Les wasn't the only one who'd noticed her wan appearance. When Lily got back from dinner, Miss Frobisher took her to one side. She looked at her in the same way Lily had seen her examine the seams on baby leggings at Ward and Keppler. Critically.

'You're not yourself at the moment, Lily.'

Lily bit her lip. She might have known there'd be no fooling Miss Frobisher.

'You've had the best news possible about your brother, but you're not happy, are you? I realise the worry doesn't stop as long as he's out there, but you've lived with that sort of worry all year. So I presume it's to do with Mr Goodridge's situation.'

Lily gasped and Eileen Frobisher had to bite back

a smile. Surely Lily must have realised that she wouldn't have missed their covert glances, the mouthed 'see you laters' and the smiles? Even so, her tone was firm.

'I know he's lost his mother, but you know very well that as a member of staff at Marlow's you must leave your troubles at the door. Those who eat the honey don't need to see the bees! Customers don't want to see a miserable face. You need to pull yourself together.'

Tears sprang to Lily's eyes and she concentrated very hard on a speck on the carpet. Miss Frobisher had never spoken to her so severely before and Lily was mortified.

'I'm sorry, Miss Frobisher,' she said. 'I truly am. I've let you down over the past few days. I will pull myself together, I promise.'

Miss Frobisher nodded approval.

'Good. Now buck yourself up!'

Miss Frobisher's reprimand was the push she needed and during the afternoon Lily threw herself into re-dressing the mannequins that greeted customers on arrival. She togged the boy and girl up in matching dungarees and pullovers, sat knitted hats on their ludicrously tidy painted hair, begged a toy dog on wheels from Gladys and looped its string round the girl's stiff plaster fingers. Miss Frobisher smiled encouragingly.

'That's more like it!' she said.

Keeping busy at least stopped Lily's mind whirring fruitlessly in its usual Jim-scarf-Margaret-sketch cycle, but once the mannequins were done, off it went again, and by the end of the day she was completely washed out. Gladys had asked her to the early show at the pictures with herself and Brenda, but Lily had declined. Instead, she waved them off for their evening and in the almost empty cloakroom, slung her gas mask over her shoulder and closed her locker door. She trudged off to clock out with the timekeeper and pushed through the swing door into the street.

'About time! I'd almost given up!'

In the gathering gloom, a figure peeled away from a lamp post.

'Frank! What are you doing here?'

Frank Bryant ground out his cigarette and came forward.

'Charming! Is that the warm Hinton welcome approved of by the Chamber of Commerce?'

'No, I mean . . . you're back here, then?'

'Old Marlow sent you on a course in the blindingly obvious while I've been away?' grinned Frank. He crooked his arm. 'Come on. I thought the flicks, with a bite to eat first. Or the other way round, your wish is my—'

'Oh . . . no, Frank, no!' interrupted Lily. 'I can't!'

'Oh, don't give me all that "boyfriend" stuff.' He rolled his eyes. 'You know it doesn't wash with me.

If a girl can't go out with a pal in all innocence—'

It was 'innocence' that did it. Suddenly she was crying, and even more suddenly, into Frank's shoulder, as he pulled her towards him.

'Hey, what's been going on? The boyfriend hasn't given you the heave-ho, has he?'

Lily sobbed some more. Where were all these tears coming from? Surely she'd cried them all out by now.

'No . . . it's my brother!' she gulped. 'He was missing and we thought he was dead or . . . then just last week we heard he's OK!'

That wasn't it, of course, but it was enough to explain why she'd dissolved so pathetically

'You poor girl,' Frank tutted. 'No wonder you're all churned up.'

'I'm sorry,' she said, fumbling for her hanky. 'You must think I'm such an idiot.'

'You're just a very nice person who cares about things. And people,' said Frank. 'Deeply. I can tell.'

He wasn't wrong there. Lily blew her nose.

'Look,' he went on. 'Scrap the pictures. Why don't I walk you home? Seems to me you need a quiet night in.'

Lily thought quickly. It was nice to have someone to walk with, especially these dark evenings, and she could always get Frank to leave her well before Brook Street, so none of the neighbours saw.

'Well . . . all right,' she said. 'If you want to. Though I'm not sure I'll be very good company.'

'You couldn't be anything else,' said Frank gallantly, tucking her arm through his and setting off. 'Right,' he continued. 'My mission for this evening is Operation Cheer Up Lily. You haven't heard the latest from Bryant's Bumper Book of Jokes, have you?'

All the way he never stopped talking, and Lily even managed a half-smile at some of his terrible jokes – the salesman's stock-in-trade, apparently.

They'd crossed the park now and were nearing home. Suddenly Lily remembered – her mum wouldn't be in: it was the night of her knitting circle. So once Frank had left her, she'd be on her own till bedtime, mooning round the house, going over things again and again, while he . . . what? Went to the cinema on his own, had a stale sandwich and a glass of beer in a pub and went back to his digs?

'Look,' she said impulsively. 'You've been so kind. Why don't you come back to mine? My mum's out. I'll make us something to eat and we'll – I don't know, play Ludo or something. But you can at least spend the evening in . . . well, in a home.'

'Really?' The moon had peeked out from behind a cloud and Frank's eyes shone. 'I'd love that! I always said you were a nice girl!'

An evening hadn't passed so quickly since . . . Lily couldn't remember when. She made them sardines on toast, and there was some leftover milk jelly on the cold shelf in the larder. Frank insisted on washing up, making her laugh by tying on Dora's pinny and clowning about with the dish mop.

'You weren't serious about Ludo, were you?' he asked when the kitchen was tidy.

'Well . . . ' She had been, actually.

'Oh, come on,' said Frank, taking her hand and leading her through into the living room. 'There's far more interesting ways to spend our time. Let me lead you astray!'

Lily had a moment of alarm. Here he was in her home, where she'd invited him – a boy she hardly knew. What she did know was that he was older – twenty – very good-looking, and very charming. What exactly did he mean?

So it was a huge relief when he went to the sideboard and started pulling out drawers.

'Make yourself at home, why don't you?' she laughed as he explained he was looking for a pack of cards and directing him to where they were kept.

'Thanks! I will!'

He sat at the table and started shuffling the pack; he'd decided to teach her three card brag. Lily knew enough about poker from her brothers to realise it was much the same, but Frank laughed at her attempts at a poker face – his was inscrutable. All part of the sales technique, he explained. You had to see who blinked first.

At about nine o'clock, they came to the end of a

game – he'd won hands down, of course. As he counted up his winnings – buttons from Dora's button box – he caught Lily looking at the clock. Another part of being a salesman, he'd told her, was being able to read the signs.

'When's your mum get back?'

'Well . . . not usually till about ten, but you never know . . . '

'I can take a hint.'

Frank stood up and Lily stood up too. He'd taken off his jacket and loosened his tie; she'd changed out of her work clothes into her good fawn skirt and a jumper that Sid had called aquamarine and said brought out the colour of her eyes.

'It's been a lovely evening.'

'Pretty boring for you, I'm afraid,' she apologised. 'But mission accomplished. You did cheer me up.'

'It was far from boring.' Frank touched her arm briefly. 'I meant it. It's been lovely. And I'm glad if it was for you too. You've got a gorgeous smile, Lily. You must learn how to use it again.'

Lily could feel herself blushing. He was nice.

'Have a try,' he urged.

Lily looked up at him with his crisp curling hair and his clear blue eyes. She gave a tiny smile.

'Better?' she asked.

'Better. And very tempting.'

Suddenly she was in his arms and his mouth was against hers. It happened so quickly that Lily didn't have time to protest, but she had time to register that he was an expert kisser before she started to struggle and pull away.

'Frank – no! No!'

He wasn't listening. The more she struggled, the tighter he held her and the more passionate his kisses became. Lily writhed in his arms, trying to tear her mouth away, but he was stronger than she was, far stronger – she could feel the muscles he'd talked about under his shirt. He pulled her closer and kissed her harder, his hands starting to roam into places Jim had never explored.

Horrified, and starting to feel quite frightened, Lily prayed with all her heart for her mother to come back. She'd be scandalised, but Lily couldn't see any other way this could end. She tried harder to wriggle away, to get an arm free so she could push him off, slap him or even scratch his face. But Frank had her pinned tightly against him and she could feel his excitement. Her own blood was pounding in her head: would he never come up for air? Then, prayers answered, she heard the back door open, and feet cross the kitchen floor. Frank had tipped her head so far back that she could only see the ceiling, but she sensed another person in the room and all at once Frank was being pulled roughly off her. Released, she staggered back, and saw not her mother, but Jim.

'It all happened at once' was what they said in

books, but it really did. One second they were all standing there, the next Jim was taking a swing at Frank.

'No!' cried Lily. 'He boxed for the county! Jim! Don't!'

Too late. Jim's fist met Frank's jaw and now he was the one staggering back, catching the standard lamp with his shoulder. It crashed to the floor and Frank sprawled into the armchair, clutching his face.

'Get out!' shouted Jim. 'Now! Before I do it again!'

Again? Was he mad? It must have been a lucky punch that had caught Frank off his guard. Jim could never repeat it: he had no chance if Frank fought back! Lily tugged on Jim's arm, fully expecting Frank to leap up and flatten him.

'Stop it, both of you!' she cried. 'Frank, just go!'

'Oh, Frank, is it?' sneered Jim. 'I'm glad you know his name at least, since he had his hands all over you and his tongue down your throat!'

Lily reeled back again. She had never heard Jim use such crude language. Frank had picked up his jacket and was dabbing at the blood on his split lip with the back of his hand. But he wasn't going just yet.

'You want to keep a better eye on her, pal,' he said to Jim. 'Inviting strange men round when there's no one home. I dare say I'm not the first.'

He leant across to Lily, so close she could smell the blood.

'Night, Lily. It was good while it lasted.' He turned to Jim again. 'Good luck with her.'

He went out through the kitchen and the door slammed behind him.

'Care to explain?' asked Jim.

Chapter 17

He righted the standard lamp – thank goodness, the bulb wasn't broken and the shade only slightly dented – while Lily shakily rearranged her disordered clothes. Then, a condemned woman, she stood to face him.

She told him the truth – who Frank was and how she'd met him on her trip to Ward and Keppler. She told him that she'd seen Frank once before in Hinton, when he'd had taken her to Lyons, and how this evening he'd been waiting for her again outside work, and that, yes, she'd let him walk her home and had invited him in. That much she got out in a low voice, wincing at every word, feeling how cheap it made her sound. Then her emotions took over.

'But it was only because he was . . . I'm sorry, Jim, I know it was weak, but he was nice to me, I thought he was just being friendly! And Mum was going to be out, and I didn't want to be on my own . . . and . . . and it was only because Frank was there and you weren't!'

'Oh, so it's my fault, is it? Because my mother died?'

Lily had expected some rebuke, but she hadn't anticipated quite such cold fury.

'No!' she cried. 'I didn't mean that!'

'I wonder what you do mean,' said Jim icily. 'And what you really want.' Then his tone changed. Now it was hurt, pure and simple. 'I'm . . . what am I supposed to think, Lily? I thought we had an understanding.'

'We do!'

'Really? I wonder. And it's not just that.' His voice shook. 'To come in and find you . . . like that . . . when I've always behaved so . . . so decently with you. We agreed we wouldn't go too far. Do you think that's been easy for me?'

'No,' said Lily in a small voice.

She knew it hadn't; there'd been times when they'd both nearly got carried away.

'So how am I supposed to feel when I come back and find another bloke slobbering all over you?'

'I didn't want him to! I didn't encourage him! He grabbed me, there was nothing I could do! Jim, if

175

you knew how I didn't want it – I was frightened – I was trying to push him off!'

'Looked like it!' Jim scorned. 'You seemed to be writhing with passion to me.'

'What? Don't you believe me? Don't you trust me at all?'

'Trust? Why should I? How can I? You say you've only seen him a couple of times – for all I know you've seen him every weekend I've been away. Him – or other blokes!'

'What?' Lily was horrified. 'You're not going to take his word over mine? I know I was wrong – very wrong to ask him back here. I was stupid! But, Jim, you must know I'd never – I'm not like that!

'Oh, yes? I don't know what I know any more! All I do know is, I've been away every weekend since the summer, how do I know how you've been carrying on? Deceiving me? And now . . . when things are so black for me at home? It's despicable.'

'Me, despicable?'

Lily's blood was up. Goodness knew, she'd been in the wrong and she'd admitted it, but she'd taken enough.

'You talk about trust – what about you?' she flared. 'You've been playing the devoted son when it's been a nice cover for dallying with that Margaret Povey!'

Now it was Jim who reeled back.

'I know, Jim! I know!' Lily cried. 'That scarf? She made it for you and you hid it in your pocket and you swap it for mine once you've left the house. You talk about me being despicable and deceitful – what about you?'

Jim had paled.

'Oh, God.'

'Yes, you may well call on God!'

It was a phrase of her mother's, and Lily rapped it out just as Dora would have done.

'All right,' said Jim quietly. He seemed to have folded in on himself. 'All right. Yes, she made it. She gave it to me, and I wore it, like you say. I admit it. I didn't want to hurt her feelings. It was stupid of me not to tell you, but I thought you might be hurt.'

'And I'm not now?'

'Look.' He spread his hands. 'Me and Margaret are friends, that's all. I've known her since school. Maybe she quite likes me, but it's all one-sided. I've never encouraged her.'

'Are you sure?' Lily had a good hand now and she was going to play it. 'That's not the impression I got from that portrait.'

Jim recoiled and Lily felt a smug sort of satisfaction that came from wounding him just as he'd wounded her.

'See,' she went on. 'I know about that too. You kept that quiet as well, and no wonder. Signed, "Affectionately, Margaret"? "Affectionately"?'

Jim didn't ask her how she'd found the drawing, or what she'd been doing in his room. He hung his head. It was all the answer Lily needed. She drew breath, and out it came.

'You did encourage her, Jim, or at least you didn't discourage her. And why? To pacify your mother. That's what she had against me – that's why I was never asked back. She had nothing to hold against me, but she wanted you back, and married to Margaret, and by not making a stand, you let them both believe it could happen!'

Jim's head came up and he looked her in the eye.

'Oh, that's what you think, is it?' he countered. 'Well, I did stand up to my mother over it, if you must know. We fell out over it – over you – and we never really made up, and now she's gone! I'm her only child, and she went to her grave unhappy about me! So I hope you're happy, anyway!'

Lily opened her mouth to apologise. She knew she'd gone too far.

'I came home tonight,' Jim said, his voice shaking, 'just for you, to tell you how things are at home. I could have stayed with my father, I should have stayed. I could have written, but I thought we could at least have a bit of time together. I wanted so much to see you, and I thought you'd want to see me. But you've been stewing about Margaret, and you decided to pay me back with that . . . that spiv! It's pathetic. I thought better of you. I think we're through.'

'What, Jim – no! Don't say that!'

Jim picked up his bag.

'I'll stay the night as I planned. There'll be plenty for me to do tomorrow anyway. But I'll keep out of your way. I don't think we should see each other again.'

With that, he went out of the room and she heard him climb the stairs.

Lily realised her legs were shaking. She fumbled behind her for the chair and almost fell into it. The fire was fading fast, but on the mantelpiece the clock ticked away, the old oak clock with the gas bill behind it, and Sid's latest postcard alongside. A framed photo of Reg in khaki shorts and of Sid in his uniform; of the three children when they were young, seated like ducks in a row on a chaise longue with a potted palm behind them. There was a china dog, one of a pair – the other had got broken – and a small lustre vase, a present from Dora's cousin Ida after a holiday in Cornwall. Lily stared at them. She'd dusted them so many times; they were all so familiar, but she felt as if she'd never handled them, and never would again. She might never do anything again, just sit there and wither away.

Above her, all was quiet. Jim must have gone to bed. She wondered if he was asleep or if he was lying there, fuming, turning things over in his mind. The old Lily would have rushed up, banged on the door and demanded to be heard, but all her usual spirit had drained away. There was no more she could say to him anyway, not that he'd listen to. The only person she wanted to talk to at this moment was her mum. The clock ticked. Ten . . . ten past . . . where was she?

Finally, at twenty past, she appeared.

'What a night!' said Dora. And she didn't even know yet! She crossed the room, and, ever economical, bent to unplug the standard lamp that Lily had switched off after its ordeal. Dora was convinced that electricity somehow leaked through the socket in the night, at a cost to both her and the country. 'Mrs Arkwright had one of her funny turns. I had to take her home and put her to bed, and could I find her *sal volatile*? I could not, and she was in no state to help me, poor dear!' She unbuttoned her coat. 'Sorry if you were worried, love. You shouldn't have waited up.'

'Oh, Mum!'

Her mother's presence, her comforting bustle, were more than Lily could take.

'Hey, hey, what's all this?'

Lily's face had crumpled: sick shock had stopped her tears before, but now her shoulders sagged and she put her hands to her face.

Still in her coat, Dora knelt beside her.

'What is it?' she asked gently. 'If this is about Reg . . . oh, Lily. You know it could be weeks before we hear from him and know exactly what went on. You haven't started worrying about him again, have you?'

'Oh, Mum, no! It's not about Reg! I only wish it was!'

'Well, what, then? Is it Jim? Have you heard from him?'

At the mention of Jim's name, more tears.

'He's here! And he came back when . . . when . . . when I was . . . '

Dora sat back on her heels. Something was up, and some of her usual briskness returned. Kindness alone wouldn't do it. This was something that was going to need coping with.

'Lily, now listen to me. Listen.' She felt in her pocket. 'Here's my hanky. You're going to stop this crying and I'm going to make us both a cup of tea. Then I think you'd better tell me all about it, don't you?'

Bit by bit, over cooling cups of tea, the story came out. Jim and Lily, Lily and Frank, Jim and Margaret, and finally, horribly, Frank and Lily and Jim.

'It's all a mess, and it's all my fault!' Lily wept. 'Jim says we're through! He'll leave me, and Hinton, and he'll end up with Margaret anyway, and it won't even be his mum's doing! It's all my fault and I deserve it!'

'Now, now,' said Dora. 'That's enough. You're running ahead a bit, aren't you?'

'Well, why wouldn't he, Mum? I've lost him, and through my own stupidity! His mum will get her way

after all, and maybe it's the least I owe her!' She wept
again. 'Even if she's not here to see it!'

'Dear, oh dear, you've got yourself in a right old
state, haven't you?'

Lily swiped at her eyes with the back of her hand.

'I know. And I'm so sorry. To have . . . to have
behaved so badly and let you down and to load all
this onto you on top of . . . on top of Reg and
everything.'

'Good grief!' exclaimed Dora. 'You don't need to
worry about me! Don't you think I'd rather know?
The state you're in there'd be no hiding it anyway,
would there?'

'I suppose not.'

Dora took a deep breath, usually the prelude to
one of her homilies. Lily braced herself, but her mum's
tone was far from harsh.

'You've been a very silly girl, but you know that.
You've let your head be turned, and even if things
were a bit trying between you and Jim, that's no
excuse.'

'I know. I'm so ashamed.'

'And so you should be. But nothing I say's going
to make you feel any worse than you do already, or
any better, so I'll save my breath for this. If it had
been me who'd walked in when this Frank was getting
fresh, he might have had worse than a split lip, I can
tell you. Has it occurred to you, Lily, that you had
a lucky escape? He could have done anything to you!'

There was a tremor in her mother's voice. Lily remembered her own panic when Frank had been kissing her so violently, and how she'd prayed for Dora to come home.

'I know. I realise that now. If I could do things differently, Mum—'

Dora shook her head.

'The saddest words in the language! There's no point, love. What's done is done. What matters now is how you carry on.'

'That's what I don't know!' Lily burst out. 'How do I carry on? How do I face Jim? He doesn't want to see me and even if he did, what can I say to change his mind?'

'Well, hang on a minute now! I'm not having you take all the blame! That young man's got some explaining of his own to do. When things have calmed down a bit—'

'Oh, Mum, not that! Please don't say everything'll look better in the morning!'

'No,' said Dora mildly. 'It'll look just the same, but you'll at least be a little bit rested. So will Jim. Some of the heat will have gone out of the situation.'

'You really think so?'

'I know so. You'll apologise to Jim, and if he's misled you, he'll apologise to you. You'll both have more chance to explain. Lay it all out between you. And if you do part . . .' Lily had started forward in her chair, 'no, hear me out – if you do part, it's a lesson learnt. A hard lesson, especially when you're both so young, but one everyone has to learn sooner or later. So you learn from it, and you don't let it happen again.' Dora paused to make sure her daughter had taken this in. 'And if you stay together, you'll have to put this behind you, both of you. Things maybe won't feel right, or be right, between you straight away, but it'll be a start. And you'll build things back up again.'

Lily had longed for her mum to tell her what to do. Now she had, it sounded as if it might just be possible, put plainly like that, but, but . . .

'I wish I could believe you, Mum! About Jim and me staying together! And maybe we could, if . . . if there was nothing else to think about. But what about his dad? Who's going to look after him, if not Jim? It's just another reason for him to call it a day between us!'

'There you go again,' tutted her mother, 'borrowing trouble. One thing at a time. First, get yourself back on speaking terms with Jim. Then you might hear what his plans are.'

'I don't see what else they can be!'

'Right,' said Dora, firmly. 'That's enough. There's no point in you saying the same thing over and over and me saying something just for the sake of it. I'm tired and you're exhausted. Go and wash your face, then it's bed for both of us.'

Lily sniffed again and dabbed her smarting eyes for one last time.

'It'll all look better in the morning?'

Dora got up. With her kindest smile she pushed a strand of Lily's hair behind her ear. 'I thought I wasn't allowed to say that! But remember, Lily, it's always darkest just before the dawn.'

Chapter 18

Dawn, thought Lily the next day when she opened her eyes on a blackness that wasn't just the fault of the blackout, *what dawn*?

She turned her hot head on the hot pillow. She'd finally fallen into a shallow sleep, her waking dreams replaying the previous evening in all its horror and humiliation. Now it was morning – or soon would be. She reached out and switched on the light. To her amazement it was after seven o'clock. If she wasn't careful, she'd be late!

Her eyes were still burning and she pressed them with the backs of her hands, cold because the room was cold. Her mum saying 'talk to Jim' was all very well, but she had to go to work. Jim had said he'd stay out of her way, and if he went back to Bidbury during the day, the chance would be lost. Her only hope was that her mum could keep him in Hinton – by force if necessary.

The thought of Jim lassoed with the washing line and lashed to a kitchen chair almost made her smile and gave her some resolve. Shivering as her feet touched the boards beyond the rag rug, she dressed and sped downstairs. She'd write her mum a note and shove it under her bedroom door.

But there was no need. On the table downstairs, a note in her mother's writing was propped up against the cruet. Lily snatched it up.

Get to work and don't worry. I'll make sure Jim stays till you can see him. You two must sort yourselves out – I can't do that for you. But I've had an idea that might help. Remember, 'head down, chin up!' Love, Mum. x

P.S. Gone to queue. A rumour of corned beef!

Lily read the note again. And again. An idea? What could that be?

At least it was Wednesday – half day – and on the way in, Lily worked out a way to put the famous family motto into practice. Miss Frobisher noted a face as pale as the collar and cuffs on Lily's uniform dress but looked approving when Lily proposed swapping two of the four-arm rails for three-arm to show the thicker winter coats off to better advantage and offered to get up and dust the top of the glass-fronted cabinets where the cleaners' feather dusters didn't reach. Anything to keep busy – and keep Miss Frobisher's all-seeing eyes off her.

If Lily had but known it Miss Frobisher had another victim in mind for her gimlet gaze that day. Gladys might not have seen Lily leave with Frank yesterday evening, but in the boardroom, early for the buyers' meeting, Miss Frobisher had been standing by the window – and had not been impressed with what she saw happen below.

So by mid-morning, as Lily lugged rails and coats about, Eileen Frobisher had Frank Bryant in front of her – in fact almost knee-to-knee – in the cubby hole Mr Simmonds called his office. She allowed Frank to run through his patter about difficulties in the supply of stockinette and explain why, sadly, there'd be a shortfall in her most recent order. He smiled winningly at her – as winningly, she noted, as his cut and swollen lip would allow.

'But I can promise you, Marlow's will be top of the list when we get our hands on some!'

Miss Frobisher smiled too.

'That's excellent. Thank you.' Her smile expired. 'But it seems to me that's not all you have a mind to get your hands on.'

Frank gave a little shake of his head, as if to clear it.

'I'm sorry?'

'I think,' Miss Frobisher said coolly, 'your interest in Marlow's goes a bit beyond fulfilling our orders. I think it extends to my staff.'

Frank gave another little shake of his head. Perhaps, she thought, it was a little muzzy this morning. He'd obviously been in some kind of altercation: someone had thumped him – perhaps even Lily. It wasn't the kind of behaviour Marlow's would usually encourage in their staff but on this occasion, if so, good for her! 'Oh, I think you do. You're not stupid. You can see when a young girl's a bit bedazzled.'

Eileen could almost see his brain whirring as he tried to work out how she knew, how much she knew, and how he could wriggle out of it.

'If you mean Lily Collins, Miss Frobisher, I admit I walked her home. She's been anxious about her brother, as you probably know. If she . . . well, I think what you're getting at is that . . . look, this is a bit embarrassing, but she seems to have developed rather a crush on me.'

'Oh, it's that way round, is it? Strange, then, that you were here of your own free will yesterday evening and obviously waiting for her.'

Still he tried to brazen it out. 'There's nothing wrong with that, is there? I was in town ahead of my calls and popped by – as a friend – to say hello.'

189

Joanna Toye

'That's a good one!' Miss Frobisher's marcasite brooch glinted evilly under the overhead bulb. 'You've got all the lines, haven't you? Perhaps you'd like to explain, then, how you came by that split lip of yours. It wouldn't be a jealous boyfriend, by any chance? Or did Lily have the sense to tell you where to get off?'

'This?' Frank touched his mouth. 'I walked into a lamp post in the blackout. It comes of not knowing the lie of the land.'

'The only kind of lie you're not familiar with!' snapped Eileen. 'I know your type, I've been in this business long enough. Lily has a young man, as I'm sure you know. And I know her. She's not the sort to two-time him. Whereas you – well, a girl in every store wouldn't be putting it too strongly, I dare say!'

Frank smirked, though she could see he wished he hadn't; it must have pulled at his sore mouth.

'I saw you waiting,' she said coldly. 'I saw you eyeing up pretty much every girl who came out, even giving some a bit of chat. I dare say if Lily hadn't come out at the moment she did you might well have settled on someone else entirely.'

He hadn't bothered with Gladys and Brenda, she'd observed, both of them too deep in conversation to notice him anyway. She was thinking of Gloria, a saucy piece from Cosmetics, who'd emerged in a jaunty hat and provoked a wolf whistle and a wink.

Finally, Frank dropped the pretence.

190

'I won't deny it,' he shrugged. 'I can't help it if girls find me irresistible.'

'Irresponsible, more like!' Eileen Frobisher raked him with her most contemptuous glare. 'If I find out that you're paying attention – wanted or unwanted – to any of the staff at Marlow's, I shall be complaining directly to Mr Ward.'

Frank stood up, causing her to swivel her legs swiftly away. He snapped shut the locks on his case of samples. He pinched the creases in his trousers and tightened his tie with its flashy gold pin.

'You won't need to,' he said. 'I haven't put in my resignation yet, but I will.'

It was Miss Frobisher's turn to look shocked: she hadn't expected her lecture to have quite such an immediate effect.

'I was going to resign anyway,' he said. 'I've got another job. Babywear – you can keep it! I'm going to a fancy goods firm. In London.'

'Fancy goods,' Miss Frobisher said slowly. 'Well, congratulations, Mr Bryant. That should suit you down to the ground.'

Chapter 19

Across town, another, rather friendlier, discussion was taking place. After the grocer's – and, yes, a tin of corned beef! – Dora had called on Ivy.

'Well you've caught me with my drawers down all right!' Ivy clucked as she ushered Dora through to the back room. Susan was, as usual these days, looking wary, but beamed when she saw who it was. Dora held out her arms and Susan rushed into them, jabbering something indistinct.

'Pleased to see you, isn't she?' Ivy smiled wearily. 'Let Auntie Dora sit down, Susan, there's a love.'

Susan did so, plumping the cushion on the best chair for Dora, who accepted it politely. Ivy established Susan at the table with her picture books and sank into her own chair opposite her guest. Beryl, she informed her, had taken Bobby to the baby clinic.

Ivy picked up a pair of bloomers she was mending.

'Gone at the seat and the seam!' she lamented. 'I've had to cut the bottom off a slip to let in down the side. And a piece off one of Eddie's hankies for the patch. Let me finish off and I'll brew up.'

'Don't worry about that,' said Dora. 'I've . . . I've got a proposition for you.'

'Oh, ar? It's been a long time since I had one of them!' Ivy bit off a length of cotton. 'Go on!'

So Dora began. Without going into detail about the previous evening, she said Jim had come back on a flying visit and was in a bind about taking care of his father.

'He's been there himself till now, of course, and there's the woman who's been coming in since Alice was first taken ill. But she can't do any more hours – she's got a family of her own – so what happens next is a problem.'

'A problem for your Lily, as well,' remarked Ivy shrewdly, rolling a knot in the end of the thread. 'If Jim leaves Hinton.'

'I won't deny it, she's worried sick he will. She doesn't want to leave her job, and if she did, what'd she do out there? Work on the land? I don't see it. And she's no housewife! Or a nurse!'

'They'd have to get married,' mused Ivy. 'The way people talk. We think it's bad here, but in a village—'

193

'Jim and Lily are a long way off marriage, I can tell you,' said Dora firmly.

A very long way at the moment, she thought.

'Well, I don't know,' mused Ivy. 'Gladys is your best bet, if you're looking for a nursemaid, the way that old besom of a gran of hers has her running around.'

'More of a housekeeper, really,' replied Dora. 'Jim's dad doesn't need nursing as such. But it wasn't Gladys I was thinking of.'

Ivy paused in her stitching.

'Who were you thinking of?'

'You, Ivy. That's the proposition.'

'Me?'

Dora took the plunge.

'Why not? You've been saying for months this place is too crowded with you and Beryl not really getting on. Susan's a prisoner since that affair on the rec, it's hard for you to get out – wouldn't a move to the country solve all your problems?'

Ivy laid aside her mending. She put her hand to her chest.

'You've quite winded me!' she exclaimed. 'I don't know what to say!'

'I didn't expect an answer straight away. It'd be a big step. But it'd be a new start as well, for you and for Susan. She'd thrive in the country, I'm sure. Lots of new things for her to see and do. And as for Jim's dad—'

'Tom, isn't it?'

'That's right.' Dora was encouraged by what sounded like interest. 'I don't think he's any trouble. He's just slow, and not too steady on his legs, and got a weak chest—'

'Well, I've had years of dealing with that!' Ivy looked across lovingly at Susan. She'd abandoned her books and was tracing her finger equally lovingly along the Rupert Bear strip in the *Express*, pretending to read the words.

'Will you think about it, then?' asked Dora hopefully. 'No one'd expect you take it on sight unseen. You'd have to go and meet Jim's dad, see if you like the idea once you're there. And check there'd be suitable accommodation. There'd be no question of anything improper. You'd be his housekeeper and Jim'd pay you. You'd have to ask Eddie, all the same . . . '

Ivy tossed her head.

'Him! There'll be a man on the moon before you get an answer if you involve him! I haven't heard a dicky bird in nearly six months! He's never been much of a correspondent, but this is rich, even for him.'

'I see!'

Dora never liked to ask about other people's marriages. Her own had been blissfully happy till her husband's early death, and though she knew full well not everyone was as lucky, she'd never have pried. Only the wearer knows where the shoe pinches, and

Ivy didn't talk much about Eddie, except sometimes to comment that the monthly payment that kept her and Susan was late. Dora had thought it best not to probe.

'What do you reckon, then?' she hazarded.

Ivy levered herself up from her chair, making clear the daily strain her bloomers were under.

'I'm going to put the kettle on,' she announced.

'You'll consider it, though?'

'I'll consider it,' said Ivy graciously.

She wheezed off to the scullery and Dora breathed a deep sigh. She'd have a cup of tea and then she'd better get home and leave Ivy to her 'considering'. There was still plenty to sort out. She'd left Jim a note telling him not to go anywhere till they'd had a word – she could only hope he'd think her idea was worth considering as well. And then there was the little matter of him and Lily.

Jim was hunched over the table when she got back, writing a letter. He stood up respectfully when Dora came in.

'Mrs Collins.'

Jim had never been anything but proper with her. He'd never been anything but proper with Lily, Dora was sure, so she didn't underestimate the shock and revulsion he must have felt when he'd walked in and seen Lily – how her daughter had blushed to tell her – being kissed and fondled by another man.

'Jim.' Dora put down her bag and took off her headscarf. She unbuttoned her coat and draped it over the back of a chair. 'I'm so glad you're still here.'

'You asked me to wait. I paid Mrs Dawkins to stay over with my father last night and she'll be there all day, so I don't need to leave till later.'

He looked so miserable that Dora felt for him – almost as much as she'd felt for Lily last night.

'I'm very sorry about your mother, Jim,' she said. 'There's been no chance to say it, really, with you coming and going so quick, but it must have been a terrible shock for you. And your father. We all knew she hadn't been well, but – I suppose we all thought she was going along all right. Even if she wasn't getting any better.'

'Yes. And she could have gone on like it for years. So in a way, maybe it was a mercy another stroke took her so quickly. But it doesn't alter things. My dad can't fend for himself, there's no one else, so the only option is for me to move back and—'

'Before you go any further,' interrupted Dora, moving to the table, 'I think we need a little chat.'

'I'm sorry, but I'm not sure there's any more to say.' Jim waited for her to sit down before he sat himself. 'I could hear you and Lily down here last night, so I assume she's told you what happened. And it's only made my decision easier. I'm writing to Marlow's to resign. I'll move back to Bidbury, take work on the land, and look after my father myself.'

'Is that so?'

'Look,' said Jim. 'I assume she's given you her version of events. I wouldn't expect you to do anything else but take her side.'

'It's not about sides, Jim,' said Dora. 'You know that. It's about trying to get to the truth.'

'Mrs Collins. My eyesight may have kept me out of the Army, but I can see what's in front of me! I could see perfectly well last night!'

'Well, you need to look again,' said Dora, 'and a bit harder. What you'd see is a girl who loves you to pieces. A girl who's been lonely without you, much as she understands why you've had to be away, and aches for what you've been going through. Lily was lonely and confused, and when this fellow Frank turned up and started paying her attention – well, she admits, she was flattered. And it was stupid, she can see that now. She could probably see it all along. But till last night all she'd ever done was have a cup of tea with him – once! She never intended to get involved with him, let alone allow him to—' Dora searched for an expression that would not embarrass herself or Jim, 'misbehave like that. It wouldn't have occurred to her! He forced himself on her!'

'That's fine as far as it goes,' said Jim coolly. 'But if it was all so innocent on her part, how come she didn't mention him?'

Dora was ready for this. 'That's a good question,' she fired back. 'And I've got one for you. This

Margaret back home. She's been around rather more than you've led Lily to believe, and seems fonder of you, too. How come you didn't mention her? Or the presents she'd given you?'

Jim reddened and lowered his eyes. He didn't reply.

'I think you've both been rather guilty of behaving as if truth was on the ration, don't you?'

Jim sighed. 'Look, Mrs Collins. There's truly nothing between me and Margaret but an old friendship. On my part, anyway. Lily need have had no worries there. But I agree I haven't exactly covered myself in glory – with either of them. I'll apologise to Lily, of course. But sadly, there are other things in play anyhow.'

'I know. And I know you only want to do the best by your dad. You're a good boy, Jim. Lily doesn't want you to go. I don't want you to go. So – I hope you don't mind – I've got a suggestion.'

'Oh yes?'

'It's for Ivy Bulpitt to go and housekeep for him.'

Jim's head jerked back.

'What?'

'That's where I've been. Your dad needs looking after, and Ivy and Susan need to get away from that house and that neighbourhood. I hope you don't mind, I've put it to her and she's said she'll think about it. We'd have to sort out the details, of course, and I'm making a lot of assumptions – whether your dad'd take to the idea – and Ivy, when he meets her.

And vice versa . . . You'd need to talk to her if you're interested, but . . . '

She tailed off. Jim was looking down at the cloth. 'Well, what do you think?'

When he looked up, his eyes were full.

'I think this is the kindest thing anyone's ever done for me. I couldn't see a way out. I thought I'd have to leave here and Marlow's and I really didn't want to. I can't tell you what a relief it would be to have someone I know and who I feel I could trust to look after him. I mean – he's all I've got left, really, and . . .' It was his turn to tail off. He collected himself. 'It'd remove a huge burden of guilt. I was writing to Marlow's to resign. But I may not need to now! Of course I'll talk to Ivy – oh, I hope she'll do it! And that they take to each other!'

'If Ivy says yes, I'll make sure she's on her best behaviour when they meet,' Dora assured him. 'None of her near-the-knuckle cracks. And I'll make sure she dresses respectable, too.'

Ivy's bold taste in clothes, combined with her sizeable physical presence and personality, could be a little overwhelming. As could her sometimes salty language.

'It might be an idea!' Then Jim's smile faded, and he said, 'About Lily. I feel such a heel. I said some dreadful things. As she probably told you.'

'That's between you and her. I've said my piece.'

'I owe both of them an apology, Lily and Margaret.

I left Lily in the dark and I didn't make it clear to Margaret that . . . that nothing was going to happen. And last night when I came back . . . oh, I don't know. Things seemed so bleak and hopeless at home and I was so looking forward to seeing Lily and talking it through and trying to work things out and to come in and find—'

'You don't have to explain, Jim,' said Dora. 'Not to me, anyhow.'

He gave her a brief smile.

'Thank you.'

Dora straightened the tablecloth, then looked at him sidelong.

'But tell me one thing. You're . . . well, you're no Charles Atlas, if you don't mind me saying, and from what I can gather, this Frank's a well-set-up kind of lad. Heat of the moment or not, how on earth did you manage to land a punch that nearly floored him?'

Chapter 20

'Made your mind up yet?'

The assistant in the flower shop, a surly girl who'd never have cut it at Marlow's, leant on the counter, tapping her teeth with her pencil.

Jim was stuck. He knew what he wanted, but the roses in a tall metal vase were priced by the stem and way beyond his pocket. Chrysanthemums or carnations were the only things he could afford, but the carnations looked constipated with their closed buds that might never open, and the chrysanths had an odd, pungent smell. The bronze ones were a bit drab, but there were some smaller white ones with greenish centres . . . maybe those . . .

The girl sighed heavily and looked at her watch.

'I'm going early dinner. Closing at half twelve.'

Jim hated to be hurried. He picked up a bunch of white chrysanths and stood there with them dripping on to his shoes.

The girl was already ringing up the till.

'That'll be—'

'Hang on.' Jim interrupted her. There were more flowers standing at the back of the shop. 'What about those?'

'Them?' She looked at him shrewdly. 'They're even more than the roses. Hothouse, see.'

Jim gulped. Who was it who'd said, 'if you have to ask the price, you can't afford it'? 'I'll take five, please,' he said determinedly. 'But give me a minute. I need to nip to the bank.'

It would be worth it.

Ten minutes later he was crossing the street and entering Marlow's by the front doors. They were forbidden to staff, but for once he didn't care. He wasn't staff today, Jim reasoned, knowing full well he'd be in hot water. Not caring that they were staring, he strode past the salesgirls on Cosmetics, past Gloves and Accessories, past Handbags, up the carpeted main staircase to the first floor. Past Model Gowns and Exclusives and Ladies' Fashions . . . and there was Lily, positioning a rail of little velvet-collared coats. Miss Thomas was with a customer at the counter but Miss Frobisher didn't seem to be around, not that it would have made any difference to Jim's resolve. He tapped Lily on the shoulder and she wheeled around.

'Jim!'

Jim said nothing but pushed the flowers towards her. She took them, eyes wide.

'Lilies!'

'What else?'

And then she was in his arms, the flowers crushed between them.

'Oh, Jim, I'm sorry, I'm so, so, sorry!' she cried.

He took in the scent of her hair, and the wonderful feel of her close to him.

'I'm sorry, too. Very sorry.'

'No, I'm sorrier! I must be, I really am!'

Jim released her and took a step back, amused, exasperated. Everything he was used to feeling about Lily was back. And the love, too – though that had never truly gone away.

'You always have to have the last word!'

'So?'

She'd done it again. Probably without even realising.

'How did we get away with it?' she asked him at one o'clock when the store had closed and they were outside.

'All the world loves a lover?' suggested Jim.

They were both grinning like idiots. Neither could believe the wrath of God in the shape of Miss

Frobisher or Mr Simmonds hadn't descended on them. Instead, Miss Thomas had quickly shooed them both towards the back stairs, past open-mouthed staff and mostly indulgent-looking customers. A couple of them had even applauded; maybe Jim was right.

'I don't know where Miss Frobisher was,' Lily marvelled. 'It's not often she leaves Miss Thomas to cash up.'

'Lucky break then. She's a nice old stick, isn't she, Thomas?'

'She was nice at the time, but word'll get back, Jim. We'll pay for it somehow!'

'Worth every penny.'

Lily sighed and lifted her flowers to her face.

'And these? They're so beautiful, Jim.' She inhaled the scent of the half-open blooms. 'They must have cost a fortune.'

'Also worth every penny if we're friends again.'

'I thought we were more than friends? I hope we are.' Lily slipped her free hand into his. 'I'm so sorry for—'

'Enough! It's not a competition, Lily, to see who's sorrier.'

'I know, but—'

'Shut up!' he said affectionately. 'We both made mistakes, but you have to make mistakes to learn from them. And I think we have. So no more sorries. Not like that, anyway. Let's head for the park and I can show you how sorry I really am.'

Lily knew what he meant. There was a little rustic shelter where they went when they wanted to be on their own.

'So?' she asked him sometime later when they had properly, and several times over, proved to each other just how sorry they were. Now they were cuddled together on the bench in the shelter, Lily stroking the petals of her flowers with one hand and Jim's long fingers with the other. 'If we're not allowed to talk about what happened, are we allowed to talk about what happens next?'

'Very much so.'

'Well?'

Did he have a plan? Was he going to carry on commuting to Bidbury or was he going to try to persuade her to move there too? Much as she'd wanted everything between them to be right again, Lily wasn't sure she was ready for that.

'Your mum's come up with an idea.'

Of course! Dora's note! Jim's unexpected appearance on the shop floor had wiped it from Lily's mind. 'What? What is it?'

Jim told her about Dora's proposal to solve two problems in one – his and Ivy's. Even for her mother, Lily had to concede, this was a masterstroke.

'I'm going to sound Ivy out myself,' explained Jim. 'There'll be lots she wants to ask, I'm sure, but my dad's no trouble. He never has been and – I'll say it

– unlike my mother, he'd never expect me to give up my life here to be with him. It was me who was feeling I had to do that.'

'And I know you'd have done it, that's what terrified me! So it all depends on Ivy?'

'It does, really. They'd have to meet and see how they like each other. But I've got a good feeling about it, Lily.' He caught her hand in his. 'It suits her as well. They may be a bit of an odd couple, but she may make life better for my dad. Jolly him along. My mother wasn't the sunniest of characters even when she was well.'

You said it, thought Lily.

Instead, she asked quietly, 'When's the funeral?'

'Next week. Monday. If you can get the time off, I'd like you to come.'

Lily's heart lurched. She'd desperately wanted to be there, but after all that had happened, she hadn't dared ask.

'Of course I will. Of course.' She gave him a hug. 'Jim?'

'Yes?' He lifted his face from her hair.

'Last night. I know you said we weren't to talk about it again, but you have to tell me just one thing.'

'Go on.'

'Where did you learn to throw a punch like that?'

Jim threw back his head and laughed.

'Your mum asked me the same question. You can't

spend all the time I have with Peter Simmonds without picking up a few tips.'

'Mr Simmonds taught you to box?'

'Not exactly. More of a demo really. But we did a bit of sparring.'

'When? Where?'

'Just messing about when we got bored of trying to overhaul the inventory system.'

'So you decided to knock seven bells out of each other?'

'I told you, it wasn't like that! All he did was give me some tips. Throw the punch straight out from your shoulder with your leading arm. Then your shoulder comes up automatically and protects your chin from a punch in return.'

'Thank goodness last night never got that far!'

'I half wish it had!' said Jim sadly. 'I never got chance to unleash my cross.'

Lily punched him now, on the arm.

'You're an idiot,' she said. 'If he'd fought back, he could have killed you!'

'Huh, not got much faith in me, have you?' grinned Jim. 'You'd be surprised what I can do when I'm roused.'

'Surprise me,' said Lily, and lifted her face.

They had to part soon after. Jim had an appointment to see Mr Marlow that he'd arranged when he'd planned to resign, and he might as well keep it. He thought he'd try to see Mr Simmonds, too.

'Straight back into the lion's den?' queried Lily.

'Putting my head right in its mouth.' Jim grimaced. 'But look, if anyone's for the high jump after my big romantic gesture it should be me.' Having mixed two metaphors already he threw caution to the winds and added another. 'I might as well face the music.'

Lion's den or not, Jim couldn't help smiling to himself about the way things had turned out as he waited to be admitted to his uncle's office. Cedric was in a meeting with the buyers from Gentlemen's Outfitting. What was the collective name for a group of menswear buyers, he wondered. A swatch? A bolt? A yard? Just when he'd decided on 'swatch', the door to the inner office opened and the buyers trooped out. Men's clothing hadn't escaped Utility regulations. There were no double-breasted suits any more, no waistcoats, no turn-ups. No wonder the buyers, who'd given their lives to the width of a lapel or the lining of a jacket, looked glum.

Mr Marlow had come to the door with them and motioned Jim inside. Cedric was still wearing a three-piece suit, but CC41 – Controlled Commodity 1941 – clothing made no difference to a man like him. He must have had about twenty suits in his wardrobe, enough to see him through any war. Jim had only one. Still, Jim thought, he was hardly here to pick a fight.

Nor, it seemed, was his uncle, though by now he must have heard all about what had gone on with the flowers – and Jim's use of the customer entrance.

'Sit down,' Cedric urged, moving back behind his desk. 'I want to say how sorry I am, Jim, for your loss.'

Jim dipped his head in acknowledgement. 'Thank you, sir. And I'm sorry for the time I've had to take off. I'll make it up.'

Cedric looked pained. 'There's really no need.'

'There is. The funeral's next week and I'm afraid I'll need the next couple of days to finalise arrangements.'

'Jim,' said Cedric quietly. 'I know you've never wanted to trade on our . . . association, and I respect that, but I'm only saying what I'd say to any employee. In these circumstances, compassionate leave is entirely appropriate.'

'A week, sir. That's what it says in the staff manual. I've had that already. Any more should be unpaid.'

Cedric sighed. He looked at the young man in front of him in his shiny suit and much-mended shoes. Stubborn, in his own way, just like his mother. He'd gathered that much about Alice Goodridge from his late wife, Alice's younger sister. Jim had a look of her about the eyes, he thought.

He tried a different tack.

'Things can't be easy with your father.' He wasn't in the best of health, Cedric knew. 'I'm not sure how you propose to manage him, but I'd like to help. A nurse, perhaps?' It was over-compensation and too late in the day. He should have been far more generous to Jim's family and offered more practical help sooner; months if not years before. And he might have guessed what the answer would be.

'That's very kind, sir. But there's no need. There's a woman in the village taking care of him at the moment, and I think I may have a permanent solution. Some live-in help.'

'At a cost, I'm sure. Look, Jim, the wages for someone at your level aren't very much – you must have been stinting yourself already.'

Staff salaries had been frozen since the start of the war and Jim's Mondays off, unpaid, again at his own insistence, must have been eating into his income. No wonder his suit was shiny.

'The extra day's been very helpful, sir, and very good of you to let me take it, but I'm hoping that once things settle down I shan't need to go as often.'

'Hoping? Why don't we both stop hoping and do something to solve the problem altogether?'

What now?

'I have a suggestion,' said Cedric. 'In fact it's not a suggestion, it's an instruction.'

Jim sat up a little straighter. When his uncle Cedric talked like this he meant business. He might be nearly seventy and a bit out of touch with the pace of change, but he still had a shrewd brain in that bald head.

'Let me pay for a telephone to be installed at home in Bidbury. Then you can check on your father – daily, if you want – using a telephone here, in the office, without having to traipse all the way out to the country.'

He smiled, and so did Jim, to himself. Uncle Cedric was shrewd, all right. Jim knew that Furniture and Household had been stretched without him – absent staff weren't replaced, and with Christmas coming up . . . But it was a generous offer and he had to admit it was a brilliant solution. It wouldn't come cheap, with the cottage being some way out of the village, but it would be a godsend, and for Ivy as well, to keep in touch with Les and Beryl. And there came a point when you could perhaps be too proud.

'That would be a huge help, sir,' he said. 'Thank you. I accept.'

Cedric sat back, satisfied.

'Good,' he said. 'Now there's one other matter. There's a young lady, I understand. Lily Collins.'

Jim looked at him straight. Here we go.

'You mean what happened earlier, sir, on the sales floor. I realise it was totally out of order, and I'd like to say I apologise, and I do – but I have to say that, in the circumstances, I'd do it all over again!'

Cedric took this in. 'She means that much to you?' he asked quietly.

'She does. We'd had a misunderstanding, and I had

to make things up to her. But I took Lily totally by surprise. That was the point. So if there's any blame attached, and any disciplinary—'

'Blame? Who's talking about blame? And disciplinaries?'

'Well, I thought you might be.'

'Oh, for goodness' sake!'

Cedric Marlow wasn't a demonstrative man and he'd had cause to regret it with his own son, Robert. He'd made mistakes when the boy was growing up without a mother, had never really tried to get to know him and had then tried to force him into a life as his successor – a life in shopkeeping that Robert had no feel for. His son was far happier – they both were – now that Robert was working in Birmingham for his prospective father-in-law. Cedric couldn't help admiring – almost envying – Jim's passion.

'Let's just say,' he began, 'that you've had a difficult time. Been under a lot of strain. Rules and regulations weren't at the front of your mind.'

'You can't let me get away with it, sir. It ought to go on my record.'

'As what exactly?'

That stumped Jim.

'You see my problem,' Cedric continued with the faintest of smiles. 'The staff manual doesn't cover it.'

'Maybe we should insert a clause.'

Jim dared a half-smile in return.

'Yes, well, you can speak to Mr Simmonds about that. He'd like to see you, I think.'

Cedric uncapped his pen and drew his correspond-ence file towards him. Jim stood up, dismissed.

'I was hoping to see him, too.' That might not be such an easy ride. 'Thank you sir. Thank you very much.'

Chapter 21

Even though the shop was closed for the afternoon, Jim automatically took the back stairs in search of Peter Simmonds. But as he emerged through the double doors on to the first floor, the first person he saw was Eileen Frobisher. So it was going to be the lioness's den.

'Mr Goodridge!' she greeted him, folding her arms. 'Or do we call you Romeo from now on?'

Jim didn't like to say that the jealous Othello might be more accurate. But if she was taking that tone, could it mean she actually wasn't too cross?

'With respect, Miss Frobisher,' he began. Nothing ventured . . . 'You know Lily; it's more like *The Taming of the Shrew*. But, um, we've resolved our differences now.'

Eileen Frobisher took this in. So there'd been doubts, difficulties, a falling-out on top of the loss of his mother – no wonder Lily had been so subdued. And all credit to her, given how young she was, for not letting her feelings show more than they had.

'I see. But after your grand gesture, there's been a happy outcome?'

'Yes.' Jim was more serious now. 'I know it was out of order, and I apologise. It won't happen again. That is, there'll be no need, I'll make sure of that. And please – none of it was Lily's fault. She's blameless.'

Eileen Frobisher looked at the young man in front of her, sincerity shining out of him, so different from the flashy Frank Bryant.

'Oh . . . run along!' she said. 'I've got invoices to check. You can tell Miss Collins we'll say no more about it. The truth is, for Marlow's, the two of you are far too useful to let go!'

Jim could breathe again – but his encounters with formidable women weren't over for the day. First Lily, then Miss Frobisher, and he still had to see Ivy Bulpitt. But when he arrived at Alma Terrace, it was Beryl who opened the door.

'My hero!' she cried. Before he knew it, he was enveloped in a waft of sour milk, only partly covered by something that smelt like a combination of stewed plums and jasmine – one of the sickly fake perfumes from Ivy's black-market contacts. He wondered what Ivy would make of the rural black market in red diesel and dung.

Beryl let him go just in time for him to take a breath, and stood back to let him in.

'It's a godsend!' she exclaimed as she shut the door. 'Me and Les getting the house to ourselves! Oh, Jim, I didn't mean . . . I'm sorry about your mum. Really. We all are.'

'It's all right.' Jim gave a brief smile. 'I know what you mean. It's a godsend to me, to tell you the truth. But you're jumping ahead a bit, aren't you? Is Ivy in? Will she really do it?'

'She's practically packing! Come on through.'

Bobby was kicking on a rug and Jim bent to make the obligatory fuss of him, so was off his guard when Ivy appeared from the kitchen. In a surprisingly swift movement for someone her size, he found himself clasped to her pillow-like chest. Susan, not wanting to be left out, wrapped her arms around him from behind and refused to let go.

'Does that mean it's a yes?' he asked when he'd finally peeled both of them off.

'Yes, it is,' said Ivy, tears in her eyes. 'It's a wonderful opportunity, Jim. Thank you!'

'Don't go thanking me!' said Jim, when he was finally sitting at the table being fed tea and bread and scrape, as he'd had no dinner. 'It was Dora's idea. And who's doing who the favour?'

Susan still had her arm round his shoulder and had brought him her rag doll. While he alternately ate, drank and plaited its stringy hair, he outlined his plan.

'I thought, Ivy, you could come out to Bidbury on Monday with Lily. She's done the journey before and I'll get a dog cart to meet you at the station at the other end. Then while we're at the funeral, you can have a chat with Mrs Dawkins, who's been helping out till now. She can give you the run-down.'

'Ooh, hear that, Beryl? What an adventure!' crowed Ivy. 'I can't wait to see the place! Susan, leave Jim alone now, he's done your dolly.' Susan took no notice. 'And I can't wait to meet your dad. If he's anything like you, he'll be a proper gentleman.'

Jim blushed while Susan waved her doll gleefully in his face.

'I don't know about that, but he's pretty easy-going. He might be a bit distracted on Monday, but you'll get a sense of how he is.'

'Bless him, the funeral's bound to knock him back,' clucked Ivy. 'But if I can cope with our Susan, I can cope with anything. Susan! I won't tell you again! Go and show your dolly to the babby!'

Meekly, Susan trotted off to kneel by the baby.

'I'll still come over some Sundays,' Jim offered. 'To keep on top of the veg plot. And, um, I'll be getting a telephone installed. So I can keep in touch.'

'A phone!' shrieked Beryl. 'How about that, Ivy? Proper posh! You've got it made, you have!'

Over the next hour, the two of them plied him with more tea and more questions. When Jim finally managed to escape their fevered excitement, he found a mercifully calmer atmosphere back at Brook Street. Lily had been arranging her flowers – four stems in Dora's prized cut-glass vase while the fifth, cut down and in a milk bottle, was destined for her own room.

'I can't take my eyes off them!' she said, and then, 'Are you all right?'

Jim had sunk down in the armchair.

'I'm shattered,' he said. 'Where's your mum?'

'WVS, where else? But I gave her the biggest hug before she went—'

'Don't even talk about it. I've been hugged to death at Ivy's!' exclaimed Jim. 'But your mum deserves one. She's an amazing woman, Lily.'

'And?'

'Sorry?'

'Now you say, "like mother like daughter". Don't you?'

'Oh, come here!' grinned Jim.

Maybe all his hugs for the day hadn't quite been used up.

He had a lot to tell her about his afternoon, but as they waited at the station for his train, the part that Lily was most intrigued about was how Miss Frobisher had reacted. She'd have expected her boss to give Jim a rocket.

'You know what it is, don't you?' Jim shrugged. 'Underneath that cool, collected exterior, she's a romantic at heart. And you know why? A secret sorrow in her life.'

'Don't be daft!' Lily countered. 'She's married with a little boy! Where's the sorrow in that, except her husband's away in the war.'

Jim made a scornful noise.

'You and Gladys may buy that story but Simmonds doesn't.'

'What? What's it to do with him? You mean you spent all those evenings with him when you weren't boxing having a good old gossip?'

'Discussing personnel matters,' said Jim blithely. 'Quite justified.'

'Huh! So what's his theory?'

'He reckons there *is* no husband.'

'What? He's dead? Well, why wouldn't she say?'

'Oh, Lily,' Jim sighed. 'I know you're dotty about Miss Frobisher and she's been very good to you, but if you'd take off your rosy specs for a minute . . . he's not dead! He's disappeared. Gone. Vanished. Run off and left her.'

'No!'

Jim was right; Lily had such a bad case of heroine-worship, she couldn't believe anyone could possibly abandon her idol.

'Think about it,' Jim went on. 'Why do we know nothing about him? Why does she never talk about him? I know you and Gladys have come up with this crazy idea he's some top-level spy, but that's about as likely as . . . as me winning a bare-knuckle boxing bout! She's been let down. Her heart's been battered and broken and that's why, out of character as it seems, she was soft about you and me.'

Lily gaped. 'Honestly, Jim, you're wasted on *The Messenger*,' she retorted. 'You should be writing those sloppy novels that Beryl reads!'

'A possible career option,' mused Jim. 'There were moments today when I thought I might need one.' As he spoke, he was scrutinising the information board, where something was being chalked up. 'Ah! My train at last.'

He took her in his arms. One thing had come out of the Frank episode – Jim was a lot more demonstrative, and Lily wasn't complaining.

But she pondered what he'd said about Miss Frobisher all the way home. She had to acknowledge it was a possibility. Maybe that was the real reason Miss Frobisher had come back to Hinton, too ashamed to stay where she'd been living, with the gossip and the pointing fingers. She could imagine her being too proud to admit it, and pretending her husband was simply away at war, but if that was the case . . . poor Miss Frobisher! It made Lily feel even luckier that things had worked out for her and Jim as they had.

*   *   *

221

'So romantic!' breathed Gladys dreamily. She hadn't noticed Frank Bryant waiting for Lily on Tuesday evening, so she'd naturally assumed Jim's big gesture with the flowers was simply because he'd been away. 'He missed you that much! So much for all your worries about that Margaret! Have you asked him about her?'

Lily smiled uneasily.

'Oh, that was just me being silly,' she said. 'Yes she made the scarf and did the sketch, but she's just a friend. I believe that now.'

She felt guilty at letting Gladys believe it, but she was too ashamed to admit her foolishness over Frank as well – and telling the whole story wouldn't do Jim any favours either.

'I don't deserve him,' she said. At least she felt that was the truth.

'Of course you do!'

It was a shame, though. Of the three of them, herself, Gladys and Beryl, it was Gladys who was the incurable romantic, yet she was the one whose fiancé was on ship thousands of miles away. Gladys hadn't seen him for months, and weeks went by between letters. Lily could only hope that when Bill did get some leave, he'd come up with a big romantic gesture of his own. She might even drop a few hints.

On the other hand, Miss Frobisher's heart seemed perfectly sound under her suit jacket – navy worsted today. She signed Lily's leave request for the funeral as if she had no idea about the scene on the sales floor, and Lily was hardly going to bring it up. Instead, she redoubled her efforts to be attentive and helpful (sales staff manual section two, paragraph one) – so much so that Mrs Pope, always a difficult customer, actually bought a boy's flannelette shirt without any of her usual dithering.

On Monday, accompanied by an animated Ivy, Lily set off on the lengthy journey to Bidbury. Ivy rattled on like a pea in a colander the entire time and as the final train pulled away, Lily's head was buzzing as the carter hauled her companion up into the promised trap while Lily shoved Ivy up as tactfully as she could from behind.

At the cottage, though, Ivy was on her best behaviour, and her dress for the occasion was as sober as anyone could have wished – a drooping black frock borrowed from a neighbour. The neighbour, however, must have been even more well-built than Ivy, and in a nod to decorum she'd pinned the gaping bodice with a vast satin poppy – bright, but at least vaguely connected with remembrance.

Jim's father seemed quite fascinated by her, and when Ivy declared that he was no more than a strip of wind but she'd soon have him doing laps of the garden, he even seemed amused. Ivy was enchanted with the cottage ('Like a storybook! Wait till Susan sees it!'), and though she was slightly dubious about the chickens that roamed freely under the apple trees – and in and out of the kitchen, if you weren't careful, Mrs Dawkins had warned – and the pig in its sty, Jim assured her that a lad from the village took care of the pig and did the heavy work in the garden. In truth, the rented cottage was pretty dilapidated and the garden overgrown – the 'lad' was the village idiot – but for Ivy, after the back streets of Hinton, it was an escape to paradise.

'I think it's going to work,' whispered Lily when she finally got Jim to herself.

'My fingers are cramped from crossing them,' he whispered back. 'But I think I agree.'

They left Ivy and Mrs Dawkins chuntering over apple versus tomato chutney for the post-funeral sandwiches and went to ready themselves for the arrival of the cortege – a pony and trap for the coffin, and the dog-cart again for Lily, Jim and his father.

It was a day of unexpected November sunshine. Tiny birds flitted in the hedgerows and pigeons patrolled the fallow fields for any remaining grain. Some of the trees were still holding onto their coppery leaves while others stretched their bare limbs to the sky. Lily squeezed Jim's hand; with the other he was holding his father's. In the village, women looking through vegetables outside the little shop stopped what they were doing and a couple of old men took off their caps as they passed. When they pulled up outside the church, the young vicar, all Adam's apple and eagerness, met them at the lichgate, asking anxiously if any more mourners were expected. There were only eight, he said, inside, mostly ladies from the WI. Jim reassured him he hadn't expected any more. Lily could see he was quite pleased by even that number, and the vicar seemed relieved.

Leaving Jim to help his father down, and the undertakers to shoulder the coffin, Lily went in. The church was small, whitewashed, and hung with tattered pennants and banners – battle honours from the Great War and before. Stone tablets in the walls commemorated important local families and the patterns thrown by the stained glass were made even more complex by the chicken wire stretched over them, not that any bombs were going to fall out here, surely? Another thing Ivy and Susan could look forward to.

Lily took a seat in the third row of pews. In front of her was a girl of about her own age sitting with what must be her parents, and Lily's heart gave a leap. The only other mourners were older ladies – presumably the WI. – so this had to be Margaret Povey. Lily wished she'd taken a seat on the other side of the aisle for a better view – all she could see were short curls under a small hat and the nape of a brown neck between them and the worn collar of her coat. When the organ stopped its twiddling and began something more sombre they all stood up and the girl stooped to pick up a fallen glove. Straightening, she half-turned and smiled. Her face was freckled and entirely free of make-up. Hard, Lily had to admit, to see her as a *femme fatale*.

The coffin came slowly down the aisle, the vicar intoning, Jim and his father following. The service was brief. Jim read the lesson, the one that started 'To every thing there is a season' and when he got to the bit about 'a time to mourn, and a time to dance' he looked up and caught Lily's eye and she couldn't believe she had ever, for one single second, doubted him.

After the burial, they all stood around awkwardly in the churchyard. The WI ladies said they wouldn't come back to the cottage – they had their own families to feed. Three of them were looking after evacuees; one had a son who'd been invalided home. Jim thanked them for coming, then turned to Margaret and her parents. He introduced Lily and they all shook hands. Lily smiled awkwardly at Margaret, wondering what they'd have to say to each other if the Poveys came back for the wake, but thankfully they too said they had to get back to the farm. After wishing Jim well, the parents moved off, but Margaret lingered while Jim went to thank the vicar.

'So you're Lily,' she said.

Lily couldn't deny it. 'I saw the scarf you made for Jim,' she replied. It had once seemed like something possessed by an evil spell but now it had lost all its power. 'You're a far better knitter than I'll ever be.'

Margaret's mouth twitched. 'You made the other one, did you?'

'Yes.' Lily heard her voice go up a notch. It always did when she was feeling defensive.

This time, it was Margaret's eyebrows that twitched. 'What did you use for needles? Cricket bats?'

Lily opened her mouth to reply but then she saw the other girl was smiling.

'Sorry,' said Margaret. 'I didn't mean—'

'No, it's a fair comment,' admitted Lily, smiling herself now. 'My mum despairs of my craft skills. Or lack of them.'

'Oh, well. I'm sure you have other talents. There's not much else to do out here,' said Margaret. 'And Jim's a . . . a very old friend.'

'I know. You'll still be seeing him.' Lily could afford to be generous. 'He'll still come out some weekends.'

She didn't add that she might now, as well.

'I dare say.' Margaret tapped her gloves against the palm of her hand. 'But I gather he's got a housekeeper for his dad, so that should spare him a lot of worry.'

'I hope so.' Lily felt a rush of warmth for her rival. After all, they had a lot in common – they both had Jim's wellbeing at heart. In different circumstances, they might even have been friends.

A car hooted in the lane and Margaret looked

across. 'That's Dad. I must go,' she said. 'Butter to make!' She took a step off. 'Goodbye, Lily.' Then she added, 'Look after him, won't you?'

'I will,' said Lily. 'I promise.'

Chapter 22

Back at the cottage, a ton weight seemed to have lifted from everyone. Ivy and Mrs Dawkins had obviously hit it off and there was a fire in the grate, sandwiches on the table and the kettle on the hob.

As predicted, Ivy did seem able to jolly Jim's dad along ('Come on, Tom, you can manage another sandwich, what you've had wouldn't fill a flea!') and after a couple of hours – Tom was visibly exhausted – Lily and Jim practically had to drag her away. Keen to maximise her income while she could, Mrs Dawkins had agreed to fill in till Ivy and Susan were installed.

'How are you going to pay for it, though?' Lily asked Jim when Ivy had gone to spend a penny ('Too much excitement!') at the station. 'There's always my Post Office account—'

'Lily, I can't take your money, and anyway, there's no need,' said Jim. 'Dad told me the other night. Turns out my mother had been putting money into an insurance scheme for years. So when that comes through, it's going to make things much easier.'

As usual, he knew what Lily would be thinking.

'Strange, isn't it? The family's going to be better off with her dead than alive.'

There was a sense in which he didn't mean only financially. Much as he'd loved his mother as his mother, and tried to please her, she'd exasperated him beyond measure, and frankly, made his life difficult. He was sorry to have disappointed her, but he had an inkling that even if he'd moved back to the country, married Margaret and become a farmer, she'd still have found fault – he didn't call round often enough, didn't produce children quickly enough – there'd have been something. Nothing would ever have been enough. She was just made that way.

It was mid-evening by the time they got back to Hinton. They managed to get Ivy a seat on the train, but Lily and Jim had to stand. At least it meant they could have their arms round each other with impunity as the carriages rocked and jolted – there was no money now to improve tracks or rolling stock – and when they got off at Hinton the newspaper placards reminded them why. The news from North Africa was still good, though, and Jim bought a copy of the *Hinton Chronicle*.

By the time they'd seen Ivy home, got home themselves, and told Dora about the day, it was nearly ten. Lily sat at the table with the paper, too restless to go to bed. Jim always mocked the *Chronicle* for its lack of news sense and it was running true to form. While the other papers gave stirring accounts of the triumphant march west of the Allied army, the *Chronicle's* lead story was 'Wedding Breakfast Brawl: Groom Bound Over'. But inside, beneath 'Owners Most Like Their Pet: Enter Our New Photographic Competition!' it had been forced to acknowledge the wider world. It had printed in full the Prime Minister's Mansion House speech – and only a week after he'd given it.

Lily read it again.

'Now this is not the end. It is not even the beginning of the end. But it is, perhaps, the end of the beginning.'

Which could also, she felt, apply to herself and Jim.

Once a funeral was over, things could get back to normal – that was what everybody said, and after all that had gone on, Dora welcomed it. Cooking, washing, cleaning – even queuing – why had they ever seemed a chore? Now she wasn't riven with worry over Reg, over Jim, over Lily, they seemed a perfectly reasonable way to pass the time, and opening up the WVS tea bar was a positive pleasure. Raising the flap on its struts, lugging up the milk crate, getting the water to boil, setting out the cups – after all the disruption, there was nothing more soothing than routine.

It was a crisp late autumn morning and nearby the Salvation Army band was getting ready to play, which always lifted Dora's heart – the first sign that Christmas was on the way. She'd been planning her gift-giving for a while. She'd eked out last month's soap ration so she could spend this month's coupons on the last day of their allocation, and next month's on the first day of theirs. That'd be Gladys, Ivy and Cousin Ida sorted, but Lily was still a problem. She badly needed a new nightie – six coupons – but then Dora's own was nearly past it too . . .

Lost in this dilemma, she was trailing the milk jug over the row of cups in a continuous stream when a voice made her jump and made the milk jug jump too.

'Well, hello again!'

'Oh! Good morning!'

It was him. Major Anderson. Hugh. And she'd been thinking about nighties! Had she conjured him up? She quickly put down the jug and smoothed her hair, not that it needed it.

He grinned his easy grin and gestured towards the band.

'Looks like you've got *Music While You Work* today.'

'Yes!' There was a pause. Why couldn't she think of anything to say? She was like a lovestruck puppy. That was a thought. 'Not got Buddy with you?'

Hugh pulled a tragic face. 'He's in the doghouse. Chewed a blanket. Well, I say chewed – shredded more like.'

'Oh, no!' Now things were getting better. 'I suppose that's what they call collateral damage.'

He smiled again. 'Right – and it wasn't even my blanket! I've disciplined guys for less, so I had to be seen to be doing something. But I guess I'll give in pretty soon and he'll still get his walk.'

'He's got you where he wants you!' Conversation seemed a bit easier now; Buddy was a safe subject. 'I said he'd landed on his paws, didn't I?'

Hugh spread his hands in a broad gesture.

'I kinda think we have to do what we can in this old world. Like you giving up your time to do what you do here.'

'Oh!' Dora checked herself. 'I'm sorry, I was . . . did you want a cup of tea? Something to eat? A sandwich?'

'No, I didn't mean that!' Hugh shook his head. 'That's not why I'm here. I called by a couple of times but you weren't on duty.'

The way he said it, it sounded more like more like 'doody'.

233

He felt in his pocket and produced a folded packet. 'I thought these might be of use to you.'

He held the packet out across the counter and Dora looked at it. Stockings!

'I'm guessing you had to junk that other pair. And I know they're hard to come by.'

Dora's heart was tumbling like a tombola drum, and she wasn't quite sure what to say, but she knew what she had to do. She put her hands behind her back to underline it.

'Thank you, it's very kind, but I can't possibly accept.'

What sort of signal would it be giving? What did he think she was?

Hugh gave a short laugh.

'You think it's too forward of me, right? Please don't get the wrong idea. I only thought as these are easy for me to get hold of and tricky for you . . . look, why not see them as an early Christmas present? From a friend.'

A friend? He was a complete stranger! Dora looked down at the stockings. They lay on the counter between them in their shiny packet. Nylons. They were actual nylons. By DuPont. Beryl would have killed for them: any woman would.

'You know,' Hugh went on, 'they showed us a little movie when we arrived, called *Welcome to Britain*. Showed a Yank having a drink in one of your pubs and trying to talk to people, to force himself onto them. He couldn't understand it when everyone stared at him like he was some crazy. The message was look, the Brits might seem standoffish, but they're just a bit buttoned up. So come on, Dora, loosen your stays, for once?'

The band had been tuning up with scales and exploratory toots on their instruments, and they suddenly burst into a rendition of 'God Rest Ye Merry, Gentlemen'. Hugh and Dora both jumped – and it broke the tension.

'See?' he said. 'Christmas is coming. "Let nothing you dismay".'

Dora sighed. She knew now she was going to accept.

'It's very, very kind of you,' she said. 'Too kind.'

'You'll take them?'

In reply, Dora picked up the stockings and held them for a moment, feeling their luxury seep through the Cellophane.

'Thank you,' she said. 'Most sincerely.'

It was what she felt him to be – sincere.

'Some sense at last!' he exclaimed. 'But there's one condition. You're not to give them to your daughter!'

He must be telepathic – that was exactly what Dora had intended, and her face showed it.

'I knew it!' he crowed. 'I got that last time. It's family first with you. Think about yourself for once, Dora. Just try it. You might be pleasantly surprised.'

He replaced his cap and held out his hand, as he

had when they'd parted before in the street. She reached across the counter and shook it.

'There's one other thing,' he began.

'Oh, yes?'

'I'm afraid this is goodbye.'

Dora looked at him blankly as the band continued its merry tune.

'You know some of our guys took a bit of a hit back in the summer, in that raid on Dieppe?'

Dora did know. The 2nd Canadian Infantry had mounted a cross-Channel raid – six thousand men in all. Fierce enemy fire on the beaches had killed half of them – half! – within yards of their landing craft.

'So my unit's being transferred,' Hugh went on. 'But you mustn't worry about Buddy. My batman's staying behind, he'll take good care of him.'

'That's all right then.'

It was far from all right: Buddy's welfare hadn't even crossed her mind. So much for the British being a nation of animal lovers!

'Where are they sending you?' she asked. She knew as soon as the words were out of her mouth it was a stupid question, and she cursed herself. He'd think she was a right idiot. Or a spy!

But, bless him, Hugh smiled. 'Down to – well, I shouldn't say – still in England, but . . . down south. And after that, who knows?' He smiled again. 'But it was good meeting you, Dora.'

'You too!' she replied automatically before she'd

had time to take in what he'd said. And after that
. . . what? Active service? Her heart rolled again and
she could feel her hand shaking slightly in his. He
released his grip.

'Goodbye, Dora. Don't forget what I said!'

He raised his hand in a brief salute and was gone.

Dora looked after him, imprinting the image in
her mind. She knew she wasn't going to forget
anything he'd said – or anything about him.

He paused to drop a coin in the Salvation Army's
tin, but he didn't look back. The band played on.

Lily, too, was relishing being 'back to normal' –
though at first she could hardly remember what
'normal' was. Gradually her awareness of it returned:
a ginger cat's pink tongue as it washed its paw; the
swish of tyres on a wet road; the stinging fire of the
chilblain on her little toe. Most of all, though,
normality was Marlow's – serving customers, tidying
stock – and the readying for Christmas. Lily climbed
up to the top shelf in the stockroom to look through
the department's dusty decorations and stretched a
display of socks round a hoop she'd begged from the
display team. But nothing spelt Christmas like the
news of the Christmas grotto.

All year, Jim had been lobbying Mr Marlow to
reinstate what had once been a fixture of the store's
– and Hinton's – calendar: the arrival of Father
Christmas in his grotto on Toys. At first Cedric had

Joanna Toye

come up with the usual objections – it had never been a great money-spinner, and with a war on, what were they going to give each child as a present, let alone find the paper to wrap it in?

Jim and Mr Simmonds had insisted the grotto would bring in customers who'd then browse other departments: Cedric remained unmoved. But Alice Goodridge's death had seemed to unlock something in him and suddenly it was all systems go.

'I found a couple of painted wood backdrops in the stores,' Jim told Lily triumphantly as they walked home. 'Last used for an Easter display, before the war, by the look of them. But with a coat of white-wash and some imagination—'

'The walls of the grotto?' supplied Lily.

'I've got Les looking out for old pallets and packing cases for the roof,' Jim went on. 'And if the handymen say they're too busy, I'll make the thing myself!'

Lily was impressed, but Jim had made their henhouse, after all.

By next day, he was mulling the next problem – how to fit the grotto in. Toys and Childrenswear had already shrunk to make way for Jim's depart-ment, which had had to move when half the second floor had been requisitioned by the Air Ministry for storing parts. In the end the only – and the obvious – thing to do was to scrap the Toy department's Play Corner for the Christmas season, and put the grotto in its place.

But that created another problem, and one that no one could have foreseen: the future of Dobbin.

Back in the summer, it was Gladys who'd suggested a Play Corner on Toys to occupy children whose mothers were shopping. Unusually, Mr Marlow had agreed at once – no cost involved – and even more surprisingly, he'd made an immediate contribution. He donated his own son's rocking horse, a beautiful, hand-carved creature, dapple-grey, with a proper leather saddle and reins and a real horsehair mane and tail. No one quite knew how, but the horse had been christened Dobbin and the children loved him. He'd become one of the store's biggest attractions, but now his paddock was needed for the grotto.

'And you'll never guess!' an incensed Gladys told Lily at dinner. 'Miss Naylor's only trying to half-inch him for Schoolwear!'

'What? You mean over Christmas?' Lily forked up a mouthful of lumpy mash.

'No! That's the point! She says he'd keep little brothers and sisters quiet while the older ones are being measured for their uniforms! She wants him for ever!'

'That's daft!' Lily rested her knife and fork on her plate. 'Dobbin belongs on Toys! It's the obvious place!'

'I know! And what's my Play Corner without him? A couple of mingy jigsaws, a doll and a spinning top!'

Gladys was so worked up she'd hardly touched her food.

'What does Mr Bunting say?'

'You know what he's like!' The buyer on Toys looked like the kindly woodcarver in *The Adventures of Pinocchio* and was about as much of a soft touch. 'He'll go along with anything. And even if I can persuade him to tell her she can only have Dobbin on loan, you know what she's like, too! We'll never get him back! I mean, I'm all for the grotto, but not if we end up sending Dobbin to the knacker, which is what Miss Naylor is!'

It was a long and passionate speech for Gladys, so Lily knew how strongly she felt.

'We'll have to do something,' she said. 'Maybe we can throw ourselves under Dobbin's hooves like that suffragette at the races.'

'Be sensible, Lily,' said Gladys. The grand gesture wasn't in her nature.

'Well, we'll think of something,' Lily consoled her. 'Now eat up, Gladys. Cottage pie! Your favourite.'

'I can't touch it,' Gladys shuddered. 'You know it's horsemeat. I'd feel like I was eating Dobbin himself.'

Chapter 23

Lily went back after dinner fired up on Gladys's behalf. On their trip to Ward and Keppler, she'd got the firm impression that Miss Frobisher wasn't sorry that Miss Naylor had had to drop out. They obviously knew each other of old – maybe her boss might have some idea of how to get round her. But Lily was startled by the vehemence of Miss Frobisher's reaction.

'The nerve!' she exclaimed. 'It's a craven bid for power!'

In Marlow's terms, this was clearly the equivalent of Hitler annexing Austria.

'But what can we do?' asked Lily. 'Mr Bunting's already sort of said yes. Or at least, not no.'

'Well, Lily, you disappoint me,' rapped Miss Frobisher. 'We'll make room for Dobbin here! We're right next door to his usual spot, for goodness' sake! I'll go and see Miss Naylor now!'

'Really? You don't think Mr Bunting should do it?' ventured Lily. 'Or Mr Simmonds?'

'I don't need a man to fight my battles!' snorted Miss Frobisher. 'Look what happened when this whole thing was left to Bunting! And Mr Simmonds'll only put her back up!'

She swished off impatiently, pulling down her suit jacket. The bad feeling between Miss Frobisher and Miss Naylor was obviously stronger than Lily had suspected. Wondering what she'd started, she concentrated on tidying the rails, her ears straining for the sound of a catfight and cursing when the tannoy pinged a lengthy announcement about Accessories offering suede gloves at 'very special prices'.

So she was highly relieved when, barely ten minutes later, Miss Frobisher was back without a scratch – and preening her whiskers.

'I don't think we'll be having any more trouble from her,' she purred.

'Really?' breathed Lily. 'Why? How did you do it?'

Lily had been right to sense the hostility between Miss Frobisher and Miss Naylor, and it went back years.

They'd both been juniors together on Ladies' Fashions – Ladies' Modes, as they were called in those days. Jennifer Naylor – never Jenny, oh no – was a year older, and six months more experienced than Eileen Frobisher – the same gap as between Lily and Gladys when they'd both been juniors on Childrenswear. The difference was that Gladys had welcomed Lily and happily shared her knowledge. Jennifer Naylor had resented the new arrival from the start.

There'd been all sorts of little things – difficult at first to trace to Jennifer, then blindingly obvious. The pins that Eileen knew she'd removed after a trial fitting before putting the dresses back on their hangers, only to find them there again, and likely to scratch a customer . . . The way Lady Harcourt's navy marocain and Mrs Vellacott's ivory crêpe had somehow got mixed up in the packing, when Eileen knew she'd addressed the boxes correctly . . . too many incidents to recall. Poor Eileen had been carpeted by their unbending buyer many times, and in those days was less likely to stand up for herself than she'd later learnt to be. She didn't like to point the finger at Jennifer, but she had to be on her guard. Double-checking everything made her days even harder work than they were already, but it had to be done.

The crunch had come when Eileen had flown into the workroom with a silk tea gown for pressing. Jennifer was on her way down to Despatch with a parcel.

'I've just been ironing one like that,' she said. 'The pressing cloth's there.'

Eileen was in a tearing hurry – the customer was waiting. She spread the dress on the board, laid the pressing cloth over it and lifted the iron when something made her check. The iron had three settings – low, medium, and high – and sure enough, the setting was high. If she'd used it, it would have scorched the cloth and possibly the dress. Whatever Jennifer had been ironing, it hadn't been silk – linen, perhaps.

Enough was enough. When Jennifer came back, Eileen told her she wasn't standing for it any longer.

'If you'd been ironing silk, why was the iron on high?' she demanded. 'What is your problem with me? When we could work together so much better!'

'I didn't say I'd been ironing silk, did I?' replied Jennifer smugly. 'I said I'd been ironing something like it. I meant a similar style. You ought to listen.'

'I shouldn't have to!' cried Eileen. 'I shouldn't have to treat everything you say like a – a crossword clue!'

She was too young then to understand that under Jennifer's surface confidence, she felt threatened. They were both bright and quick, but Jennifer's was a brittle brightness; she had no real feeling for customers or for clothes – and she'd realised from the start that Eileen had.

'I think you're a bit barmy,' Jennifer retorted. 'The only problem is in your head.'

Eileen could see only one way out: she went to the buyer and asked for a transfer to another department.

'But why?' asked Madame. '*Pourquoi?*'

To give Ladies' Modes the whiff of Paris couture, the three buyers – dresses, suits and coats, and model gowns – were addressed as Madame or Mademoiselle – but the dress buyer actually was French.

'Now you have learnt to take more care, you are doing very well. You have a feel for fashions. It's not always the case.'

Eileen didn't say that taking more care while Jennifer tried to undermine her was nearly costing her her sanity. But her boss was perceptive.

'I had in mind,' Madame went on, 'to make some changes in *personnel* anyway. I hear there is a vacancy on Luggage and Travel Goods. I think perhaps Miss Naylor might be better suited there. Would that make a difference to your decision?'

Eileen didn't have to answer. The relief in her face was enough.

Miss Frobisher wasn't going to tell Lily any of that, nor that Jennifer Naylor still seemed to seethe at her transfer all those years ago. Miss Frobisher had gone to London and got her experience there; Miss Naylor had gained her experience on different departments in Marlow's. Lots of different departments, because she was often moved sideways before being moved up. She'd made life unpleasant for every staff member she'd come into contact with, and in the end she'd been promoted to buyer on longevity rather than merit, and in the department where the least flair was required. She might as well have had 'Bitter and Twisted' tattooed on her forehead.

'Ah, well,' Miss Frobisher said now. 'I told Miss Naylor we could easily have Dobbin here. We were, er, discussing it when Mr Marlow passed by. He was very clear that, in his view, Schoolwear should remain educational, not recreational. He said it was no place for Dobbin, but instead he offered to get some letters and numbers stencilled on the walls.' Mr Marlow obviously knew what he was up against with Jennifer Naylor too, and Eileen admired the way he'd cunningly bought her off. 'I must say,' she added, 'the paintwork over there is especially tired.'

Lily beamed and Miss Frobisher sent her off to tell Gladys the good news. In her long-running feud with Miss Naylor it was a significant victory, but she was braced for retaliation. Eileen had thought when she came back after her time away in London that things might be different, but Jennifer Naylor was expert at holding a grudge. There'd be a backlash at some point, she was sure. But for now, the triumph was hers.

* * *

Sid roared with laughter.

'Hang on,' he said when he'd finally stopped. 'There's a war going on and you're telling me the biggest excitement round here is two old birds at Marlow's coming to blows over a rocking horse?'

Lily bristled at her beloved Miss Frobisher being referred to as a 'bird' – let alone 'old' – though the image wasn't far off for the beaky, bony Miss Naylor.

'All right, smart Alec,' she retorted.

She was sitting opposite him at the small kitchen table. Sid had just been there when Lily and Jim had got back from work, unexpected and unannounced.

'No time for a letter,' he'd explained, once Lily had finished smothering him with hugs. 'Thought I'd catch you all out.'

'And then he's got the nerve to complain because there's no cake! I ask you!' Dora tried to look cross and failed, so pleased was she to see him.

'So?' Lily continued. Initial excitement over, they were back to being siblings, pure and simple. 'What's the excitement been in your work? Mixed up two movement orders? Issued the wrong travel rations?'

'I deal with pay scales and re-grading, as you well know,' said Sid loftily. 'Very responsible task. And since you ask, I have got news, actually. Lots of it.'

Dora was whipping up a junket to make up for the cake crisis and Jim had started on an Everest of potatoes to stretch the precious tin of Fray Bentos into a bigger corned beef hash. Both stopped what they were doing and looked up. Sid knew how to grab an audience.

He bent and undid the drawstring on his kitbag, extracted some small, folded sheets of paper and slapped them down on the table.

'That do you?'

Lily snatched up the letter – Reg's writing!

'But there's—' Lily turned the sheets over in her hand. 'There's three sheets here! A proper letter! How come he could write that much? And to you, not us?'

'Those evening classes in etiquette are really paying off, Lil,' quipped Sid. 'Charming! I am his brother!'

'I know, but why not to Mum? We've had nothing, not even a miserable letter card! You can go off people, you know!'

Jim and Dora had come to the table as if drawn by a magnet and Jim, as ever the voice of reason, made a suggestion.

'Why not just read it, Lily?'

Sid stood up to let his mum have his chair and stood with his hands on her shoulders.

'Yeah, go on,' he said. 'It's quite a tale.'

So Lily began.

'Dear Sid

Real sorry for the worry you've all had. It's a long story, as they say, but I'll do my best. We start the attack the night of the 23rd October, as you know. Monty's been round the day before,

*and we're all raring to go. Day 2 I get the order
to pick a couple of good blokes and take three
trucks forward – two with supplies, and one
with special kit artillery. We set off OK but the
road's mined, we have to go off road and by
the time we get there, this . . .'*

Lily paused, then continued. It was what Reg had
written after all.

' . . . this arsey Captain says where the . . .'

She glanced at her mother but Dora just nodded
to her to go on.

*' . . . where the blinding hell have we been,
the battle's moved on, the stuff's no . . . '*

She paused again, looking nervously at her mother.
This was awful lot of what Dora would call 'language'.
This time Sid gave her a nod.
'He's got to tell it like it was.'
Lily took a deep breath and read on.

*' . . . the stuff's no effing use now! He only
goes and sends us back again. So we turn round
but the fighting's still all over everywhere and
we're coming under fire, not very handy. Then,
blow me, the artillery truck that I'm driving*

249

springs a leak – radiator – we're crawling along now. One of the privates, older bloke, says 'Look, at this rate, we're going to be picked off by a gunner – we've got to get back and fast. Ditch that truck and torch it, it'll get us all killed.' Well, Sid, I didn't know what to do, I'm the Corporal, it's my decision. And ditching that truck didn't feel right – all that kit? So I sent them on ahead, said I'd follow in the dud truck. Then at least it was only me that'd cop it.'

Dora closed her eyes and let out a little sound. Even if it hadn't happened, it was hard for a mother to hear. Sid squeezed her shoulder and nodded to Lily to carry on.

'But life's not like that, is it? On the way back I pass their trucks, burnt out. Airstrike, I suppose. They've had it, poor devils, and as far as base is concerned, I'm missing and most likely a goner too.'

Another squeeze from Sid on Dora's shoulders. 'It's all right,' he said. 'You know there's a happy ending. Go on, Lil.'

'So when I finally show up back at base,' Lily continued, *'all hell breaks loose. Had to go before the brass hats, account for myself,*

expected a right . . . ' She gave a little warning cough, *'. . . a right bollocking, travelling alone and that – but the kit was all they cared about! Blow me if I didn't get a pat on the back! And I'm going to get another stripe, how about that?'*

Lily lowered the sheets of paper, stunned.

'Our Reg, a sergeant!' grinned Sid. 'How *about* that?'

It was all right for him; he'd had the letter for days and had had time to take it in. For the rest of them, the news was almost too much to absorb. Jim had his thoughtful face on; Dora was dabbing the corners of her eyes with her apron.

'Turn over,' urged Sid. 'There's more.'

Lily did as she was told. Reg was clearly getting tired or had added the end later, quickly, because the pen was different, the writing more wiggly and the sense more choppy.

'I know Mum had a telegram and I'm sorry. I've written home but God knows when or if they'll get it, and I couldn't say much. I'm sending this with one of the nurses who's coming home with a medical airlift so it should get to you fairly pronto. Can't wait till we're having a pint together or even a cup of tea. We're pressing on, we're going to win this, Sid, we've

> got to. *Tell them at home I love them and to
> keep writing.*
>   Reg.

There was quiet in the kitchen when Lily had finished, then Dora took the letter from her – she wanted to read it herself, to see Reg's writing for herself; it made him feel that little bit closer. When she laid the letter down, Jim picked it up and read it too. There were still a lot of unanswered questions, and they could only guess how much Reg must have spared them in the telling.

'You were right,' Jim said to Sid. 'Quite a tale.'

Chapter 24

Lily had time on her own with her brother next morning, when Jim headed off early to check on the progress of the famous grotto. Sid wanted a shave and a haircut from a barber who wasn't a modern-day Sweeney Todd, he said, so he offered to walk Lily to work. The late November morning was dark, but at least it was dry and she linked her arm happily through his.

'You're looking better than when I last saw you, anyway,' she began, meaning in Liverpool. 'Did you get into trouble for your poor bashed-up face?'

'Not really,' shrugged Sid. 'The tutor made more fuss over a slip-up I'd made in some accrued expenses. Typical accountant!'

'That's one good thing. And you haven't had any more trouble?'

'No. Though I won't be falling out with Jim anytime soon!'

Lily stiffened.

'Jim? Why would you? And why not?'

'Because he's likely to land one on me! Boxing? Him? It's about as likely as Rita Hayworth pulling pints down the local!'

Lily withdrew her arm and stopped.

'What's he said?'

The two of them had stayed downstairs last night with a couple of bottles of pale ale but surely Jim wouldn't have told Sid about Frank?

'He told me he'd had some lessons from that supervisor bloke, Simmonds.'

That was all right, then, thought Lily.

'He didn't tell you how he put them into practice?'

Sid was nonplussed.

'No. Did he? I got the impression it was just for fun.'

'Fun!' Lily tutted. 'Oh, look, Sid, I was going to tell you. I want you to know. Even though I acted so stupid and I don't come out of it very well.'

'I can't believe that!'

Dear Sid, dear, loyal Sid.

'You'd better. I was a right idiot.'

'Go on.' Sid still sounded as if he couldn't believe it. 'But we'd better keep moving, or you'll be late.'

Lily was grateful. Not having to look straight at Sid made it easier, somehow, to confess. And out it came – her suspicions about Jim and Margaret and her encounters with Frank. How it had all played out in the awfulness and anxiety of Reg being missing and Jim's mother struck down, and the final, surprising, surprisingly violent outcome.

When she'd finished he stopped and turned her to face him.

'Hell's bells, Lily! All this has been going on! And you didn't say?'

'I couldn't put it in letters! How could I? I wouldn't have known where to start! I had to tell you in person, whatever you might think of me.'

'Oh, Lil.' Sid's voice was wearily kind. 'Don't be daft. I'm not going to judge you. You're only young and . . . how do any of us know what we'd do in any situation till it happens?'

'But I was such a fool! Sid, you mustn't let me off!'

'You let your imagination run away with you. That's not a crime. Jim didn't help matters, and from what you've said, he admits it. But from what I've seen of the pair of you these past twenty-four hours I think it's brought you closer.'

'You're right,' Lily acknowledged. 'It has.'

'It would. Anything like that . . . you'd never want it to happen. But it doesn't half make you grow up.'

Lily looked at him standing there, tall, blond,

clear-eyed, broad-shouldered, brave. He'd had it far tougher – the person he'd loved, Anthony, a pilot in the Fleet Air Arm, was gone for ever, his plane shot down in the summer.

'What about you, Sid?' she asked gently. 'Have you . . . have you met anyone else?'

Sid's forehead creased.

'Lil, I'm not ready. It hasn't been six months.'

'Yes – I didn't mean you didn't care or were hard-hearted or anything.'

'I know you didn't. You just want me to be happy. But where I'm posted, up in Scotland, it's such a tiny place . . . there's no chance of meeting anyone even if I wanted it, let alone getting away with it if I did. But it's no good wallowing either, so I've done something about it.'

'What?'

'This is my other bit of news. I put in for a transfer. And I got it.'

'Oh, Sid, where?'

'London,' said Sid. 'It's a big place. Anonymous. It'll be easier for me to start again there.'

When Sid got back, spruced by a Hinton barber, Dora was mixing suet into flour for a no-steak and not-much-kidney-either pudding.

'London!' she exclaimed when Sid told her about his new posting. 'Well!'

Sid smiled to himself. From his mum's face, he

might as well have announced he was off to Mars in a hot air balloon, or to walk the Great Wall of China on stilts.

'At the Admiralty!'

'Yeah,' he teased. 'Next time I come home it'll be in a staff car with scrambled egg on my shoulders and a high hat with plumes! It's still only clerking, Mum.'

'Even so. It's a step up, Sidney.'

Sid smiled, outwardly this time. She was his mother; she was allowed to be proud. Dora went back to her pastry, adding water little by little.

'London, eh?' she reflected. 'Well, I think it'll suit you. You'll be able to live the life you want better there.'

Sid's senses crackled. What was she saying? Had she guessed all along that he wasn't like other men, that the girls he'd dutifully gone out with had all been for show? Was it possible that his mother had always known that he wasn't the marrying kind?

He wondered whether to say anything more. He watched her skilfully mixing the dough with the flat-bladed knife, and realised how little he actually knew about her, how little he'd ever thought about her as a person, and not simply as his mother.

'What about you, Mum? Are you living the life you want? Have you ever?'

Dora looked up, startled.

'I don't know what you mean! What's what I want got to do with it?'

'It's got everything to do with it! You've given your whole life over to us kids, haven't you, since Dad died. How about doing something for yourself for a change?'

Her reaction surprised him.

'You're the second person to say that to me in as many weeks!'

'Am I? Who was the other?'

Dora was concentrating on her mixing bowl again.

'Oh . . . someone I met through the WVS.'

'Really? Well, good! She's right!'

Dora added a few more drops of water and bent her head to the bowl to cover her amusement. If that didn't just say it all – the assumption it'd have to be a woman. But as she abandoned the knife and started to mix the pastry by hand, she gave the idea more thought than she'd allowed herself since Hugh had first raised it.

Life had been hard for so long, since Arthur had died, that she could barely remember the days when she'd been young, working as a machinist at the corset factory, and they'd been courting. Or newly married and living with his mum and dad. Then Reg had come along, and they'd managed to get a place of their own, one room at first, then two, and then the house, thanks to Arthur's job with the council. Setting up home, more babies, being a family – all gone in a heartbeat – or the lack of one. Arthur had simply collapsed in the yard one day, a fragment of shrapnel lodged near his heart since his time in the trenches having finally done its work. The small pension, the scrimping, the weariness and the terror of coping alone . . . and when things might have got easier, with all the children earning – another war.

The dough was leaving the sides of the bowl, a smooth ball now. Dora lifted it out onto the board. There'd been no time or money for fripperies or fun. Or had she forgotten how to have fun anyway?

'Mum?'

Dora looked up, bemused: she'd been so far away. 'Don't you think I'm right? Not now, but when the war's over, and we're all off your hands – maybe you can start to live a bit.'

'If it's not too late!'

The words were out before she could stop them.

'It's never too late.'

'Isn't it?' Dora gave a faint smile. 'This is real life, not one of your Hollywood films, you know, Sid.'

'I do know,' said Sid. 'That's why it's even more important.'

'You're a good boy,' said Dora, dusting the rolling pin with flour. She had to head off this line of conversation. 'It's been worth it because you've turned out so well, the three of you. That's all I ever wanted. And now all I want is the three of you safe and well and happy in whatever you're doing, and wherever and whoever you're doing it with. That's all I care about.'

There was no doubt in Sid's mind now. She knew.

'Put that rolling pin down and let's have a hug,' he said, getting to his feet. Dora did as she was told. As they hugged, she felt the tension leave both their bodies. She knew, and he knew that she knew.

When he pulled away he held her face in his hands.

'Thank you, Mum,' he said. 'For everything. We can never thank you enough. I can never thank you enough.'

'Oh, get away!' This was getting too emotional for Dora. 'I'll never get this pastry done, and then there'll be trouble!'

'Yes, and there'll be trouble from me,' retorted Sid, 'if you don't start taking a bit of time for yourself and doing a few things for yourself.' He wasn't going to let her get away with it. 'Think up some things to do, if necessary! Or I'll think of them for you!'

'There's a threat!' exclaimed Dora. 'I dread to think what you'd have me do, looping the loop, probably, or standing for parliament! No wonder I want to stick to my knitting!'

Chapter 25

Sid's leave was over too soon, as it always was, and at last it was almost December. They could leave all that had happened in the autumn behind them, call it winter, and properly start to think about Christmas.

Sid made the move to London and quickly wrote to say he was 'settling in nicely' at the Admiralty, though the hours were long. The promised letter from Reg arrived from North Africa, but censored of course, so gave them no real information and made them all the more grateful for the letter he'd managed to get smuggled out. In Hinton, though, there was plenty of excitement to be going on with.

Cedric Marlow was old-fashioned: he wouldn't let the store's Christmas decorations go up till the first

Sunday in Advent had passed. Jim's appeal in *The Messenger* for volunteers to stay late on the Monday after to help put them up hadn't exactly resulted in a stampede, so he'd press-ganged Lily and Gladys, not that they needed much persuasion. Gladys had been full of the Christmas spirit since their triumph in the Dobbin drama. She was busy making up a special parcel for Bill: chocolate, cigarettes, the latest Eric Ambler and a special card, 'For my Fiancé at Christmas'. For Lily there was no contest between spending time with Jim or not.

When the store closed that night, though, Jim wasn't interested in the huge Christmas tree that was going to greet customers as they came through the doors. He hurried them through hanging the paper chains and strips of lametta printed with 'Merry Christmas' on their own departments and wasn't even very impressed by the little robins – admittedly in the last stages of moult – that Lily had found at the bottom of a box and was fixing between the fingers of the Childrenswear mannequins.

'Hurry up!' he urged.

The decorations on Furniture and Household hadn't taken him five minutes: a few wizened fabric poinsettias in whatever receptacle he could find and some balding strips of tinsel.

'All you care about is your precious grotto!' complained Lily.

Les was going to bring the sides and roof up to

the first floor for assembly. The next day, Father Christmas, in other words Albert, one of the store's retired carpenters, would arrive. Padded up and decked out in a somewhat limp red velvet suit, he would wave and smile to the popping of the *Chronicle*'s flashbulbs and the eager anticipation of a throng of small children.

As Les and Jim unloaded the boards from a trolley, Lily nudged Gladys. She didn't like to say that she could still see the outlines of Easter bunnies and spring flowers through the thin coat of whitewash. Gladys could see what she meant.

'Perhaps we could paint over them . . . turn them into penguins?' she whispered.

'I think that's the wrong Pole,' Lily mouthed back.

Oh well. Maybe when the thing was erected and tinsel hung around the outside, no one would notice. The children would be too excited as they waited behind the red rope or rode on Dobbin, now grazing happily in Childrenswear, while their mother or a nanny kept their place in the queue.

'Good, isn't it?' enthused Jim, blind to any faults.

Lily and Gladys nodded obligingly as Jim and Les paced out the space where Play Corner had been and Dobbin had stood and decided, with much relief, that the grotto would fit.

Miss Frobisher had stayed for an hour but had then left – she had her little boy to see to. Mr Bunting had bustled off too, keen to get home to his tea, but

Mr Simmonds was still pacing about, checking that the decorations were fairly distributed and the tinsel wound round the pillars was evenly spaced before he nodded to the staff concerned that they could go.

Now he strode over to Toys. 'Baubles going spare,' he offered, holding out a box. 'Some tinsel . . . and anyone short of an angel?'

Lily and Gladys fell on the tatty treasures while Mr Simmonds took off his jacket and helped Les and Jim get the sides and roof of the little house in place. Jim had found an ex-display velvet curtain for the fourth wall, and a carver chair from the boardroom was going to be Father Christmas's seat, draped with remnants of gold and silver lamé, which Haberdashery had stitched into a coverlet. It was far from the pre-war days when, Miss Temple had told Lily, the grotto really was a place of wonder, Father Christmas on a padded velvet throne attended by elves in costume and a mechanical toy as each child's present. But this was 1942, and anything was better than nothing.

In an hour, the nailing and hammering and banging was over and the basic structure was up. The men stood back sweatily while Lily and Gladys shook out their arms, tired from holding up the roof and walls while they were fixed in place. Now all that remained was to drape the grubby cotton wool that Lily had unearthed over the roof for snow and hang tinsel and baubles round the walls.

Peter Simmonds looked at his watch.

'It's nearly nine,' he said. 'Wouldn't you like to get off home? We can come in early in the morning to finish it off.'

Gladys and Les looked keen, but Jim glanced at Lily. 'I'd rather know it's done,' he said.

She knew he'd say that: he was such a perfectionist.

'I'll stay,' she offered. 'It won't take long.'

'Whatever you prefer.' Peter Simmonds wasn't surprised: he knew what Jim was like as well. 'You others get off, though. I'll tell the night watchman there's still two of you left on the first floor. Make sure you let him know when you leave.'

'Will do,' agreed Jim. 'Oh, and we don't need all the lights on – just this section.'

The store's blackout blinds were down, of course, but there was no point in wasting electricity.

Gladys gave a cheery wave – she was off to finish packing Bill's Christmas parcel – and Les gave them a thumbs-up as Mr Simmonds escorted them off the sales floor. At the doors to the back stairs he flicked off the lights in every section but Toys and Childrenswear, and the sales floor settled into darkness.

Jim turned to Lily.

'I think this is where I say, "alone at last",' he grinned.

'Yes,' said Lily. 'And instead of a moonlit beach and a tropical moon, we've got a plywood grotto and a box of baubles! Let's get on with it, can we?'

'No romance in your soul, that's your trouble!

Don't say I didn't try!' Jim bent to the boxes of decorations. 'Tinsel first, is it?'

They worked happily for twenty minutes decking the grotto, Lily tactfully using the shabby scrim that had been wrapped round some of the baubles to build heaps of 'snow' over the most visible rabbits.

'I was hoping for a little picket fence,' mourned Jim as he put the retaining ropes, normally used to keep the crowds in check at the sales, in place. 'But the carpenters told me to take a running jump and I didn't have time to—'

Aaaoo . . . Aaooo . . . Aaooo . . .

No. It couldn't be? The sirens!

'Typical!' Jim stopped what he was doing. 'Nothing for months and there's a raid tonight!'

'It must be a false alarm,' said Lily. 'Like the last one Mum told me about, the day I was in Liverpool with Sid.'

'Probably. Look, what do you want to do? Go down to the shelter?'

Lily sighed.

'Is there any point? By the time we get down there, the all clear'll probably have gone!'

Aaooo . . . Aaooo . . . Aaooo . . .

Lily had come to hate the way the notes repeated themselves, followed by a fractional pause before they started again, as if the siren was taking a breath.

'Even so, Jim, we could take some sort of cover? Get under a table or something?'

Jim came close and put his arms round her.

'So there is some romance in your soul! What are you suggesting?'

'Oh, you're hopeless!' But she lifted her face and let him kiss her. 'This is all your fault! You and your blooming grotto!'

'Ah, wait till you see what Father Christmas is bringing you. You won't say that then!'

He was looking down at her, smiling, his brown eyes catching the little light there was. He bent his head to kiss her again when—

At first it was a whistling whoosh then a screaming then a great booming crump as the bomb fell. It blew them clean off their feet as shards of glass, spars of wood, bits of plaster, limbs of mannequins, flying metal rails and shredded – what? clothes? – rushed past and around and rained all over them. Lily tried to clutch at Jim as she went down – she couldn't see him as the lights had gone out – but either she couldn't reach him or he wasn't there. As she hit the floor, she covered her head with her arms and tried to throw herself flat, feeling something at once light and heavy knock her sideways against something hard and solid. Then it was all clatter and crackle and creak and trickle and dust – thick, choking dust filling her eyes and nose and mouth.

Gasping, she lay there in the darkness, shaking, while the fabric of the building settled around her. From far, far away she heard the clanging of bells, and knew what they meant – fire, ambulance, police. Fire! Please, God, no. But at least help was coming.

A minute or two – maybe longer – passed. Struggling, choking, retching, and against sickening stabs in her shoulder where she'd been flung, Lily groped slowly into a semi-sitting position. When she stretched out her left hand – her right arm was too painful to move – all she could feel were wooden beams and lumps of plaster. There was something on her legs too, but at least she could feel them, and she could sit up; thank God she wasn't trapped. She must be in some kind of air pocket. She wriggled her legs experimentally to see if she could get them free.

'Jim!' she called helplessly. 'Jim? Are you there? Are you all right?'

'Lily?' His voice came back to her, sounding small and far away.

'Oh, Jim, thank God! Are you – are you hurt?'

'No . . . no, not really. I'm a bit stuck, though.'

'Where are you? Keep talking, I'll try to get to you.'

'No!' Don't move, you might make things worse. What about you? Are you hurt?'

'My shoulder's a bit sore, I crashed into something. Oh, Jim, why would they bomb Marlow's?'

There was a pause before he answered.

'I don't think they did. It just felt like it. If they had, I don't think we'd be here at all.'

That was probably true. Not a good thought.

'But why Hinton then?'

'Probably didn't mean to. Probably had the map upside down.'

'Jim!' Only he could joke about it. 'You sound like you're over to my left,' she added. 'I'm going to try to come over. Keep talking.'

'Lily, don't . . . '

'I'm coming.'

He could say what he liked, she was going to get to him, whatever. Slowly, inch by inch, she wriggled her legs from their sharp, scratchy casing. Debris slipped and she jabbed her knee into a jutting edge that hurt. She waited a moment, then tried again, easing her leg round the obstruction.

'Keep talking!' she urged. 'Sing to me if you have to.'

'Sing!' He gave a feeble laugh. 'I was kicked out of choir, you know.'

'Never!'

'Mm hmm. The choirmaster caught me smoking behind the rood screen.'

'Smoking? You! How old were you?'

She had her legs free now. She just had to fumble her way to Jim, if there was a way. A bit of light would have been nice.

The sirens were still howling, but over them, or under them, she thought she could hear shouting.

'Was that someone calling?'

'I didn't hear anything.'

Inch by painful inch, groping her way, dislodging debris, the electric shocks of pain in her shoulder making her feel sick and her knee where she'd caught it throbbing, she crawled and clawed in what seemed to be Jim's direction. He'd gone quiet.

'Jim? Keep talking, go on. We'll have to shout in a bit, so the rescue men can find us. Jim!'

'Hmm . . . what?'

'Rescue men!'

'Yes . . . ' There was a pause.

'People know we're here. The night watchman. Mr Simmonds.'

'Gladys . . . Les.'

It was strange. The nearer she thought she was getting, the smaller his voice sounded.

'They'll be at home though, by now,' she realised. 'Or in a shelter. They won't know Marlow's has been hit. And the watchman . . . '

He could have been anywhere in the store. He could be hurt himself, or worse. Not to mention the firewatchers on the roof.

'Jim?'

Lily's hand had met something. She was on her stomach now, edging forwards on her elbows – mostly her left elbow as her wretched shoulder was making her whole right arm useless.

'Is that your foot?'

It had lost its shoe, but it felt like a foot.

'Is it?'

'Can't you feel it? It must be! It's too human for a mannequin!'

She groped this way and that, trying to find what was above, beyond, trying to gauge which way was best, safest for them both.

'Are you . . . are you sitting up or lying down?'

'Lying . . . I think.'

'You think?'

While she was talking Lily had been creeping forwards. Ahead, she felt something smooth – a great slab seemed to be wedged. If she dislodged that, they were both done for.

'Jim? Am I anywhere close?'

Suddenly she felt a touch on the top of her head. Jim's hand was resting on her hair. She put up her good hand and clutched at it.

'At last!'

She squirmed forwards, moving in half- and quarter-inches now. For the first time she appreciated what the rescue men were up against, and why it took so long, sifting and shifting the rubble of bombed-out buildings piece by piece, trying not to make things worse. And how incredibly brave they were to put their own lives at risk.

Lily stretched out her hand again and at last – Jim's face! She wiggled and wriggled till she was lying next to him, or as close as she could get.

'What's all this on top of you?' she asked. She was

271

lying on her left side, so only had her pitifully painful right arm to explore with.

'Don't know. Feels heavy.'

'I thought you said you weren't hurt?'

'I'm not!' he insisted. 'I'm . . . '

'Hello? Hello? Anyone there?'

The rescue men! Oh thank God! They must have put ladders up already.

'Yes!' cried Lily. 'Yes! We're here! Two of us! Alive!' The word stuck in her throat. 'Oh, get us out! Please get us out! Please!'

Chapter 26

'Lily? Lily!'

Someone was calling her name. But she was so tired.

'Lily? Can you hear me?'

The voice was more insistent, and now they were touching her, touching her hand. Why couldn't they leave her alone?

'Lily. Speak to me, please!'

It was no good: whoever it was wasn't going to give up. Slowly, painfully, Lily opened her eyes, then promptly shut them again. Where everything had been black, now everything was bright, bright white. A white ceiling with a row of lights down the centre. Where was she? She was lying on something soft – a bed? – but her body was pinned down and her right arm felt funny; stiff and strapped across her chest. She opened her eyes again and tried to lift her head to look at it, but pain shot through her shoulder and her head fell back.

'Don't move,' said the voice. 'You're all right.'

She knew that voice. She turned her head to the left, but cautiously this time.

'Sid?' It hurt her throat to speak. 'What are you doing here? What's the matter?'

'Oh, Lily! You're the matter, you dozy duck! Don't you remember?'

Well, there was a question. Remember what? And then all at once, she did.

Marlow's . . . the Christmas grotto . . . she'd been finishing it off with Jim. And he'd been looking at her, and talking about Christmas, and then . . . She swallowed. Her throat was sore, raw.

'There was a bomb.'

'Thank God! You do remember! Yes, there was a bomb.'

'And it fell on Marlow's.'

'No, Sis, it didn't. It fell down the street. Outside Burrell's. But Marlow's – or a bit of Marlow's – the bit you and Jim were in, took some of the blast.'

'Jim! How is he? Can I see him? Is he coming to see me?'

'All in good time,' said Sid. Then he added quickly, 'And if you're wondering about Mum . . . I sent her home to get some rest. She'd been here without a break since they brought you in.'

'What? How long have I been here? When did you get here? I'm in hospital, am I?'

Sid's face creased. 'Oh Lily, you don't know, of course. It was midnight before they got you out. Mum was there, she'd got word. She came in the ambulance with you. Then they knocked you out so they could have a look at your shoulder. Mum managed to get through to me at work first thing and I came up straight up. It's three in the afternoon now.'

'Oh, poor Mum. But my shoulder hurts, Sid. What have I done to it?'

'No wonder. You've given it a good thump, sprained it and broken your collarbone. And—' He picked up her other hand so she could see it, and her arm, where the hospital nightgown fell back. It was livid with bruises, cuts and scratches. 'You're pretty battered all over. But I tell you, you were . . . '

'Don't say it. I was lucky.'

'You were.' He laid her hand back down on the covers. 'Mum'll be back soon. She's going to look for grapes.'

'Grapes! I couldn't be *that* lucky!'

'Oh, Lily!' Sid almost looked as if he might cry. 'It'd take more than a bomb to keep you down! I want to give you a hug, but I don't want to hurt you!'

'Oh, please don't. I hurt all over.'

'You've had Lord only knows what on top of you, chick. But us Collinses are tough nuts. You'll be all right.'

'I hope so.' Lily swallowed painfully through a throat like barbed wire and tried to wriggle her legs under the covers. 'Why do they tuck you in so tight? This is worse than last night.'

Even as she said it she knew it wasn't. Not the gut-twisting terror when she'd heard the bomb descend and the flash and the smash and being flung off her feet and the dust and the rubble pelting her and Jim . . . Suddenly she knew she had to see him, she knew it as urgently now as she'd known she had to be near him last night. Sid tried to stop her, but she struggled to sit up, biting her lip against the pain and the sick, giddy feeling it gave her. Her knee jabbed as it pulled against the sheet, just like it had when – she remembered now – she'd hit it in the dark against something sharp.

'Where's Jim?' she said. 'Why isn't he here? He's all right, isn't he? Is he coming?'

'He's, um . . . no, not straight away. He's in hospital as well.'

'What?' Lily yanked herself up the bed, disregarding the pain. 'He told me he wasn't hurt!'

He'd said he didn't think he was, anyway.

'No, he . . . well, maybe he couldn't feel it.'

It was fear that was making her nauseous now,

not her shoulder. Jim hadn't told her the truth. He'd known he was hurt.

'What? How bad is he?'

Sid didn't reply and Lily had her answer. She pushed at the stiff sheet with her good hand.

'Get me out of here, Sid, I've got to see him!'

'Lily – they won't let you.'

'Let them stop me! Help me, Sid! I've got to see him!'

Sid would never know how they got out without the nurses noticing. It could only have been because visiting time proper had started and the ward was filling up, the ward sister was showing a student nurse how to book in a new arrival, and someone was shouting for a commode. Sid put his arm round Lily as gently as he could, partly to shield her, partly to hold her up. He got her through the double doors, but outside she leant palely, almost green, against the wall.

'You'll never make it. The men's ward's upstairs and right along the corridor.'

'I'm going to see him if I have to crawl. Please, Sid, help me!'

Sid knew when his sister had him beaten.

'Wait here.'

Lily clung to the wall as Sid strode off, returning two minutes later with a wheelchair.

'Don't ask,' was all he said. 'Hop in and we'll go for a spin.'

* * *

Jim was lying as Lily had been, pinioned by sheets, which almost matched his face. From a bag on a stand, colourless liquid dripped through a tube into his arm. Before Sid had put the brake on the chair, Lily had scrambled out, clutching at Jim's hand with her free one.

'Jim! It's me! Lily! Jim, say something! Tell me you're all right!'

Jim lay there unmoving, unmoved. Now Lily understood how Sid must have felt, trying to get her to open her eyes.

'Jim,' she said, trying to keep her voice steady. 'Jim! We didn't go through all that for you to . . . Tell me you can hear me, please.'

Sid touched her arm softly.

'Lily. He's had quite a big op. Leave him be.'

Lily turned on her brother.

'An operation? What operation? How big is big?'

'Well, you see—'

'Lily . . . ' Jim spoke faintly from the bed.

Lily spun back round.

'You could hear me! Oh, Jim!' She fell back into the wheelchair and, not knowing where he was hurt, touched her forehead to his hand. 'Thank God you're all right!'

Jim gave a faint nod of his head.

'I'm fine.'

That did it!

'You'd better be! You told me you weren't hurt!

How dare you say that when you were obviously worse off than me! And then tell the rescue men to get me out first! You idiot!'

'That's right.' Jim's voice was very faint and he had to keep catching his breath. 'No sympathy. Just tell me off.'

'Oh, I didn't mean—'

'What on earth . . . can't you read?' The ward sister, starched apron, frilled cap, was standing at the end of the bed and pointing to a sign above it. It said 'No Visitors', beside another reading 'Nil by Mouth'.

Lily tried to object and Sid to explain, but the sister shooed them away from Jim's bedside and told them not to think about coming back.

'Please,' said Lily from her wheelchair as the sister held the ward door open for them. She didn't have to try very hard to look pathetic. 'I was trapped with him and I don't even know . . . how bad is he?'

'Are you a relative?' rapped the sister.

'As good as,' said Sid. 'He's our lodger. We're the only family he's got.'

The sister gave a quick glance left and right as if she was about to spill a state secret.

'You should really speak to the house surgeon,' she said, 'but just this once. It was a ruptured spleen, it had to come out. And broken ribs, several. He was lucky they didn't puncture a lung. Now be off, the pair of you!'

All the way back, Lily didn't speak: there was too much to take in. While she'd been inching through the rubble and making him make conversation, Jim must have been in agony, chest crushed, every word a huge effort. Trust him not to admit it! Now Lily had to feel guilty as well as sore!

When they got back to her ward, they were in trouble there as well. Sid had some explaining to do about his half-inching of a wheelchair and the kidnap of a patient, but when Lily was imprisoned in bed again, pulse and blood pressure checked, she wanted him to tell her everything he knew about the last twenty-four hours to get it clear in her own mind.

'I remember the rescue men coming,' she said. 'We heard them shouting. And I remember Jim telling them to get me out first.' She tutted, knowing now what she hadn't then. 'I know it seemed to take a very long time. And they were talking to me all the while, asking me what I could feel, telling me to keep talking so they knew exactly where I was and the best way to get to me.'

'Right.' Sid nodded. 'You've got Les to thank for that.'

'Les?'

'Seems Beryl's been on to him to distemper their scullery. Well, he wasn't in a great rush to start, so he stopped for a quick one in town. When the sirens started everyone piled into the pub cellar, but he heard the bomb drop and he realised it was close. He knew you and Jim had stayed back, so he got out and headed back towards Marlow's. He was the one who told the wardens who was in there and where to start looking. And he was the one who ran to get Mum.'

'Les!' breathed Lily.

Sid had always teased Les for the short time he'd spent in the Army before being discharged ('The only action you saw was a fight in the NAAFI queue!') but to head back into the thick of a blast was bravery verging on foolishness. Not quite George Cross level bravery, but bravery even so.

'Go on, Lil,' said Sid gently. 'Best you talk about it. What else do you remember?'

'Well, I know I kept on to the men about Jim. Telling them to make a bigger hole and get him out at the same time, but they said it wasn't safe, better to do us one at a time. It seemed to take for ever. And I know when they pulled me out . . . they couldn't help it but it was by my bad arm and it hurt so much . . . and Jim . . . I suppose he'd passed out. I didn't even say goodbye to him. If anything had happened to him . . . did I pass out too?'

'Yes. Mum said you were unconscious when you came out. Covered in dust, your clothes all torn, and grey from head to foot.'

'Oh, poor Mum!'

'You were alive, that's all she cared about.'

'And what about Jim? What's your spleen anyway? How can they just whip it out?'

One of Sid's first lectures in training had been about casualties with serious internal injuries but he didn't think he'd mention that.

'It's a bit of a spare part really. Like your appendix.'

'It must do something!'

'It's a bit like your liver or kidneys, I think, sort of filters things. But if it's gone, the rest of your organs muck in and work a bit harder.'

Lily looked doubtful.

'You're not just saying that, are you? To shut me up?'

'Lily, you can ask the medics if you like. It's the truth. And as if I'd try to shut you up! All these years of living with you . . . I like to think I've learnt something!'

Lily closed her eyes. Broken bones would mend. Jim hadn't punctured a lung. He could live without his spleen. He was going to be all right, they both were. It was more than either of them had a right to expect.

'Sid . . . did – did anyone die?'

'Thank God, not at Marlow's. I'm afraid Burrell's nightwatchman copped it, and one of their fire-watchers. The other was injured. Otherwise, a couple of ARPs were blown off their feet, and people who stupidly hadn't bothered getting to a shelter, but your nightwatchman got out without a scratch. And the firewatchers – they'd taken cover on the far side of the roof.'

'And Marlow's itself? The shop?'

Sid paused and looked down. Marlow's was such a big thing in their lives: like Jim, it was almost another member of the family.

'It's looked better. But by the time you and Jim are back on your feet I'm sure it'll all be ship-shape.'

Sid hadn't seen it for himself, but he'd bought the *Chronicle* at the station and seen the photo on the front page, taken even before the all clear had sounded. Part of the elegant 1920s façade of Marlow's was crumbled like a fallen cliff, while further down the street, a fire raged. Searchlights still scanning the sky lit up plumes of water as firemen directed their hoses and a dazed casualty was being helped into an ambulance. Sid had stuffed the paper into the pocket of his greatcoat. There was no need for Lily to see it – certainly not yet.

'Can I have a drink of water, Sid?' said Lily. Her throat was dry, her shoulder ached, and she was feeling impossibly tired. 'Then I think I might close my eyes for a bit.'

'Good idea.' Sid got up and began to pour a glass of water. 'And here's something to think about as you drift off. There is a silver lining. The Army won't ever bother itself with Jim now.'

Chapter 27

After all the fuss about her adventure with Sid, and overtiring herself, the next day Lily was hauled out of bed by the ward sister anyway.

'But I shall be watching you,' she warned, settling her in a high-backed chair. 'No more young men! No more escapades!'

Lily wouldn't have had time anyway: the morning was taken up with the doctor's rounds, thermometers and bedpans, and the moment the bell rang for afternoon visiting, Gladys burst through the door, bringing not grapes but a bar of ration chocolate, which she promptly unwrapped and started absent-mindedly eating.

'Sat under the stairs with my gran, I was!' she

wailed. 'I didn't know a thing about Marlow's and you and Jim till I turned up for work!'

'Why aren't you there now?' asked Lily.

Gladys smoothed out the chocolate paper. For once she decided not to go into detail.

'They're assessing the damage,' she said briefly. 'We'll be notified when we can come back.'

Lily went quiet. It was that bad, then.

When Sid and Dora arrived, Gladys had to go – only two visitors were allowed at a time. Dora was reassured to see Lily sitting out and with a bit more colour in her cheeks.

'That's 'cos they've washed the dust off!' said Lily. 'The flannel was filthy when they'd finished!'

Dora didn't need reminding of the state her daughter had been in, but all Lily wanted to know was how Jim was doing. There was good news there: Sid had been up to the ward and chatted up the staff nurse. Jim still wasn't allowed visitors, but the nurse had said his condition was 'comfortable', which, Sid said, actually meant he was doing well – possibly better than the doctors had expected.

'Doesn't dare otherwise, with you breathing down his neck!' he joked.

'You will phone and tell his dad, won't you?' worried Lily. 'He'll want to know.' Lily had spent all morning fretting about Tom Goodridge, hearing about Jim's injuries so soon after his wife's death.

'Already done,' Dora reassured her. 'Beryl phoned

285

to let Ivy know, so Tom knows all about it. And one of us is going to call them every day and tell them the latest.'

Visiting time was coming to an end. Dora didn't want to go, but she could see that Lily was getting tired, and she hurried Sid through one of his anecdotes.

'Let her get some rest,' she warned, kissing Lily on top of her still dusty hair. 'We'll get off now, Lily. We'll be back tomorrow. There's no grapes to be had, love, but I'm hopeful of at least finding some barley water for you.'

Lily was grateful when they'd gone. Talking was surprisingly tiring and she'd be glad when the nurses came to help her back into bed. But just as she felt herself nodding off, she felt a light touch on her arm. She opened her eyes and saw someone she took a full minute to recognise – Miss Frobisher!

Lily had never seen her out of work clothes, or in anything but a dark or neutral colour, but now she was in lovat-green trousers – trousers! – with a lemon V-necked sweater and a bottle-green leather – leather! – jacket. Instead of the usual chignon or French pleat, her hair was loose on her shoulders, held back by a folded scarf printed with what looked like scenes of some foreign city – wasn't that the Eiffel Tower?

'I shan't stay long, I can't stay long,' she said, perching on the edge of the bed. 'That ward sister makes me look quite a kitten, doesn't she?'

'Miss Frobisher,' squeaked Lily, wishing the dressing gown her mum had brought from home was a bit less shabby. 'Thank you for coming.'

'Lily, how could I not? You're much liked at Marlow's. Everyone sends their love. And Mr Marlow particularly wanted me to ask if there's anything you need?'

A useable arm, thought Lily, but she shook her head.

'Nothing I can think of, thank you,' she said. 'I hope I won't be in here long. I want to get back to work!'

'I feel so responsible, Peter,' said Eileen Frobisher. The bomb and its aftermath had catapulted them onto first name terms and they were sitting at a table in the hospital tea bar. Peter Simmonds had been to ask after Jim. 'She's so young . . . Leaving a junior member of staff, however competent . . . what was I thinking?'

'The same as me, I expect,' he said gruffly. 'That it had been a long day, all days were going to be long leading up to Christmas, and you might as well scoot off while the going was good. At least you had good reason – your little boy.'

Eileen shook her head impatiently. 'No, I didn't. My neighbour was putting him to bed and staying with him. I knew that. He wouldn't have known if I was there or not.'

Peter Simmonds had seen this before, in the Army – the guilt and self-reproach in those who'd survived unscathed. There, the answer had been easy: 'Do a hundred press-ups and get a grip, you sloppy article!' but that was hardly the answer here. Eileen needed sympathy; a shoulder to lean on, to cry on if necessary, and after months of being daunted by her, then fascinated, all the time strongly attracted, his shoulder was ready and waiting.

'If it's any consolation,' he admitted, and this was the truth, 'I feel the same. I'm the captain who deserted his ship. So we're both in the same boat.'

It was a weak joke but she smiled anyway.

'Thank you,' she said. And then suddenly: 'I'm glad I've got you to talk to.'

And she was. She'd been wary of him at first, an unknown quantity who'd come from outside and hadn't spent long as buyer on Sportswear before being promoted to first floor supervisor. He'd seemed stand-offish and abrupt – much the same as she'd seemed to him, ironically. But over time, she'd come to see it was just his manner, and no one could deny it had got results. The improvements he'd made along with young Jim in efficiency savings and stock control had seen profits hold remarkably steady despite the shortages.

And as she'd relaxed and begun to see him as a colleague instead of a threat, she'd had time to consider him as a man. No one knew anything about his private life, but there were rumours of a broken engagement in his twenties, and the usual excuse – that a career as a professional soldier didn't help to foster permanent relationships. Nor, perhaps, did his off-duty dress sense, she thought mischievously. Regimental blazer . . . cravat . . . They'd have to go! Hang on – was she seriously considering . . . ?

'I'm glad you feel you can,' he said quietly. 'Talk to me, that is. And if you've finished your tea, Eileen . . . it's dark already. If it's all right with you, I think I should see you home.'

They let Lily out after three days. Jim was making steady progress, but to his fury, he'd been told he'd be kept in for at least a week in case of infection.

'Serves you right,' Lily said. She'd been first through the doors when she'd found out visiting was allowed. 'This is what you get for not telling the truth!'

It helped her to make light of what she was really feeling – huge surges of relief and gratitude that he was alive alternating with the sickening realisation that she might have lost him.

'And after all that stupid business with Frank and being jealous of Margaret!' she sobbed to her mother when her feelings overtook her.

'Shh,' Dora soothed. 'You've had a big shock, love. You cry it out.'

Dora had dropped her WVS and Red Cross duties to look after her daughter. 'Charity begins at home', as Ivy had said when Dora had phoned to give her the latest bulletin.

Little by little, more had emerged about the night of the bomb. The main shopping street might have been devastated but there was one beneficiary – the much mocked *Hinton Chronicle*. It was the most exciting event in the town since a local gardener's giant marrow had won first prize in a national gardening competition.

'Local Stores Razed in Surprise Raid' screamed the front page the day after the blast, closely followed by 'Miracle Not More Killed' and 'Praise for Rescue Services'. A reporter had tried to get to Lily and Jim in the hospital, but with Sid and Dora guarding Lily's privacy, and the Gorgon ward sister guarding Jim, the paper had to make do with, 'Night Watchman's Lucky Escape: A Survivor's Story' before finally asking, 'That Bomb – Why Hinton?'

Good question. Even at the height of the Blitz, the town hadn't been a target. Hinton's factories, like the corset factory that now made webbing, and Tatchell's, the former car parts place making altimeters for planes, were hardly going to have Hitler's henchmen tapping their noses with their pencils and sticking a pin in a map.

'What about the aircraft parts Marlow's is storing, though?' asked Beryl, who'd come round to see Lily at home. 'Maybe they were the target.'

'If they were, their aim was all to cock,' scorned

Les. 'Burrell's copped the worst of it! Anyway, not worth their while. Tip and run,' he added. 'Some Jerry who ran out of fuel and offloaded the extra weight.'

It was true there'd been a raid on northern cities the same night. The planes would have passed Hinton on their way back.

Beryl shrugged and smiled at Dora, who was stitching the beads back on a Juliet cap for one of Beryl's brides. Dora smiled in return. Beryl had had her own torment on the night of the bomb: when he didn't appear at home, she was convinced Les had been caught up in the blast himself. Now Ivy was in the country, Dora had pretty much adopted Les, Beryl and Bobby as her own – so much for making more time for herself!

Once Jim was discharged and they were both back at Brook Street, it didn't take long for Lily and Jim to get restive. They chafed against the doctor's certificates that would keep them off work till mid-January and the restrictions their injuries imposed.

'I wish I'd been more sympathetic to my mum,' Jim reflected. 'I know how she felt now.'

'Me too,' Lily agreed. 'Trying to clean my teeth and brush my hair, let alone get dressed trussed up like this . . . '

Jim was strapped up too. He was trying to take deep breaths although it was painful: if he didn't, fluid could collect in his lungs and he'd get a chest infection. But he was moving more easily every day, and seemed to be managing fine without his spleen, though he'd lost weight he couldn't afford to lose. Dora's new mission in life was to put it back on him, but Lily and Jim's only aim was to get back to work, whatever the doctors said.

First, though, they had to convince their bosses, which meant a trip into town. To prepare themselves, they looked at the papers again – the back copies of the *Chronicle* that, at their request, but with very mixed feelings, Dora had put to one side instead of bundling them up for salvage.

Lily sighed as she looked at the photographs.

'Isn't it terrible . . . such a mess.'

'These were taken straight after,' said Jim. 'They'll have restored some order by now.'

Both fell silent: Lily touched the now grubby sling, which kept her right arm pinned across her chest.

'We were here, weren't we, Jim?' With her good hand, Lily pointed to the first floor. 'Think what could have come down on us.'

Jim touched his head to hers.

'It hadn't got our names on it, that bomb. It was never meant for Hinton, so it was never meant for us.'

'Maybe.' Lily was bent over the photograph again, peering. 'Is that . . . ?' she straightened up. 'You know what that is, don't you?' She pointed to a tiny dot. 'That, there . . . it's a horse's head! It's Dobbin! Oh, I hope they got him out!'

'They better had!' grinned Jim. 'Robert Marlow's own rocking horse – almost the store's mascot! Maybe even its lucky charm.'

When they got there, though, Marlow's looked anything but lucky. The street outside was looking better than in the *Chronicle*'s blurry photographs: shoppers had returned and traffic was skirting the potholes in the road. But the boarded-up frontages of Burrell's and Boots, the pitiful Christmas decorations in the undamaged windows of Marlow's and the brave 'Merry Christmas' signs on the entrance doors brought tears to Lily's eyes.

'Oh, Jim. Our lovely shop!'

One by one Cedric and his father had acquired the shops on either side of J. Marlow and Co. (Capes, Mantles and Bonnets) – until Marlow's was made up of no less than fifteen different premises. The commanding corner span had been the last piece of the jigsaw, when Montague Burton, the self-styled 'Tailor of Taste', had moved their premises to an even more splendid site. Thankfully that section was undamaged, but down the right-hand side, the bomb had wrecked four of the ground floor windows and blown in those on the floor above – where Lily and Jim had been. Next door, Boots the Chemist had suffered even worse damage, while Burrell's, down the street, had absorbed the worst of the blast. Their building was more than half burnt out.

'Let's go in.'

'Jim.' Lily's throat had closed up. 'I'm not sure I can.'

Jim took her good arm and led her away, so they weren't facing the worst of the damage. He pulled her towards him – cautiously, because it hurt him, and because he didn't want to hurt her.

'Look,' he said gently. 'I feel it too. Sick. Disbelieving – that it could happen at all, that it happened to us. But we got out. And unless we're going to let one night rule the rest of our lives, we've got to face it.'

'I thought I had faced it. But seeing it . . . that's different.'

'Yes. And when we get inside, it'll probably hit us even worse. But if we run away, then what? Sit at home? Find other jobs?'

Lily looked down at the pavement. Even here it was cracked and dusty.

'When we got together,' Jim went on, 'we said our future was bound up with Marlow's. We'd never have met if it wasn't for the place. It's been good to us – good for us. We can't desert it in its hour of need. Don't we owe it some loyalty?'

Lily looked up, this time, up at the white December sky, then back towards Marlow's. Two women came out of the double doors, chatting happily and examining their purchases. Marlow's was trying to put its best foot forward. Was she really not going to help it limp along till it was up and running again?

'Come on,' she said. 'What are we waiting for?'

Inside, the store was doing its best. The huge Christmas tree had been felled by the blast and the ornaments shattered, but Gladys had already told them that staff had brought in their own trinkets from home to replace them. The Cosmetics counters were offering 'Christmas coffrets' and Accessories were still proposing gloves, purses and umbrellas as 'The Perfect Gift'. Customers were browsing, some buying: Christmas was coming, nothing could change that. But the usual pre-Christmas buzz wasn't there: it was like a film with the sound turned off.

On the first floor, Lily's heart sank further. Ladies' Fashions, Model Gowns and Exclusives – even miserable Miss Naylor's Schoolwear had been left untouched. But on the other side of the sales floor, raw plywood panels sectioned off the unsafe areas. Furniture and Household was reduced to a few items with a sign saying, 'More Stock Available: Please Enquire'. Toys was a couple of trestles trying to look jaunty with crêpe paper skirts. Childrenswear wasn't even there: a sign with an arrow said it had been 'relocated'. Lily whirled around: it had moved to the area that had been Bridal. Of Dobbin the rocking horse, there was no sign – and no room for him even if there had been.

Lily reached for Jim's hand.

Joanna Toye

'It's worse than I could have imagined,' she said. 'All the stock we must have lost . . . '

'It's no good dwelling on it, Lily,' said Jim firmly. 'It's an opportunity. Most of Marlow's is sound – Burrell's are trading off a couple of stalls on the pavement. I don't want to dance on their grave, but this could be the chance of a lifetime for Marlow's.'

Chapter 28

Lily and Jim didn't stay long. Jim went to find Peter Simmonds while Lily went to Childrenswear, but Miss Frobisher was off somewhere trying to replace the ruined stock. Just as on the ground floor, there were customers around, but Miss Temple and Miss Thomas looked tired and harried and sad. Very little had been salvaged; what had was so sub-standard it was doubtful it could even go into the January Sales. The few replacements Miss Frobisher had been able to source so far were thinly spread about, looking even more pathetic against the new 'Merry Christmas' signs that had been put up.

It was the same story on Toys. Lily watched as Gladys tried to convince a customer that a dispirited-looking rag doll would be a good substitute for the baby doll with real hair that the customer's little girl had wanted for Christmas. She was making the point Jim had made, that the only other stockist in town had been Burrell's and their entire stock of toys had been blown to bits.

Lily hissed Gladys over the minute she was free, but Gladys's smile faded when Lily asked after Dobbin.

'Oh dear,' said Gladys. 'He's in pieces.'

'So he needs to go to the rocking horse hospital!'

'I don't think he's top of the list for repairs,' Gladys warned. 'Now I'm sorry, I'll have to go. It's lovely to see you and you're very brave to come, but you know we're not meant to talk to friends – even you!'

On the way home, the bus jolted over a pothole. Jim winced and clutched his ribs and was embarrassed to be offered a seat by an elderly man.

'War wounds, eh? You sit down, lad,' he said, though Jim insisted he could stand.

When they got off the bus, his mouth was set in a way Lily had come to recognise. Peter Simmonds and Jim's boss on Furniture, Mr Hooper, had told him to take his time before rushing back to work, even part time. He'd wanted to go and plead his case with Cedric Marlow as well, but they'd put him off.

'I'm not a complete crock!' he complained. 'It just makes me even more determined to get back to it!'

'Me too,' Lily agreed. She'd had the same message

from Miss Thomas and Miss Temple. 'They keep telling us we'll set ourselves back, but if you ask me, we've got more get-up-and-go than the lot of them. Gladys doesn't even seem bothered about Dobbin! Everyone's so fed up!'

'Well, we're not taking "no" for an answer.'

'What are we going to do? Stage a sit-in?'

'Let's get Christmas out of the way. But don't worry,' promised Jim, 'I've got an idea.'

Christmas came and went. There was one good thing about being signed off: Lily and Jim had the time to go and see Jim's dad. Jim wanted to show him he was well on the mend, and though it was unspoken between them, Lily knew she'd feel much more welcome in Bidbury without Alice.

It was a breath of fresh air to be in the countryside and Jim was cheered to see his father looking well. Tom was racked with his usual cough, but Ivy's feeding up regime had actually put a bit of flesh on his bones, and she and Susan were blooming. Ivy had been welcomed into the bosom of the village WI and pressed into service with the other ladies at the village hall, producing jam, chutney and rosehip syrup for the Ministry of Food. Jacob, the lad who did the garden, was, like Susan, a bit backward, but she worshipped him, following him around and helping him gather firewood or spread manure.

'It's been the making of her here,' Ivy told Jim with tears in her eyes. And to Lily she said: 'Truth be told, love, I'd like to stay here for ever.' What Eddie, her husband, might think of that wasn't mentioned; but he was away at sea for now, and if her experience of being buried alive had taught Lily anything, it was to live for the moment.

When they got back to Hinton, Lily found that she and Jim weren't the only ones keen to get on with things. On the first day of the New Year, Beryl came round to collect the presents Ivy had sent back with them and told Lily all the gossip.

'You'll never guess who's here!' she challenged. And before Lily could even try: 'Robert Marlow! The Prodigal Son! Stepped in to save the day!'

Jim would be interested to hear that, thought Lily. When he'd worked at the store before, Robert had masterminded a delivery racket for favoured customers and when it had come to light, had tried to shift the blame on to Jim. It had all got straightened out in the end – with just a little intervention from Lily – and though they'd settled their old scores, both Lily and Jim were still a bit wary of him. But Beryl had already moved on to her next piece of news: she'd heard that the Bridal department at Marlow's had all but shut down.

'They've stuck a few brides' dresses on Models and Exclusives,' she said, 'but it's nothing like it was. Good job I snapped up those frocks from that little shop in Dudley that was packing up. I've got twelve bridal now, and seven bridesmaids.'

Lily was confused.

'What are you saying? I don't mean to be funny, Beryl, but anyone who could have bought a dress from Marlow's isn't going to hire one from you, are they?'

Beryl wasn't letting that go.

'Did you get a concussion in that bomb or what? I think you've forgotten Burrell's Bridal department's out of action as well! What choice have people got? Unless they can afford to go looking in Birmingham or even London – it's an ill wind, Lily.'

Chapter 29

It was a lazy wind – the sort that goes through you, rather than round you – that was blowing as Robert Marlow, velvet collar of his overcoat turned up, cashmere scarf at his neck, stood outside Marlow's and surveyed the fragmented frontage.

He'd been back at his father's side since Christmas, working with Peter Simmonds. Together they'd agreed on the way forward. Cedric would nag the insurers, and Robert oversee the interior repairs. Peter Simmonds would take a final decision on the damaged stock – whether to knock it out cheaply to a wholesaler or somehow sell it in-store. So far, so good. But a decision had to be taken about the store's exterior – chiefly the four shattered ground-floor windows.

The demolition squad had insisted that the props and battens remained on the ground and first floors, but otherwise they'd declared the structure sound. They'd inspect monthly, but they'd credited the solid Portland stone construction with remarkable staying power.

Cedric Marlow and the staff, like the store itself, weren't the only ones who'd been shattered by the bomb. Robert had turned his back on shopkeeping but seeing the store – and his own father – brought so low had affected him more than he'd expected. He'd felt for a while that the responsibility of managing the place was getting too much for his father, and he wasn't sure that Cedric had the energy, the will, maybe not even the time left to him, to oversee its recovery.

But Robert Marlow never did anything for purely unselfish reasons. Putting in a bit of graft back at the shop, while making clear it was only temporary, would also make a welcome change from his current working life. Sure, the money was good and the work itself at Sir Douglas Brimble's Birmingham stockbroking firm was fine. His job was basically lunching private clients, tickling them along and assuring them that their portfolios were performing as well as could be expected in the circumstances, which they generally were, since they were managed by brokers far more experienced than Robert. The share dealing tips he got on the side were a bonus, too. What grated was having to toady to Sir Douglas, tell him how far sighted and talented he was and laugh at his feeble jokes. He knew it was the bride price due for Evelyn's hand in marriage, but sometimes he felt as if he'd sold his soul to the Devil.

Worse still, Robert even had to endure him in the evenings and at weekends. Because of the difficulties of transport, the Brimbles had shut up their large house in Hinton and were renting a mansion flat in Birmingham. Once Robert and Evelyn were officially engaged, Sir Douglas had suggested Robert move in too.

'Separate bedrooms, of course!' he'd boomed. 'No hanky-panky!'

No, quite – and that was another thing. Robert was a normal red-blooded male with all a young man's desires. Evelyn had been responsive enough before in their smooching sessions when they could get time alone, but since their engagement she'd turned into a regular Ice Maiden, intent on being a virgin bride.

The wedding was all she thought – and talked – about. They were going to be married in the summer – a big, lavish wedding with six attendants and two flower girls, and it had become the bane of Robert's life. When she wasn't wittering about horseshoe necklines and top hats, she was showing him fabric samples for the house that Sir Douglas was buying for them in one of Birmingham's leafy suburbs. She wanted, or said she wanted, Robert's opinion on everything, though in truth she, or she and her mother, had already made up their minds.

She hadn't been impressed when Robert had said he'd be moving back to Hinton.

'It won't be for long,' Robert had pleaded. 'But I have to help the old man out. A couple of months, tops.'

'A couple of months!' Evelyn's rosy mouth had closed into a frost-bitten bud. 'But don't you want to help me choose things for our first home? Let alone plan the wedding, please?'

'And I do! I do! I'll still be free at weekends,' urged Robert, seizing her hands. 'I'll come up to Birmingham and we can see each other and decide things together then.'

Evelyn had pouted and postured for a bit, but it was just for show. In the end she'd given in and Robert knew why. She was daddy's little girl, used to getting her own way, and she'd get her own way faster if she didn't have to go through the pretence of consulting him.

She had lifted her eyes, doe-like, to Robert.

'Oh, well. If you have to, you have to. If your father needs you . . . I mustn't be selfish.' Evelyn smiled generously, unselfishly. 'After all, we've got the rest of our lives together.'

Robert had smiled back, but thinly, as he tried to silence the bell of doom tolling away down the years.

* * *

Now in the cold light of January, Robert looked at the forlorn sight in front of him. Selfridges in London had bricked up their windows when they'd been hit – there was no plate glass that size to be had – but that seemed to Robert both ugly and defeatist. Could Marlow's use the space for some kind of display, relics of what had survived, things not worth looting, in the spirit of 'Keep Calm and Carry On'? Or would that be rubbing it in? Just posters, then, praising the Ambulance and Fire and Rescue Services?

'Shocking, isn't it?'

Robert spun round: a young woman he half-recognised was standing there. She wore a red coat, shabby but defiant. Her head was coquettishly on one side and a lock of blonde hair fell over her eye, a ration-book Veronica Lake.

'You're not sure, are you?' She came nearer and held out a gloved hand. 'Beryl. I used to work here. On Toys.'

He remembered now. Rather a fast piece. She'd always given him the eye.

'Beryl,' he said, smiling. 'Of course I know you.' She batted her eyelashes in a way he recognised too. 'You're looking very well. Married life must suit you.'

She'd married, he remembered that. Some bloke from despatch, wasn't it?

'I don't know about that,' she simpered. 'I've got a baby and all. Bobby, he's called.'

'Oh, er . . . congratulations.'

'Thank you.' The eyelashes fluttered again. 'Named after you, isn't he?'

She couldn't be serious! 'Really?'

'I've always thought it was a good name.' She lifted her shoulders and her chest rippled under the tight-fitting coat. 'And if he grows up like you he won't be doing so badly for himself, will he?'

She was shameless.

'It breaks my heart to see Marlow's like this,' she went on. 'Your father must be glad he's got you. It's going to take someone with your nous to pick things up again.'

'Well, that's very flattering,' said Robert. 'We've got a strategy worked out for inside, but out here, well, I'm not sure what we'll do.'

'If anyone can sort it out, you can,' she said firmly. 'Lovely to meet you again, Robert, but I'm sorry, you'll have to excuse me. I'm meeting friends for lunch.'

He looked after as she tripped away on what he could see were much-mended heels. Beryl! As brazen as ever. And somehow rather appealing.

Half an hour later, the cut-price Veronica Lake was sitting with those friends in Peg's Pantry. Its 'Businesswoman's Lunch' offered soup, a dry roll and a cup of tea for fourpence (margarine 1d extra).

'You *spoke* to him?' Gladys had her soup spoon halfway to her mouth.

'Glad, you don't change, do you?' Beryl dipped her roll in the thinned-down, made-from-a-cube tomato soup. 'You're engaged, you and Bill could be married by the year end and you're as green as the day you were born!'

'But Robert Marlow's the boss! Or he was! And the big boss's son!'

Lily drank her soup without comment. She'd long ago sworn not to be surprised by anything Beryl said or did.

'It's given me an idea, anyway,' said Beryl smugly, and she told them what it was.

Lily felt her previous resolve dissolve, and her mouth almost fell open. Beryl might as well have declared herself an expert in edible fungi, or that she was off to tour the world with ENSA, while Gladys couldn't have looked more shocked if the Loch Ness monster had sat down at their table and asked her to pass the salt.

Even so, Gladys spoke first.

'Beryl! You can't!'

'Nothing ventured,' said Beryl, getting out her purse. 'I don't see why he shouldn't agree. Now, how about we have a Bath bun between the three of us. My treat. I've got a good feeling about today!'

'Can you believe her, really?'

After the Bath bun had been divided and eaten and a good five minutes spent re-applying her lipstick, re-arranging her hair and re-tying the belt of her coat, Beryl had left them, and Gladys and Lily were sitting over the dregs of their tea.

Lily shook her head. 'No. Every time I think I've heard it all, she amazes me. Well, we'll see how she gets on. But listen, Gladys . . . before Beryl dropped her bombshell . . . ' Lily paused. A couple of weeks ago she might not have been able to use that expression. Now she could. It made her feel she'd made the right decision. 'I've got something to tell you as well. Jim and I will be back at work tomorrow.'

Poor Gladys. She'd had so much to take in today her eyes were rolling in her head like marbles.

'Already? It's been nowhere near six weeks!'

Patiently, Lily explained. 'We had our hospital check-ups yesterday and we've discharged ourselves. The doctors haven't got any say over us now. We can do what we like.'

'Oh, Lily. You are brave!'

'No, I'm not!'

'You are,' Gladys insisted. 'If it had been me, I don't know as I could ever have gone back to where it happened. It's been bad enough as it is, and I wasn't even there!'

'I did have a wobble,' Lily admitted. 'That day when Jim and I came in before Christmas. But seeing the shop look so down on its luck . . . We can't let this beat us. I'm going to get over it and Marlow's is going to get over it and we'll both be bigger and better and stronger than ever!'

Gladys looked almost dismayed. 'Oh, Lily, no!'

'What? Don't you want Marlow's to—'

'It's not that! Of course I do! But a bit of me quite liked it when you weren't so well, when you hadn't got quite so much energy and all these ideas all the time! You were like a normal person, like the rest of us!'

Lily laughed. Sometimes, Gladys wasn't quite the doormat Beryl made her out to be.

Beryl hoped Robert would still be outside; she didn't want to have to talk her way past the secretaries on the management floor. But as she rounded the corner, there he was with a couple of the store's handymen, debating the placing of a banner reading 'Please Excuse our Appearance . . . Business as Usual!'

Beryl hung back until its position was decided and the handymen were angling their ladder. Then, as Robert turned to go inside, she materialised at his elbow.

'Good move,' she began. 'Your idea, I expect.'

'It was,' he said. 'Though it should have gone up long ago.'

'Well, I wasn't going to say it. But better late than never, eh?'

'Quite. Um, well, I'd better get on.'

'Don't go,' she interrupted. A hand – gloveless this

time – flashed out and rested on his arm. 'I'm sorry I had to rush off before. There's something I'd like to put to you.'

It was cold in the wind, but she gave off a kind of warmth that he'd never experienced with Evelyn. Maybe it was the way she stood so close. She delved in her bag and produced a grubby card, which she pressed into his hand.

'Beryl's Brides, that's me, see. I've got my own little business.'

Robert was nonplussed. 'Well, what can I say? Again, congratulations. Very enterprising of you.'

'Thank you, it's doing really well. A lot of my business is word-of mouth, recommendations, so till now it's suited me to run it from home. But I've been thinking for a while that I need some premises.'

'Premises?'

'Nothing fancy, just a small lock-up sort of place. But in a good area. Passing trade. Footfall.'

She knew all the gen.

'So . . . ?'

'Well, here'd be perfect. One of these windows spaces, I mean. The glass has gone, but the shell's fine, isn't it? The floor and ceiling's secure and the sides. Clear out all the rubble, brick up quarter height, window above, door to the side – you've got a nice little unit there.'

'Hang on. You're . . . what? Offering to rent it?'

'I'm sure we could come to some arrangement.'

She smiled up at him, pushing the Veronica Lake-ish lock of hair behind her ear. 'I'd be doing you the favour. You might be able to let the others as well. But you'd never have thought of it if it wasn't for me.'

She had the brass neck of a thousand monkeys, but as someone who'd brass-necked his way through school, flown by the seat of his pants when working for his father and secured Sir Douglas's approval and Evelyn's hand by running a racket that had risked the store's reputation, Robert had to admire it.

And she was right, damn it. She'd spotted an opportunity. There were four window spaces. If they really could be made safe, they could rent the rest to other selected businesses – nothing common, not your greengrocers or fishmongers . . . Glazed and fronted as she'd imagined, Marlow's might even be able to utilise them for itself.

'I'd have to discuss it with my father.'

'Really?' Her hand rested fleetingly on his arm again. 'I thought you were the one taking the decisions these days, Robert.'

He noted her use of his name. The little minx.

'All right. Let me think about it.'

She liked that. 'So how will you let me know?'

Robert was used to Evelyn's method of getting her own way, the steamroller or the sulk, and the hopeless feeling it gave him. He knew that something similar and just as unsubtle was happening here, but he didn't mind in the least.

'Are you free in the evenings? We could meet for a drink.'

'That would be lovely.'

'Tomorrow, say? The White Lion, about seven thirty?'

'I'll be there.'

Chapter 30

'What the blinking . . . what are you doing here? Your six weeks' recuperation isn't up yet! The Sale's barely started!'

'You'd better read this.'

Peter Simmonds opened the envelope Jim held out to him and scanned the letter. It was on hospital headed paper and said that as the patient Mr J. Goodridge had discharged himself from their care, they no longer had any authority over his actions.

'And before you ask,' said Jim, 'Lily – Miss Collins – has got one too. We can't sit by when Marlow's is in this state. Neither of us can.'

Peter Simmonds shook his head. There were blokes like this in the Army. For every malingerer, there were half a dozen who couldn't wait to get back to the fray, even if they were nothing like battle-fit. Jim was one of those; he'd been like it himself. The day he'd been invalided out with a niggling injury had been the worst of his life, so he understood.

'I don't know what Mr Marlow'll think,' he said. 'As for me . . . I might have known!'

On Childrenswear, Lily had much the same response. She'd managed to get rid of the sling, but her arm was encased in an elastic bandage under the sleeve of her uniform dress – Dora had insisted. Lily had deliberately handed the letter to her boss with her right hand, though. A sudden movement could still cause a needling of pain, but she wasn't going to show any sign of weakness.

Miss Frobisher was folding the letter. 'Well, you've outwitted us all as usual. Never mind the doctors, what does your mother have to say about it?'

Dora wasn't happy, of course, but Lily passed it off.

'I'm afraid she knows me by now.'

'Don't we all!' exclaimed Miss Frobisher before she could stop herself. 'Well, whatever you say, I'm going to keep you on light duties, and I trust Mr Hooper and Mr Simmonds will do the same with Mr Goodridge and not have him lugging furniture about.'

'I think he can look after himself.'

Lily was remembering her efforts to minister to Jim and how he'd brushed away her attempts to make him more comfy with cushions or ply him with hot Bovril.

'I—' Miss Frobisher stopped. There were shadows under her eyes and new, tiny lines at the corners of her mouth. 'Oh, look. I'm not going to pretend we haven't missed you, Miss Collins. Miss Thomas and Miss Temple are worn out. Oh, Lily, I am glad to see you. Welcome back!'

Lily's answer about her mum hadn't been quite the whole truth.

'You've what?' Dora had said when Lily had explained she and Jim had discharged themselves. 'You've pushed me to the county boundary before, Lily Collins, but this time – I tell you, I'm halfway to Birmingham!'

Lily's chin went up – never a good sign. 'I'm sorry, Mum, but it's done now. We're a right couple of useless articles hanging round here and it's only making us fed up.' She smiled, trying to break the ice. 'Come on, don't tell me you don't want us out from under your feet?'

The trouble was, Dora couldn't. She didn't approve of them going back, but she'd seen how bored they were getting, squabbling over board games, fiddling with the radiogram. And while she didn't trust Lily or Jim not to try to take on too much too soon, she had every faith in Marlow's not to let them. She'd met Miss Frobisher now, at the hospital, and though she was slightly over-awed by her, as Lily herself had been, the two women had one thing in common, the only thing that mattered – their fondness for Lily.

Now on a January morning, Dora had to admit it was a relief to have the house to herself. It might be a bit early for spring cleaning, but she hadn't been able to get round properly with the two of them always there: the whole place needed a good turning out. She tied her hair up in a turban and fastened her wrap-around pinny a bit tighter. She'd start in her bedroom with her chest of drawers: she'd been stuffing things in any old how, most unlike the usual tidy piles.

Upstairs, she pulled out the top right-hand drawer and tipped its contents on the bed. Stockings, her better brassiere, knickers, all jumbled up together. She began to sort them, then slowly she sat down. The stockings that Hugh had given her. She'd tucked them right at the back.

He'd teased her about not giving them to her daughter, but that was exactly what Dora had planned. She'd been going to give them to Lily for Christmas – her first pair of proper nylons. But what with the bomb, and that long night with Lily in the hospital, and Jim hurt as well, and next morning having to get hold of Sid, and Sid coming straight away, bless him, and him cabling Reg and phoning Bidbury and getting Ivy to tell Jim's dad the news, so soon after he'd lost his wife . . . And later that day Lily waking up and seeing her there, and bursting into tears and saying she was sorry, so sorry, for all the worry she'd ever caused her, and she'd never cause her any ever again . . . Some hope!

Dora sat there, the packet cool and slippery in her hands. Hugh had held it in his hands too. He was miles away from the Midlands now, down south, maybe further, maybe hundreds of miles, maybe thousands, abroad. Hinton's bomb might have occupied the *Chronicle* for days but it had been a tiny paragraph in the *Sketch* and the *Mirror*. They probably weren't the sort of papers he'd get to see anyhow in the officers' mess, more likely *The Times* or the *Telegraph*. Had they even mentioned it? What could or would he have done if he'd known? Lily's name had been in the *Chronicle* but not in the national papers, and even if it had been, Collins was a common enough surname. Even if Hugh had suspected the connection, he couldn't have got in touch; he didn't know her address.

It would have been nice to hear from him, though, and to have known that he was thinking of her. Sid had been wonderful, and friends, and neighbours, but it would have been nice to know that someone outside the family – and a man – was concerned for her.

Dora looked round the room; the faded wallpaper, the darned pillowslip. It was ridiculous, thinking like this. He wasn't coming back – and if he had been, what then? Hugh Anderson was miles out of her league, socially and in every other way. He was from a completely different world – a world away! And for goodness' sake, he was surely married! A lovely chap like him, he'd have a wife, she could see her now, small and dark and pretty. There'd be children, two of them, twins maybe – the perfect family – a boy for him and a girl for her. Hugh would build his daughter a doll's house and he'd take the boy fishing at the weekends. Together he and his son would sweep leaves in the garden – they were sure to have a big garden, all the space there was in Canada – and they'd build a bonfire and his wife and daughter would come out with steaming cups of hot chocolate and cookies – that was what they called biscuits over there, wasn't it? – that they'd been baking together. Dora could see it all.

What a fool she was. They'd been ships in the night, that was all, and the sooner she gave Lily the stockings the better. But for now, she'd tuck them back in the drawer. Right at the back.

'Oh, he does look sorry for himself!'

Lily had always thought the rocking horse had an expressive face. When a child was on his back, he had an eager look, the bit between his teeth, the wind in his mane, racing down the home straight. Standing idle, you could convince yourself his eye was less bright, his head not quite so proud. Now, with his head severed, ears chipped, teeth knocked out, back leg hanging off and the struts of the frame splintered and bent, he looked thoroughly miserable.

Miss Frobisher and Mr Simmonds had conferred. They had to accept that they'd been victims of a stealth attack, but they were fighting back. Lily and Jim weren't quite confined to barracks, but they were put on light duties. Peter Simmonds explained the division of labour he and Robert Marlow had worked out, and immediately delegated the damaged stock assessment to Jim, while Miss Frobisher gave Lily a clipboard and exactly the same task. They both knew they were being fobbed off so they quickly did what they'd been asked to do in their respective stock-rooms, then went exploring, which was how they'd found Dobbin in a dusty corner.

'There's no chance of getting him fixed,' said Jim. 'There's no money for fripperies.'

Lily hugged Dobbin's roughly beheaded neck.

'He's not a frippery! He's part of the furniture! The heart of the store!'

'Lily,' said Jim reasonably. She hated it when he took that tone, though he often had to when she worked herself up. 'There's no money for the rocking horse hospital – if one even exists. And we can't ask the handymen. They're run off their feet.'

They were: cutting and sticking bits of carpet, mending panelling, making good.

Lily stroked Dobbin's dappled coat, even more dappled now, pocked with chips and scratches.

'There must be someone! I know . . . Father Christmas!'

'A bit early in the year for him, isn't it?'

'No, you big dope! Albert, who was going to be Father Christmas in the grotto! He's a carpenter! Or he was, here! Maybe he could take it on!'

Jim looked at Dobbin, then at her.

'It's a big job.'

'Worth asking!'

'Well . . . you might be on to something,' Jim conceded. 'I remember Simmonds telling me Albert wasn't enjoying retirement. Felt useless. Bored.'

'There you are then!' Happier now, Lily patted Dobbin reassuringly. 'It's a good job we're back, Jim. I know no one's indispensable, but frankly I don't know how they've managed without us!'

'Let the window space out?' Cedric Marlow rubbed his face wearily. 'I'm really not sure, Robert.'

Father and son were in the middle of a discussion. Robert had expected resistance – Cedric was too old to be adventurous, and the bomb had only made him more nervous of change. To Cedric, the bomb damage was a tragedy, not an opportunity: all he hoped to do was patch up Marlow's as best they could and stagger on.

They'd clashed in the past, but Robert had learnt

– especially with his experience of Evelyn's tactics – to have another card up his sleeve.

'Look, there's only one outside enquiry at the moment – this little bridal business. You can't deny that seems a nice respectable sort of outfit. If you don't want to offer the rest of the spaces to other traders, we could put a few of our own departments in there. It'd free up space inside, make up for the space we're never going to recover, not for a while anyway, till we can get some proper building work done.'

Robert sat back and watched his father turn it over in his mind. He felt sorry for the old man. Cedric Marlow lived and breathed the store; it had been his life. He'd taken the destruction as a personal blow, as crushed by it as if he'd been under the debris himself. His mind had been fogged by it too, but he couldn't fail to see the logic of Robert's suggestion.

'You could be right,' he said slowly. 'Pipes and Tobacco, for instance, that's all the space they need.'

'The Red Cross stall, too,' suggested Robert. 'That started as a charitable gesture but it's taking up room we could be making a profit from. If we put it in one of the window spaces, it has the virtue of making us look virtuous too.'

Cedric closed his eyes. Anything would be better than seeing the windows as they were now.

'We'd have the expense of sorting the frontage,' Robert added. 'But relatively speaking . . . '

'Oh, do it, Robert,' said his father. 'You're right. We can fill three of the windows. And if you're convinced by – what is it – Beryl's Brides . . .' He winced. 'But I shall want strict terms and conditions. She must understand that.'

Robert nodded. 'Absolutely. I shall make the terms and conditions very clear.'

His father's and his own.

Chapter 31

In the lounge bar of the White Lion, Beryl looked up hopefully.

'Well, what do you think?'

Robert handed back the battered exercise book. He liked that look.

'They all seem to be in order. Thanks for bringing them.'

One of his father's conditions had been that Robert should see Beryl's accounts. Robert had agreed without ever expecting to bother, but now he had, and on her initiative – she was a smart cookie, all right – he'd seen all he needed to.

'I'm only showing a loss because of the stock I've bought lately,' she added. 'But,' she smiled, 'you've got to speculate to accumulate, haven't you?'

Robert smiled back. The returns were pitiful, really, and she'd have to boost turnover substantially to keep up with the rent, but he could afford to be generous.

'Given you haven't been trading for long, they're very impressive.' The bar wasn't busy, but he'd chosen a secluded corner, their table lit only by a red-shaded lamp. 'But then I never thought you were just a pretty face.'

It was the most clichéd of compliments, but she smiled as if she'd never heard it before, her eyelash-batting smile.

'Well? Will you give me a chance?'

'I'd like to, Beryl. I had a hard job persuading my father, I don't mind telling you, but I managed to convince him. He insisted on some conditions, though.'

She sat up a bit straighter. 'Go on.'

From his inside pocket, he produced the contract his father had made him draw up.

'These are the terms of the lease. It's pretty standard stuff – you're welcome to take it away and look it over.'

'That's all right. I'll take a look at it now.'

As she read, he took a look at her. She was wearing a dress in jade green, made from a thin, self-striped material, much too thin for January. He had a dreadful suspicion it might have started out as curtains: it was home-made and had obviously been re-made at least once. Her blonde hair was out of a bottle, her nail varnish – red, of course – had been touched up and was slightly smudged. She wasn't over made-up, but it wasn't subtle either, not the faint blush and slick of lipstick that was all Evelyn's porcelain beauty required. All the same, and though in later life she might be coarse and blowsy, for now she was in full bloom. Evelyn was, he supposed, more like the picture-book image of the perfect English Rose, but beside Beryl she was tight and closed – the stiff forced roses of a florist's shop. Beryl was a rambling rose in a summer garden – open, voluptuous, spreading herself generously everywhere.

She was chewing her lip as she read, her hand at her throat, and he had to look away, wanting to snatch at her hand and pull her towards him.

She looked up, frowning. 'I want to check I've got this right. Marlow's will pay for the clear-up and making good inside and out. Inside'll be distempered but I can paint over it at my expense if I want to. Outside paint's black, I can't change that. Right so far?'

'Spot on.'

'What about signage? And fitments, rails?'

'Come on, now you're asking!'

'Yes, I am,' she said defiantly. 'You want all the outside uniform, then all the sign writing's got to match. You've got the store sign writers, haven't you?'

Smart cookie, all right.

'All right,' he conceded. 'We'll do the sign writing.'

'And rails?'

'Beryl . . . '

She said nothing, just looked at him, lips slightly parted.

'You're pushing your luck! But I'll see what I can do. On the QT, OK?'

'Thank you, Robert.' Her hand flashed out and hovered over his sleeve. 'I can call you Robert, can I?'

'Well . . . when we're meeting like this, yes, you can. But at the shop—'

'Oh, don't worry. It'll be all formalities then.'

'Good. As long as we understand each other.'

He was sure they did. But they'd better get the business bit over.

'You're happy, then? I'll add a line about signage if you like. But the rent's fair, you'd agree? And Marlow's gets twenty per cent of your takings?'

Her hand went to her throat again. 'I was coming to that. I wasn't expecting that.'

'It's standard for a concessionary department. It's the same for our sportswear brands, for instance.'

'But I'm not a concession, am I? I'm independent. And they're inside. Rather more plush facilities.'

Robert gave her a sceptical look. 'Have you been inside lately? It's all make do and mend! Your place'll be brand spanking new.'

Beryl pulled down the bodice of her dress and smoothed its skirt over her thighs. She wasn't trying to be seductive; it was to buy herself time. She had too much to think about now to bother about any effect she might be having on Robert. She could still take the unit and make it work, but it would be much harder. This had gone beyond womanly wiles: she'd have to try straight talking.

'I can't afford it,' she said. 'Not twenty per cent on top of the rent. Can we say ten?'

Robert wasn't surprised. Twenty per cent was standard, but he could have persuaded his father to leave it out. He'd left it in because it gave him bargaining power.

'Why didn't you say so before? Instead of all the guff about rails and signage?'

'I wanted to get that straight. What might be included.'

'Before you started to negotiate? You've done it the wrong way round. I've thrown in more. I'm hardly going to charge you less, am I now?'

His tone was sweetly reasonable. He could play games, too, though for Beryl it wasn't a game any longer. She stood up.

'Then I'm sorry to have wasted your time.'

'Beryl.' He stood up and took her arm. 'Don't be silly.'

'What's silly about it?'

'Sit down. Let's talk about it.'

She sat again, and he sat beside her, perhaps a fraction closer than before.

'Look. I want to help you. Like I said, I admire what you've done. What you've made of yourself. Maybe we can come to some arrangement.'

'Like what?'

'I can't budge on the commission. My father'll see the returns. But I could help you with paying the rent. To start with, at least.'

'Why would you do that?'

He could hardly say, 'Because I want to sleep with you. Because Evelyn keeps me at arm's length and says it's because we're only engaged, but I know now that's how it'll always be.' He didn't say it, but she knew.

'Hang on. You think I'd . . . What do you take me for?'

'That's choice! Don't play me for a fool!' Robert saw the barman look over and lowered his voice. He hardly wanted a report of this little rendezvous flying round town. 'You made up to me! It was obvious!'

Beryl drew herself up and somehow drew into herself as well. 'If you saw it like that . . . I approached you, I don't deny it, but with a business proposition, that was all. Any other kind of proposition never entered my head!'

'Oh, really?'

'Yes, really.'

Evelyn wasn't the only one who could sulk: Robert had his petulant side and now it was on display. This wasn't going the way he'd planned.

Joanna Toye

'I've stuck my neck out for you. I talked my father round. I've been on the phone all afternoon after paint—' He made an effort to turn peevishness into persuasion. 'Beryl. You want that little shop. I want you to have it. You pay the twenty per cent, I'll take care of the rent. Everybody wins. We could have a nice time together and no one would ever know. Why make life difficult for yourself?'

'Why? Because I'm married! And to a man who's worth a hundred, a thousand of you!'

'Les Bulpitt? Do me a favour!'

'He is!' She stood up again and reached for her coat. 'You're right I want that shop. And I'll take it. I'll pay your rent in full and your commission. I'll work day and night to do it, if it kills me! I'll show you I can do it without having to pay you back in kind!'

She picked up the contract and stuffed it in her bag. He stood up as well.

'Fine,' he said coldly. 'Have it your own way. The unit'll be ready by the end of the month. Collect the keys from the office – oh, and you'll have your sign writing and your rails. I won't go back on that. But don't expect any more favours from me. And if the rent is ever a day late you're out on your ear.'

* * *

330

Beryl was shaking as she left the White Lion. She'd got what she wanted, at a price, though at least not the price he'd been angling for. She stood in a shop doorway until she saw Robert Marlow come out and walk off in the other direction, not trusting him not to follow her.

His offer had genuinely appalled her: she'd truly never expected he'd go that far. She wasn't even flattered. Smug so-and-so, he thought he could have anyone! There were plenty who'd have fallen for it, but not her. Les might have his limitations, but he loved her and he loved Bobby. He'd married her when she was in trouble and he'd supported her in starting her business, which a lot of husbands wouldn't. He didn't mind when his tea wasn't on the table because she'd had a bride in for a fitting; he even gave Bobby his bottle and changed the stinkiest of nappies. He hadn't minded either when she'd told him about her plan for a shop, and how she'd have to farm Bobby out to a neighbour. Instead he'd hugged her, with Bobby sandwiched between them, and told her he knew she was only doing it for all of their good. Bobby, he'd said, was the luckiest baby in Hinton to have a mother like her and he was the luckiest man in the world to have her for a wife.

Her legs were still shaking when she started the walk home, but following the quivering beam of her torch, she thought it through. She'd show Robert Marlow. She'd pay that rent every week on the nail if she had to raid Bobby's Post Office book to do it: he'd benefit in the end! She'd get hold of some paint too, and have it pink inside, like she'd always wanted. Les could bring the stock over on a barrow. She'd have the cheval glass from Ivy's and the scrap screen for the trying on, and in time, if they could get the stuff, a little rail across one corner and a curtain for a changing room. She'd need a chair for the mother of the bride . . . she'd have to work on that. There was a nice lyre-backed chair in the Collinses' front room: maybe Dora would lend it to her. As Beryl's official seamstress, she was going to have her work cut out if things needed a nip and a tuck. But a February opening was perfect – just in time for the spring brides . . .

Les was waiting up for her when she got back to Alma Terrace, and he hugged her again and got a brew on. As she told him all about her evening – well, not quite all – Beryl felt herself becoming more determined than ever. Stuff Robert Marlow! She'd make it work. Somehow.

Beryl wasn't the only one with a problem about her shop opening: it had left Jim in a quandary. He didn't know which story to lead with in the next *Marlow's Messenger*.

'Do I go with the windows scheme,' he pondered, 'or the news that Dobbin's on the mend? With a before and after photograph?'

The old carpenter, Albert, had leapt at the chance to use his skills on something more challenging than carving yet another pipe rack for a relative, and had performed miracles on poor old Dobbin. Jim and Lily had been to see him working away in his outhouse and could hardly see the joins where ears, teeth and most importantly, a hind flank had been restored. Now there was only the rocking mechanism to fix, and Albert had enlisted the help of his son-in-law, on leave from the Royal Engineers, for that.

Lily and Jim were properly on the mend too. Jim was moving and breathing easily again, and Lily was conscientiously doing the exercises the hospital had given her to restore the wasted muscles in her arm. Her grip was still shaky and she had to take extra care when she was writing out bills or lugging armfuls of clothes about, but she didn't mind, just grateful that new stock was coming through, and they had somewhere to put it.

Bit by bit, the first floor had been reclaimed. Of course they couldn't use any floor space that was deemed unsafe – the ruins recorder was a weekly visitor – but whole areas that had been out of bounds simply because they were scattered with dust and lumps of plaster were now back in use. Furniture and Toys had expanded again and Childrenswear had returned from its exile in the Bridal section. To Beryl's relief, that was now full of Sportswear for the summer season, cricket flannels and tennis shirts. The last thing she wanted was competition.

Well, that wasn't strictly true – the last thing she wanted was another encounter with Robert Marlow, so she was relieved when she took the wording for her shop sign up to the management floor and he wasn't about. She'd decided on Beryl's Brides with 'Bridal and Occasion Wear for Hire' in smaller letters underneath. She'd have liked a curly script on a pink background, but it would have to be boring old capitals, and gold on black, like the Marlow's signage, of course. There was no pink emulsion to be had either, but she'd found a roll of dusty wallpaper in a junk shop – enough, she reckoned, to paper the back wall.

'Fleur-de-lys,' she carolled triumphantly when she called round to the Collinses to show it off. 'Classy or what?'

She caught Jim as he was debating his *Messenger* headline and stood over him as he typed. She insisted that the lead story had to be the grand opening on February 1st of what she called the 'parade' of little units.

'I mean, who can get excited about a blooming rocking horse? Call yourself a journalist?'

Jim gave in. In this mood Beryl had the force of the bouncing bombs, which the military were pretending didn't exist but which everyone knew were being secretly tested. And Jim had put his own stamp on the 'parade'. He and Peter Simmonds had ousted Pipes and Tobacco and had seized the fourth window space for a Bargain Bazaar where they could sell off stock damaged in the raid.

Cedric Marlow had quailed at the thought ('Turning Marlow's into the market hall!') but Robert could see their thinking and had given Jim a quote for his newsletter.

'Bridal Hire, Red Cross, watch and clock repair and a Bargain Bazaar – all four have the same aim, in line with Government thinking: Recycle and Re-use!'

'And rejoice!' said Lily when Jim gave her the article to read. 'I can't wait to see those windows full again!'

Chapter 32

The Mayor cut the ribbon on the opening day of Marlow's parade. In the lead-up, the *Chronicle* had reached for all its superlatives, describing the move as 'the phoenix rising from the ashes', and on the day sent a reporter *and* a photographer.

In a smart new frock run up by Dora out of blackout material, Beryl made sure she was in the front of every photo – every one that Robert Marlow wasn't in, that is. She seethed when she heard him telling the *Chronicle* that the whole idea had been his, but there was nothing she could do – she had to keep her head down. And pay her rent.

There was a buzz of excitement after the opening and the *Chronicle*'s breathless coverage, and plenty of people peered in the window of Beryl's Brides. Some came in to browse, and some were tempted into paying their deposit. But even with the smart paint outside and the bold claim of the signage, and the dresses that Beryl displayed on a Marlow's dummy, damaged in the raid and rescued by Les from the incinerator, business in the first few weeks wasn't as brisk as she'd hoped.

She couldn't blame the weather: it was mild, so that wasn't keeping people away. Every day she opened up hopefully. She dressed and re-dressed the dummy and, worried that people might think she was too expensive now she was cheek-by-jowl with Marlow's, wrote a card for the window: 'A Small Deposit Secures – Ask About Our Easy Terms'. Beyond that, she couldn't think what to do; she could hardly drag people in off the street. She could try advertising, but that meant laying out more money. She had nowhere to turn for advice – or felt she didn't. Jim had helped her understand accounts when she'd first set up, and he was always full of bright ideas, but something stopped her from approaching him. It wasn't that he'd tell Lily; she knew she could trust him to keep a confidence if she asked him to. But she was ashamed to admit her failure to anyone: she'd had such big ideas.

All she could do was to try to cut her costs. She made excuses when Gladys and Lily called in to ask her to join them in Peg's Pantry, saying she couldn't leave the shop at dinner time, just when customers might pop in on their own dinner breaks. When they offered to bring her something back, she said she'd brought something with her, and she had; she was subsisting all day on a slice of bread and marg and a flask of tea from home. By mid-March she'd already had to raid Bobby's Post Office book for the rent twice.

Still she didn't confess.

'How's it going?' Lily asked her on one of the abortive dinner-time visits. Gladys was admiring a dress in white slipper satin with a heavily ruched bodice.

'Fine!' said Beryl brightly. 'My order book's filling up nicely!'

'I wish I could give you a date for me and Bill,' mourned Gladys. 'Do you think something like this'd do for me, Beryl, when my big day finally comes around?'

Gladys didn't even know where Bill's ship, the HMS *Jamaica*, was these days: though she wrote daily, she hadn't had a letter back for weeks and he couldn't have told her anyway.

Beryl looked at Lily, both of them thinking the same thing: Gladys's generous proportions would be better suited to something not quite so shiny.

'I see you in lace, Glad,' said Beryl. 'Or a nice crêpe. I haven't found anything quite right for you yet. But I'll know it when I see it.'

If I ever have the money to buy any more stock, she thought. *If I can even keep afloat.*

Time was running out for Robert Marlow as well. His work in Hinton was done, by and large, and it had been a success. He'd almost enjoyed knocking things back into shape at Marlow's, and even better, he'd had the opportunity to show his initiative in a bit of business himself. Aside from that, even Robert's selfish heart was pleased to see that by taking the distress of the damage and the stress of the restoration off his father, Cedric had rallied. He'd returned to his forensic examination of the takings and his daily tour of the store, picking staff up on faults again; an unpolished shoe, a crooked name badge or a counterside chair an inch out of true.

But if Cedric was having an easier time of it now, Robert wasn't – at least not at weekends, when he went back to Birmingham. As the weeks wore on, Evelyn pouted more and more about his absence and though he knew the answer was to return to Birmingham, something in him rebelled. But he couldn't get away with it much longer. Their first married home was bought and needed to be furnished; their wedding date was getting nearer and there were decisions to be made. He had to be seen to be involved.

So it was with great interest that he studied the weekly returns for Beryl's Brides in its first month of trading, and then looked at the returns for March. It was as he'd thought. Her cashflow position had never been strong enough to sustain the shop: she didn't have the reserves. She had orders for summer brides, but until they paid in full on the day, her takings were so low that the commission Marlow's was getting was a tiny sum. That, though, was the least of his concerns. He wondered how she'd been managing to pay the rent. Maybe it was time to ask.

He wanted to catch her on her own, so he left it till almost the end of the working day. As he approached her little unit, the blackout blinds were already down: perhaps he'd missed her. But surely she wouldn't risk missing a customer by leaving even a few minutes early? He tapped on the glass panel of the door.

'Who is it?'

'I need a word.'

She'd recognise his voice, he was sure. The door opened a crack.

'It's you.'

'Don't be like that, Beryl. Can I come in?'

Shadow of a Doubt? Tell me what it's about again.'

Lily and Jim were late leaving work. Jim had been discussing a promotion with Mr Simmonds – for goods, not himself, he explained to a disappointed Lily, who'd been waiting for him.

As they left the staff entrance, Jim was still buttoning his coat.

'No, I'm not going to tell you the plot! It's a Hitchcock, surely you can guess!'

'Not a musical then, or a nice romance?' teased Lily, hooking her arm through his. 'I don't know why you like these grim films, Jim. You seem so nice and normal. I hope you're not a secret axe murderer.'

'Aha, wait till the full moon.' Jim tried unsuccessfully to sound, and look, sinister.

'If that's you trying to look wolfish, you look more like a . . . a Pekingese choking on a fishbone.'

'Not cut out to be a villain, am I?' Jim gave her arm a squeeze as they turned onto the main road. He paused. 'So, we've got time for a cup of tea and a bun before the film. Where do you want to go?'

Beryl had opened the door. She'd turned the light off so as not to show a chink; once Robert was inside she snapped it on again and stood with her back to the door.

'Well?'

He turned to face her, smiling. 'That's not a very nice welcome. No wonder you haven't got many customers.'

'I have! Plenty!'

'Don't be silly, Beryl,' he said smoothly. 'I see the returns and the commission, remember? A small amount of a small amount isn't very much.'

'Well, I did warn you,' she shot back. 'I said it was too much. Anyway, I'm paying the rent, aren't I?'

'You have been up to now. How've you done it, eh? Going through Les's pockets for loose change? Pinching the housekeeping? Robbing Peter to pay Paul?'

Beryl closed her eyes. Robbing Bobby to pay Robert, more like.

'You're a strong woman, Beryl,' he went on. 'Independent. I admire that.' He meant it. It wasn't something you could accuse Evelyn of. 'But you can be too proud. It's silly to refuse help when it's offered.'

'Oh, yeah? I know what you were offering!'

'Well, why not take me up on it, then?' he suggested. 'It's not too late. I won't hold it against you. We could let bygones be bygones.'

Beryl closed her eyes again: the room was starting to spin. It had been a long day and she had a pounding headache. Her slice of bread and marg had been thinner than usual and it seemed a long time ago.

'Is that a yes?'

She hadn't said no. Maybe this was going to be easier than he'd thought. It was worth a try . . .

Eyes still shut, Beryl sensed rather than saw him lean forward and dip his head. His face was close to hers. Oh, God, why not? No one would ever know. He'd be going back to Birmingham soon. If it just paid this week's rent, and next, then it would be properly spring, and young men's fancy would turn to thoughts of love, and their girlfriends' thoughts would turn to orange blossom and tulle and the paste tiara that she'd given seven and six for because she was sure it'd fly out of the shop time and time again. She took a breath. He smelt lovely. Fresh and clean and – well – rich. Eyes still closed, Beryl suddenly saw her shop for what it was – a cramped cubby-hole full of second-hand clothes, second-class, second-rate. How had she ever thought she could make a go of it without his 'help'?

She felt his hand on her face. He lifted her chin.

'Beryl. Look at me.'

Beryl opened her eyes and, close to, with the shock of an ice bath, saw Robert Marlow for what he was – a spoilt, privileged toff who'd leeched off his father for years and now was leeching off Evelyn Brimble and her father. He thought he could have whatever he wanted; if he couldn't get it, he thought he could buy it, and that included her. Finding strength from somewhere, she pushed him hard in the chest.

'Get away from me!' she cried. 'Get off! How dare you!'

Robert grabbed her wrists and held them tight.

'You stupid girl,' he said. 'When it could all have been so nice.'

In one quick thrust he pushed against her. Beryl fell back against the door, trying to writhe away.

'Get off me, you bastard! Let me go!'

'Go where?' he sneered. 'Back to your hovel of a home and your hubby? I don't think so. Not yet.'

He pushed up against her again with such force that Beryl thought the door would give way. Instead, the blind flew up from its fastening, shooting up to the top of the glass like a rattlesnake into its crack.

Shocked, they both cried out at once.

'Now look what you've done!'

'Simmonds seemed to like the idea, what do you think?'

But Lily was looking across the street at Marlow's parade.

'Look!' she said. 'Beryl's shop! She was showing a light! And there's someone in there with her!'

'What? I didn't see—'

'The door blind shot up!'

Jim looked across. 'It looks fine now. Not a chink – Lily!' But she was already in the road. A passing car, its slitted headlights dipped, braked as she ran in front of it. 'You'll get yourself killed!'

'It got pulled down!' she called over her shoulder. 'But not by Beryl! There's a man in there! And it looked as if—' Jim had plunged after her, and they reached the other side together. 'They were in a clinch! And don't say it's Les. He'll be at home with Bobby!'

Jim grabbed her arm.

'Lily! If that's the case – maybe it's none of our business!'

But Lily shook him off. She marched across the pavement and started hammering on the door. There was something about what she'd seen that didn't sit right, and she knew what it was. It had reminded her horribly of her encounter with Frank Bryant.

'Beryl?' she called. 'Are you in there? Are you all right?'

Something was going on inside. Someone was grappling with the door handle, but they weren't being allowed to turn it. Jim was beside her now. They could hear little cries and protests – a man's voice and a woman's.

'See?' demanded Lily.

There was no doubt. Something was wrong.

Jim banged on the glass. 'ARP!' he said sternly. 'You were showing a light! Open up!'

There was a curse, then the door was wrenched open, and Beryl stood there, looking startled, guilty and discomposed.

'Jim! Lily!'

Light was flooding out onto the pavement. Jim quickly pushed his way in, Lily following.

Robert Marlow was perched on the little table Beryl used as a desk, examining his fingernails.

'Evening,' he said coolly. 'Correct me if I'm wrong, but isn't masquerading as the ARP an offence?'

'He *is* ARP,' said Lily.

She'd never trusted Robert Marlow and she was even more suspicious now.

'I'm off duty,' said Jim. 'But still got powers.'

'Really? Good for you.' Robert stood up as he spoke.

'What was going on in here?' asked Jim.

'Not really any of your business, old chap,' said Robert. 'But if you must know, I'm saying my good-byes. I'll be going back to Birmingham soon, so I dropped by to wish Beryl all the best. She tells me business is going very well.'

Lily looked at Beryl, waiting for confirmation. Beryl looked at Robert, and then at Lily and Jim.

'That's right,' she said. 'It is. I'm standing on my own two feet, and that's the way I like it.'

Lily was mystified. A business farewell wasn't what the scene she'd glimpsed had suggested, far from it. Something had definitely been going on. But if that was what Beryl said . . .

Robert moved towards the door. 'Well, I'll be getting along,' he said. 'It's been very nice working with you again, by the way, Jim. We must keep in touch.'

Jim very much doubted they would, especially after tonight. He'd been on his guard the past few weeks with Robert back at the store. He'd been watching him closely but hadn't noticed anything untoward. On the contrary, Robert really had seemed to have the future of the store and the welfare of his father at heart and he'd worked hard and well alongside Jim and Peter Simmonds. But there was something very off about this encounter. Beryl certainly wasn't telling the truth: she seemed both shifty and subdued. Robert had tricked Jim in the past and it was starting to look as if he'd done it again. But if that was what Beryl said . . .

They went through the usual rigmarole with the door and the light. Robert sailed into the street with a careless wave of his hand and the three of them stood there uncomfortably.

'OK, Beryl,' said Lily. 'What really happened?'

Beryl was keen to get home – Les would be worried – and they walked with her. Miserably, tearfully, she told them how Robert had propositioned her before she'd even taken the shop and how, tonight, he'd tried it on again. Even though it was what she'd suspected, Lily was appalled, and Jim was disgusted.

'This is what happens when people have things their own way all their life,' he said. 'And when money can buy whatever they want. Or they think it can.'

347

'So how did you . . . how did you get him to take his hands off you?' asked Lily as delicately as she could.

Beryl pulled a face. 'I said I'd tell his dad, but he didn't care! Said his father knew exactly what he was like.'

'I'm afraid he does,' agreed Jim.

When the truth about the delivery racket Robert had instigated had finally come to light, Jim's uncle had admitted to Jim that he'd indulged his son far too much.

'But then,' continued Beryl, starting to sound more robust, 'I said I'd tell his precious fiancée. At first he said she'd never believe me, my word against his, but he was bluffing, I could tell. He couldn't take the risk. Evelyn Brimble's a right madam, we all know that, but he's on to a nice little number with her and her dad. A soft life. He's not going to chuck that away on a cheap piece like me.'

'Beryl!' Lily objected. 'You're not cheap!'

'Oh, I am. That's how he made me feel.'

'That's rubbish, you're a good friend, a loyal wife, a loving mother—'

Beryl gave a curt laugh. 'You're very kind. Pity I'm a useless businesswoman.'

'What do you mean?'

Beryl stopped walking. 'I might as well tell you,' she said flatly. 'The reason he came sniffing round again . . . he can see I'm not doing well. He was offering to cover my rent in exchange for me giving him what he wanted.'

'Oh, no,' cried Lily. It was dreadful to see Beryl – bold, brassy, life-enhancing Beryl – brought so low. 'I had no idea! Why didn't you say?'

Chapter 33

There was no more to be said that night – it was late enough. By the time they got Beryl back to Alma Terrace, Les was beside himself.

'Where've you been?' he demanded, though in relief, not in rage. 'I had to put Bobby to bed without a kiss from his mum, your tea's all dried up, and I've been in and out like a dog at a fair looking for you!'

Les deserved an answer, but they couldn't tell him the truth. He'd have raised hell – sought out Robert Marlow and knocked his block off. So on the walk back, the three of them had agreed on the line they'd take.

'It's my fault,' Jim said now. 'Beryl's been having

trouble with her accounts, we started talking about them and – well, I'm afraid time ran on.'

It was a fib, but one on nodding terms with the truth. Once Beryl had confessed the real state the business was in, Jim had immediately offered to look through the books, and both he and Lily had promised to come up with some ideas to promote Beryl's Brides, without adding to her costs.

Les, God love him, bought the story entirely. So while he removed her plate from the oven for the umpteenth time, Lily and Jim hugged Beryl and, leaving her with her dried-up tears and dried-up tea, walked slowly back to Brook Street. Finally, Lily had chance to let off steam about Robert Marlow.

'It's incredible,' she fumed, 'the damage that bomb has done, how wide it spread! Beryl was miles away when it fell, but it went and brought him back on the scene – and look what happened! What a snake!'

Jim was quiet. No, not a snake. Robert's smart pinstriped suits were clothing a leopard, complete with the same spots as before. He was a chancer. He always had to push things too far. There was no way Jim could have known the hold that Robert had, or thought he had, over Beryl. What was worrying him was what else Robert might have been up to in his time back at the store – what Jim might have missed.

* * *

Over the next few days, Jim and Lily put their heads together. Jim pored over Beryl's accounts while Lily sketched out the wording for a leaflet. By the weekend, they had what Jim called a plan of campaign. The Army might not want him, but it didn't stop him borrowing their language.

The weather was mild and the sun was struggling to come out, so on Sunday, Lily packed up a picnic and the two of them, with Les, Beryl and Bobby, took a blanket to the park. It wasn't only her friends from whom Beryl had hidden the truth about how badly things were going financially. She hadn't told Les either, but now she'd confessed everything – except Robert Marlow's part in things, of course.

'And it's a blooming relief, I can tell you!' she declared as they lounged on the rug eating meat paste sandwiches and drinking Tizer.

'I dunno what she was thinking – that I'd think any less of her?' asked Les, feeding Bobby cubes of his sandwich. 'It was bound to be tough at the start.'

'Yeah, but I didn't allow enough to cover it, did I, Jim? What did you call it? A cushion.'

'Well, there's no point going over it,' said Jim. 'We've got to concentrate on what we can do to turn things round.'

They all looked at him expectantly, except Lily, who knew what he was going to say. She simply looked at him happily, happy that he was there at all, that he was taking charge, that the two of them were together.

'Right,' he said. 'First we do some marketing. We check the *Chronicle* to see who's announced their engagement.'

'They always give addresses, don't they?' Lily elaborated. '"The engagement is announced between Jack, son of Mr and Mrs John Jones of 1 Jubilee Terrace, and Betty, daughter of Mrs and Mrs Bert Bloggs of 2 Bridge Road" or whatever.'

'So?' asked Les.

'So,' continued Jim, 'we just happen to drop a card through the Bloggses' door, advertising Beryl's Brides. And the same for a few other houses in the street, so it doesn't look too obvious.'

Too obvious? Beryl and Les were looking at Jim as if he were a god.

'He read it in a book,' Lily put in. Jim was good at this stuff, but she didn't want him claiming a seat on Mount Olympus just yet. 'Written by some American business wizard.'

'Targeted marketing,' Jim explained. 'A lot better than randomly sticking leaflets through letterboxes.'

Beryl still looked bedazzled, but Bobby was beginning to grizzle; he was fed up with his sandwich and with all eyes on Jim, he was feeling left out. Les picked him up and let him play with his hair.

'As well as that, Simmonds and I have been talking about a spring promotion,' Jim went on. 'Including a fashion show, so people can see Utility fashions aren't all that bad. If we can get Mr Marlow to agree, we thought it could be a grand relaunch for the store as well.'

'Sounds lovely,' said Beryl. 'But how . . .?'

'Come on, Beryl,' urged Lily. 'Think! At the end of every fashion show there's a bride, isn't there?'

Beryl gasped.

'What? You'd have one of my dresses up there with proper fashions? New stuff?'

'Why not?' shrugged Jim. 'It's the only bridal wear at Marlow's now. And for miles, with Burrell's out of action.'

Les laughed. 'How about that, Bobby, eh?' He threw Bobby up in the air and caught him, to the baby's shrieking delight. 'Never mind Burrell's,' he added. 'The way you're going on, Jim, you'd better watch out. There'll be a Bulpitt's to rival Marlow's soon!'

For once Beryl wasn't crowing with him. 'My dresses . . . on a catwalk . . . ' She bit her lip. 'My mum'd be so proud.'

Lily squeezed her hand. Beryl's mum had died young after a miserable life with a violent bully of a husband. She'd been a gifted needlewoman who'd given Beryl her love of pretty things.

'We'll make your business boom,' Lily promised. 'It's been a rotten winter, one way or another . . . ' She glanced at Jim and he gave her a smile. 'But this year can only get better.'

Bobby was getting restless again, so Les made a ball out of some scrunched up greaseproof from the sandwiches and he and Jim took the baby off to play with it. Beryl and Lily packed up the rest of the picnic.

'I'm sorry there wasn't much,' Lily apologised.

'Don't be daft! There was plenty!' Beryl smiled as they made themselves comfy on the rug. 'Mind you, I bet Robert Marlow's supping brandy and smoking a cigar now after a big roast dinner!'

'I hope it chokes him!' cried Lily. 'Oh, I know it's Sunday and I'm supposed to be charitable but he'll get his comeuppance, you know, Beryl. One of these days.'

'You reckon?' said Beryl. She sounded older, sadder, and maybe even wiser. 'I think his sort usually manage to get away with it, one way or another.'

There was a bubbling shriek of laughter from the baby and they both looked across. Jim was making a great play of bowling the paper ball with whirling overarm movements. When Lily turned back, Beryl was watching her with a curving smile. 'You really love him, don't you?' she said.

'Bobby? Of course I do!'

'Not Bobby, you daft ha'porth! Jim!'

That made Lily sit up.

'What?'

'The way you look at him! For heaven's sake, Lily, it stands out a mile!'

355

Lily looked at her, dazed. Did she? Was that what it was? The fear she'd felt when she'd thought she might lose Jim to Margaret; the terror in the hospital when she'd heard he was injured; the sick relief when she'd realised he was going to be all right? All because she couldn't imagine – and didn't want to imagine – life without him? She cared about him, very much, she knew that; she preferred being with him to anyone else. He made her feel safe – she'd have trusted him with her life. If that was love . . .

Beryl was watching her, amused. 'Don't tell me you thought it was going to be some thunderbolt?' she asked. 'Eyes meet across a crowded room and Prince Charming sweeps you off your feet? Come on, Lily, you're supposed to be the clever one! This is Hinton, not Hollywood, you know!'

Lily smiled back, cautiously, as if it was the first time she'd ever tried it.

'I love being with him, I know that,' she said slowly. 'I care about him. Very much. More than I've ever cared about anyone who wasn't my family. I – I can't explain it, Beryl. I just feel right with him. Safe. Secure. If that's love . . . '

Beryl nodded. 'You've got it.'

'Then you're right. You're absolutely right. I do love him.' And, trying it out, 'I love him. I love him!'

Beryl cast her eyes up to the sky. Well, hooray!' she said. 'Corn in Egypt! Light has dawned!'

Lily looked over again towards Les and Jim. The

ball game was over. They were sitting with their arms round their knees, talking, while Bobby gleefully shredded the greaseproof into pieces.

She loved Jim. She loved him to bits.

'I don't know how to thank you for getting my Beryl straightened out,' Les was saying.

Jim tried to wave the thanks away. 'Don't be daft.'

'I mean it. You and Lily's quite a team, aren't you?'

'Yeah,' grinned Jim. 'Look out, Selfridges, here we come!'

'I wouldn't put anything past you,' observed Les. 'But I don't mean just business. You're great together, the two of you.'

Jim had been idly watching the baby in case he tried to eat the paper, but he swivelled his head sharply to look at Les.

'Do you think so?'

'Blimey, Jim, come off it! You don't need RAF night sights! Of course you are! Anyone can see the girl loves you to pieces!'

'What did you say?'

'I said the girl—'

Jim stopped him.

Yes, yes . . . sorry, I did hear.'

'What then?'

'It's just . . . nothing. Nothing.'

It wasn't nothing. Jim remembered now – Dora had used the same phrase when she'd been explaining how Lily had felt when he'd been away. In everything else she'd gone on to say and all he'd had to deal with that day, the sorting out and the emotion, it had got lost: it hadn't really registered. It had taken Les to unlock the memory, and for Jim to see that they were both right.

He remembered the misery he'd felt when he thought Lily might have been seeing someone else; how wounded that made him feel, because he'd always thought they had something special; an understanding and an unshakeable trust. And of course he'd been proved wrong, or rather right; she'd never really wavered in her feelings for him. But if she actually loved him . . .

He'd known he was fond of her; she was bright and funny – funny peculiar sometimes in the things she said, in what she knew and what she didn't, and had to have pointed out to her. But now he thought about it, how could anyone not love her energy and her generosity and her eagerness to help anyone, to get things done, sometimes to the point of interference, but only ever with good intentions?

Oh, she wasn't all sweetness and light – headstrong and impulsive, quick to anger, sometimes, but quick to laugh, positive, optimistic, teasing him if he got too serious or introspective. She annoyed, exasperated, challenged him – but he wouldn't have had it any different. Les was right. They were a good team. They balanced each other out.

'Oy, what are you up to, feller?' Les leant forward and fished out a scrap of paper that Bobby was chewing to a pulp. 'Little devil, isn't he?' he said lovingly.

Jim was thinking of other things. 'There's no need to thank me, Les. I ought to be thanking you.'

'Eh? You've really lost me now.'

'Never mind. You've made me realise something, that's all.'

'Cooee!'

They both looked towards the path. It was Gladys, but she was hailing Lily and Beryl. They were waving to her, so Les lay back, hands under his head, and Jim sat and watched Bobby happily tearing the grease-proof into confetti.

'Gladys!' called Lily, waving. 'I thought you couldn't come!'

Gladys had had to decline the picnic; there was a sale of work in aid of refugees after church.

'I can't stay!' puffed Gladys. She was in her Sunday best and her Sunday shoes, not designed for speed. 'Got to get back for Gran. But I've got news!'

Gladys never had news, at least nothing more exciting than her gran complaining her morning porridge had caught at the bottom of the pan, but her smile told them this was about more than a burnt breakfast – the sort of news that couldn't wait till Monday. Lily and Beryl scrambled to their feet.

'Bill?' Lily asked.

Gladys nodded, too overcome, or perhaps too out of breath, to speak. From her handbag she produced two letters.

'Two!' exclaimed Beryl. 'Well, you've waited long enough!'

'This is the one,' said Gladys shakily, offering the top envelope. 'You can read it.'

Lily scanned the letter, Beryl looking over her shoulder. It was on one side of the paper only, and said absolutely nothing beyond that life went on, with PT, drills and divisions (whatever those were). The main excitement had been when, on one of these, the DPO (whoever that was) had found a carelessly discarded cigarette end and had 'raised hell about it – turned out to be the chaplain's!'

Lily and Gladys glanced at each other. Was that it?

'Well, that's lovely, Gladys,' said Lily gamely. 'I'm so glad you've heard.'

'Have you read the P.S.?'

'Oh.' Lily turned the page.

'How's Lily?' Bill had written. 'And the shop?' Thrilling stuff.

'Oh,' she said again. 'Well, that's nice of him to ask.'

'No,' said Gladys, as if they were being deliberately obtuse. 'You know what it means, don't you?'

'No,' said Beryl firmly. 'We don't. How about you tell us?'

'It's code, isn't it?' said Gladys.

'Is it?'

'Our code!'

'You have a code?'

'Yes!' exclaimed Gladys. 'If Bill ever puts anything in a P.S. it means something!'

'Don't tell me he's passing you secrets!' Lily didn't know whether to be amazed by the ingenuity, or appalled. 'Telling you where he is?'

'No!' Gladys scorned. 'L for Lily – that means leave. 'And S for shop means—' Her eyes filled with tears and she swallowed. 'Soon!'

All the frustration of the protracted explanation evaporated. Bill had promised Gladys they'd get married next time he got leave.

'Oh, Gladys!' Lily threw her arms round her.

'Oh my God!' squeaked Beryl, flinging her arms round the pair of them and jumping up and down. 'At last!'

'Of course, I can't book the church, or anything, we don't know when,' quavered Gladys when the jumping had stopped. 'But at least I know! It's really going to happen! And soon!'

There was more hugging and jumping. Lily was thrilled for her friend. Gladys and Bill were made for each other, and she'd waited so long and so patiently without complaint. Beryl touched her hand.

'You are going to be the most beautiful bride ever,' she said, and with a glance at Lily. 'Beryl's Brides is going to make sure of that.'

Unable to ignore the commotion, Jim and Les brought Bobby back and the congratulations started all over again. Then Gladys realised the time, and, mindful of her gran, said she had to go. It was time for Bobby's nap, too, so Beryl stowed him in the pram and they all moved off together.

Lily took the first turn pushing. Secure in the new realisation of how she felt, and what it was, she watched Jim and Les walking ahead, the nape of Jim's neck where his hair grew in a little point, his straight stride, his long back under his shirt and the broken ribs so recently mended. She looked at her own hands on the pram handle, the right hand that had been so weak as a result of her own injury. Bobby was fast asleep now and she glanced behind. Gladys and Beryl were walking arm in arm, deep in discussion about dresses and headdresses and veils.

Such a lot had happened – again – in the last year, more than she'd ever have thought possible when she'd started at Marlow's and met all these people who'd become so important to her, as important as her own mum and brothers, the store itself as important as the four walls of her own home. And Jim more important than anyone.

At the pond, they parted to go their separate ways with more hugs and congratulations to Gladys. Hand in hand, Lily and Jim strolled slowly towards home.

Lily was quiet. Now she knew how she felt, it wasn't in her nature not to say anything, but could she – should she? – just come out with it? Perhaps not yet. Why not enjoy it for a while and find the right moment?

Jim was quiet too. 'It's been a good day, hasn't it?' he said finally.

'Perfect,' agreed Lily.

Jim stopped. They were still within the park. Sticky brown buds were breaking on the huge horse chestnut above them. Further off a couple of boys were kicking a football against the rustic shelter. Further still, a woodpecker thrummed. Jim put down the picnic basket and the rug.

'Thing is,' he said, 'I've realised something. Something I should have known a long time ago. Maybe I did. I just didn't sort of put a name to it. But there's something I want to say. Now I've realised, I can't not say it.'

Lily looked into his eyes, serious, shining, sincere, and she knew. A smile broke over her face. 'I think I might know what it is,' she said. 'I've got something to say to you, too.'

Author's Note

When I began the Shop Girls series three years ago, Beatties of Wolverhampton, the inspiration for Marlow's, was still trading as part of the House of Fraser group. Whilst I've been writing, though, House of Fraser fell into administration and several stores, including Wolverhampton, have been closed. The iconic Beatties building itself, with the imposing corner position that I borrowed for Marlow's, has been sold for redevelopment. All of which makes me sad, but at the same time delighted that the spirit of Beatties – and so many other old-established and much-loved department stores that have disappeared – can live on and be celebrated through Lily and her colleagues.

Lots of people have helped to make that celebration possible. Firstly, the relentless positivity of my agent Broo Doherty and of course the equally enthusiastic HarperCollins editorial and publicity team – Lynne Drew and Sophie Burks, Jennifer Harlow and Jeannelle Brew. My thanks again to Claire Ward and her team for another beautiful cover.

This is my chance also to acknowledge the many friends who were so supportive and encouraging when I first tentatively hinted I was attempting a novel and have been some of my first readers. So a huge thank you to Mary Cutler (again), and to Claire MacRorie as well as to Debbie Crooks, Penny Searley, Louise Gifford, Julie Jeffries and Nicky Savage and to Gudrun Smith, Jo Acha and Angela Power.

I would be nothing without the daily love and support of my family – my husband John and daughter Livi, and it would all be pretty pointless without you, the readers. Thank you! If you've got this far, I can only hope you're enjoying the Shop Girls saga. If you feel moved to, please leave a review on Amazon or GoodReads – it really does help other readers – and find me on Facebook or Twitter for news about what's next in store for Lily, her family and friends.

Don't miss the next book in
the Shop Girls series

CHRISTMAS
for the
SHOP GIRLS

Drama, courage and romance at Marlow's department store this Christmas . . .

For Lily, Beryl and Gladys, another Christmas with ration books, shortages of goods and staff – not to mention a store coping with war damage – will be a real challenge.

But with a wedding in the offing, Beryl is in her element. Gladys has a secret, one that will take her and Lily all the way to London. And Lily can't help wondering what her own future holds, as Jim is pulled into a black-market racket while the call-up posters for the women's ATS catch her eye.

But the shop girls rally round and put their worries aside to make this, the hardest wartime Christmas yet, one that their families, and their town, will never forget.

Have you read the first book in the
Shop Girls series, *A Store at War*?
Read on for a taste . . .

'So when do you start?'

'Next week. Monday.'

'That's brilliant, Sis! Well done!'

Sid folded Lily in a huge hug and she relaxed for the first time that day. He was in the garden now, in an old collarless shirt and some ancient trousers, once their dad's – nothing was ever thrown away in the Collins household. They were too big for him round the waist, so he'd found a huge leather belt which pulled them in tight and his braces were hanging down. Somehow, using the handle as a support, and putting as little weight on his bad foot as possible, he'd been hoeing between the lettuces, which were dangerously close to bolting, their mum said.

Now things were getting scarcer in the shops, Dora had taken 'Dig for Victory' to heart. She'd never done more than nurture the odd Christmas cactus or aspidistra for the front room, but now they grew what they could in a couple of small raised beds at the back of their terraced house. It had been nothing but a yard, but Lily and Sid had carted the soil in barrows half a mile from a bigger, boarded-up house with a garden. Every little bit they grew helped cheer up a diet that was becoming more and more repetitive and meagre.

Bacon, butter, sugar . . . they'd been rationed since almost the beginning of the war; even margarine had been rationed for almost a year now. Meat, tea, jam . . . sweets, of course . . . last month cheese and this month, eggs. One egg each a week!

Still, if it helped the war effort . . .

'Where's Mum?' asked Lily. 'I wanted to tell her straight away!'

'Ah. She's out,' said Sid mysteriously.

'She never goes *just* out.' Lily looked puzzled.

'She won't be long,' soothed Sid. 'Anyway, you can tell me. Who was there? What did they ask you?'

'Ohhhh,' said Lily, covering her face. 'It was dreadful. It wasn't just Miss Garner, it was Mr Marlow himself! I mean, he seemed very nice, but . . . he asked what I'd liked at school and I said "all of it" and how I'd have liked to stay on, and then I thought that was the wrong answer 'cos he'd think

I didn't want the job . . . and then I blabbered on about how I liked meeting people, and talking to them, and about how I really really wanted to work there . . .'

'Well, you do, don't you? Better than that steamy laundry any day of the week. Or the Fox and Goose, with old Pearson trying to put his hand up your skirt.'

'Sid!'

Sid grinned. 'It's true. There'll be none of that at Marlow's. Everyone there's ever so well brung up, ain't they?' He lapsed deliberately into the strong local accent.

'I suppose so,' mused Lily.

'Well, don't sound so sorry about it! So no mental arithmetic or spelling? You were dreading that.'

'Nothing like that,' said Lily. 'It's only a junior's job – in the Children's department. I don't suppose they'll let me near a customer. And anyway I don't know if I can take it. I haven't got the right clothes!'

'What, no uniform?'

'They've scrapped it 'cos of the war. A dress in a plain dark colour, they said, or dark skirt and white blouse. And plain black shoes.'

'Well, you've got those.' Sid nodded at Lily's best Sunday shoes.

'They'll never last the winter!' cried Lily. She steadied herself against Sid's shoulder and balanced stork-like to show him the soles, which were already worn. 'As for a dress—'

'Mum'll come up with something. Or we'll ask around. You know how it works in our street.'

Lily knew all too well. Hand-me-downs, making do. That was one thing the war hadn't changed.

Sid went back to his hoeing.

'Surely though, you'll get some kind of discount? Buy some decent stuff?'

'What, like a tie for you? On their prices, 90 per cent off wouldn't be enough!'

'They had some smashers,' said Sid wistfully. 'Silk. Still . . . one day, maybe . . .'

'One day,' sighed Lily. 'When the war's over . . .'

'Dear me. A nice enough girl, but no polish.'

Miss Garner was assembling Lily's staff manual, letter of engagement and terms and conditions of employment. Cedric Marlow was standing at the window of his office, looking down into the well at the back of the shop. A grimy pigeon was fluffing out its feathers in the sun and he was ashamed to realise that all he could think about was how good it would taste casseroled with bacon, mushrooms and shallots. His household could afford to buy its way out of the worst of rationing, and he could always eat out, but there was less and less variety on the menu.

'I think she'll suit very well,' he said mildly.

'She'll need a few rough edges knocked off her.' Miss Garner tapped the pages straight and pinioned them with a precious paper clip. They'd be the next thing to disappear. She'd make sure the girl gave it back once she'd signed her contract.

'I daresay. But we've had worse.'

'I'll say.'

Her thoughts swung immediately to Beryl Salter on Toys. A year at Marlow's had knocked off her rough edges, it was true, but at the expense of the girl giving herself a most uncalled-for air of superiority and what she obviously thought was a 'refined' accent.

Shaking her head, Miss Garner returned to the latest candidate.

'Miss Collins is a little too keen to pipe up, I thought. "Likes talking to people" – she'd better not try that with the customers! She'll have to learn to speak when she's spoken to. But Eileen Frobisher will keep her in line.'

Miss Frobisher was one of Miss Garner's protégées, having soared rapidly through the complex sales hierarchy to the dizzy heights of buyer on Childrenswear. They'd been so lucky to get her back. She wasn't really a 'Miss' of course, else she'd have been in a munitions factory or the services by now, but Marlow's convention was that all saleswomen were addressed as 'Miss' whether they were married or not. And Eileen was, with a husband serving overseas and a little boy of four, which excused her from war work. An elderly neighbour looked after him during store hours.

Cedric Marlow let the net drop back as the pigeon fluttered off.

'How's that new young man on Furniture and Household getting on by the way? James Something-or-other.'

'Oh! You mean Jim. Jim Goodridge,' confirmed Miss Garner. 'From what I can gather from Mr Hooper,' she named the Furniture buyer, 'he's made quite a good impression. He's rather quiet, not the most pushy, but as third sales he doesn't have to be. There's plenty of time for him to learn. And with experienced salesmen like Maurice Bishop to learn from . . . Why do you ask?'

'Oh . . . he simply popped into my head for some reason,' Cedric Marlow replied. Then: 'Did you notice that poor kid's shoes? Literally down-at-heel.'

'I'll make sure her presentation on the sales floor is up to scratch, Mr Marlow, don't you worry.'

'That's not what I meant.' He turned away from the window. 'The Queen may feel she's able to look the East End in the eye, but sometimes . . . I wonder. I mean, I don't suppose Lily Collins' family were exactly flush before the war, her mother being a widow, but so many like them are suffering more than ever now. As is anyone who can't buy their way out of it. And here we are, selling only the best . . . '

Miss Garner cleared her throat. Mr Marlow wasn't usually given to sudden enquiries about random members of staff, nor to such outpourings – and certainly not this kind of sentiment. It had been a long day, clearly.

'It's got very warm in here,' she said. 'Might I suggest you open the window? And I'll ask the restaurant to send you in a tray of tea.'

'Lay the table will you, love?'

Her mother's voice carried over the clattering coming from the scullery.

Lily went to the sideboard for the knives with the yellowed bone handles and the tarnished forks and started doling them out on the cloth.

After the elation of getting the job, it had all been a bit of a comedown. Her mum had been pleased, of course, and Lily could see the relief on her face. But on hearing of the uniform requirements, she'd jumped up, gone upstairs and come back down with a hideous dress in navy gabardine.

'Cousin Ida's,' she announced. 'I knew it'd come in useful!'

Cousin Ida. Her mother's cousin – a shrivelled spinster who worked as an assistant in a chemist's so old-fashioned they practically had leeches in jars. Hardly a fashion plate at the best of times, this particular dress was at least ten years out of date, Lily could tell from its straight up-and-down shape. It was already seated in the behind and sagging at the hem, but Dora Collins loved nothing like a challenge. Lily had had to stand while her mother forced her to put it on – smelling of camphor and itchy in the afternoon heat – and primped about with a pincushion, tucking and pinching, prodding and poking, telling Lily to stand up straight, before proclaiming that with a few darts, a nice Peter Pan collar, and cuffs if they could run to them, it would do fine. A Peter Pan collar! Cuffs! As if they'd make it look any better!

Out came the cruet, the mismatched plates . . . What was the point, thought Lily, of getting a decent job if she was going to look such a frump? She might as well have been stuck slaving over a mangle at the laundry.

Sid came downstairs, spruced up after his stint in the garden. Dora had fretted that he'd overdone it, standing all that time on his injured foot, but she and Lily knew sitting about wasn't his style – he wanted to be up and doing. He'd got to report to the local medical officer weekly, but the doctor had advised against going back to training too early. 'You'll only set yourself back' had been his advice, so it looked as though they'd have him around for a while yet. Lily was glad. She loved her mum dearly, but Dora had always been so occupied with making ends meet and keeping them fed, clothed and shod – even more so nowadays – that there wasn't much time or maybe energy left over for the smiles and cuddles which Lily had craved since she was a little girl. That was another reason she was happy to have

Sid around. He was always ready with a joke and a hug.

On trailing feet Lily carried through the breadboard and breadknife with the inevitable loaf – they seemed to live on it – the pot of dripping, the dish shaped like a lettuce leaf with, yes, lettuce on it. A few tomatoes, a dish of radishes, half a pot of green tomato chutney. Was that it? Hardly a celebration tea. She'd hoped her mum might have conjured something tasty from somewhere – potted meat? Pilchards? Or at least fried up a few potatoes – Sid had dug some up, she'd seen – but it looked as though this was going to be their lot.

Sid carried the tea things through one at a time – he used a stick inside the house – and dispensed pot, milk jug and cups and saucers. Maybe that was the celebration, no milk bottle on the table. Lily thought he was limping more than he had been at the start of the afternoon and gestured to him to sit down, bringing him the rush-topped stool.

'I could get used to this!' he smiled as she stuck a cushion under his foot.

'Well, don't!' she retorted. 'Who's going to look after you in the Navy? One of the Wrens? You hope!'

Sid winked.

'Wouldn't say no.'

Lily was pouring tea when her mother finally appeared, so she didn't notice the serving dish till it went down in front of her. She lowered the pot in wonderment.

'Oh, Mum!'

There, in all their jelly goodness, were three fat slices of pink, speckled brawn. Lily bent and sniffed the plate. It smelt heavenly.

'Meat? On a Monday tea? Where did it – how did you . . . ?'

Her mother sat down in her place with that little 'Oof' which she so often gave these days when taking the weight off her feet.

'Never you mind,' she said. 'I wanted us to have something special. To celebrate.'

'But – how could you be sure I'd get the job?'

Lily sat down too, almost in slow motion, still transfixed by the sight and smells in front of her. Sid was watching it all with amusement. Dora served a slice of brawn on to each of their plates.

'I never had a minute's doubt! I knew you'd impress them. If you ask me, they're lucky to have you!'

Lily bit her lip. It was one of the nicest things her mother had ever said.

Her mother put her hand over hers.

'You've done very well, love – and thank you.'

'You're thanking me? Why?'

'Oh, Lily,' said Dora. 'You know and I know you should have stayed on at school. And you know as well as I do that you could have gone to the grammar school back along if things had been different.'

Lily knew. But she hadn't even taken the exam,

because she also knew her mother could never have afforded the uniform.

'You've had to give up so many opportunities already,' Dora went on. 'I hope this job'll be the start of something good for you. And it could be, you know, if you work hard.'

'I know, Mum. And I will. I'll do my very best to make them like me and keep me on.'

'Course they will,' Sid assured them. 'Give her a few years, she'll be running the place, won't you, chick?'

Her mother squeezed Lily's hand and they both had to squeeze back tears.

'Oh, blimey,' said Sid, offering his handkerchief to each in turn. 'Women! Give over, will you? There's a slice of brawn with my name on it in front of me! Can we get stuck in?'